*Beneath the*
*Shattered Moons &*
*The White Otters*
*of Childhood*

**MICHAEL BISHOP**

SPHERE BOOKS LIMITED
30/32 Gray's Inn Road, London WC1X 8JL

To Jeri
*light, warmth, and love*

# Contents

# The White Otters of
## Childhood

# One

*A wind came across the ocean, sweeping with it a pall of fine
white ash. The ash fell into the sea and into the breakers. The
breakers washed dead shrimp ashore with the driftwood. Then
they washed up the whiting. The shark swam out to his deepest
waters and brooded in the cold clean currents. He was very
hungry that season.*

*– Walter M. Miller, Jr.*

It is the Year of Our Lost Lord 5309. Or so we believe.
From the sea we came, and to the sea we return.

I am chronicling both the upheavals of our ruling order
here at Windfall Last and the upheavals of my own spirit.
I have recourse to books. Although Mankind has been
diminished to the two million who dwell on this island, all
the knowledge of the past lies in the great Sunken Library
at the bottom of Pretty Coal Sack, the bay on which our
city fronts. After all, I have been the premier literary
adviser to the Sunken Library, and also one of the foremost counsellors of the Navarch of Windfall Last. The
Sunken Library contains manuscripts which not even the
first ancients – those who initiated Holocaust A well over
three thousand years ago – had at their disposal; many of
these records, of course, we owe to the archaeology and
the persistence of the Parfects. As a consequence, books
open to me almost of their own accord. I know several of
the dialects that were spoken before the first holocaust and
several of those that were spoken before the second rain of
fire, nearly fifteen hundred years later. I believe myself
well versed in the ways of men.

Another fifteen hundred years have passed since Holocaust B, since the dispersal of the all-humbling ash, since
the season of the shark's hunger. Sharks still thrive in the
world – though, for the most part, we have forgotten their
sleek flanks, their slashing undercut mouths, their piggish

and brutal eyes. We have forgotten because the sharks themselves avoid the waters that surround our native (so to speak) island of Guardian's Loop, here in the Antilles. They probably scent that this final remnant of mankind dwells here in thrall to a bestiality more terrible than their own sharkishness.

But sharks still exist. In an open boat upon the sea I have had the privilege of seeing their dorsal fins slice through the sapphirine waters. Like blades through flesh.

My name is Markcrier Rains. I am the guilty conscience of a species which has twice tried to exterminate itself.

I am Markcrier Rains: poet, horseman, sailor, antiquarian, philologist, mystic, diplomat, natural historian, counsellor, exile, lover, husband, dupe, widower, wretch and finally revenger.

For forty-eight years I lived as if integrity were the sole means towards the scarcely attainable end of conquering the bright black canker in our collective souls. In this last year, my forty-ninth (a minor climacteric, if you believe in numerology), I shoved integrity arsewards and let that deep-seated soul-bruise ulcerate into something indisputably animal. My revenge was sweet; my remorse is as bittersweet as love.

And in this Year of Our Lost Lord 5309, I, Markcrier Rains, make my general confession to whatever deity the Parfects (who have inherited the earth) bequeath their innocent and untarnished spirits to. Not having fallen, the Parfects multiply on the continents, reign over every archipelago, rejoice in the bounty of the oceans. Since we have only Guardian's Loop, I confess to that veiled deity who has freed them from the Beast.

Therefore, read my confession:

I am going back now to the final December before the turn of the new century, back nine years to the last Christmas of that departed age. It was the Year of Our Lost Lord 5299.

I had just returned from a ten-month sojourn among

the Parfects in Azteca Nueva, nearly two thousand miles across the Carib Sea, where these transcendental human beings permitted me to wander among them – just as we tolerate a pet dog to run underfoot at one of our sacramental bayside weddings. The Parfects, who enforce mankind's exile here on Guardian's Loop, the winged island, refuse to come among us; but occasionally they require detailed knowledge of our moods, our numbers, our intramural repressions. At these times they compel the Navarch to provide them with an envoy. On the past two such occasions, our Navarch, Fearing Serenos, selected me to represent the two million dying and doomed human beings of Windfall Last.

And gladly I performed the Navarch and the Parfects' will.

But on the Christmas of my second (and, I hoped, my last) return, I was a man consummately weary and dispirited. No human being can live among the Parfects for ten months without coming to feel himself a wholly contemptible creature, wanting in reason, purpose and ultimate grace. The experience enervates and destroys. Even the wisest comes back to Guardian's Loop with the stench of his own humanity suffocating him and tainting his reunion with the old friends who seek to celebrate his return. Time becomes a necessity as great as food or shelter. One must recover. One must shake off the malaise produced by nearly three hundred days among the tall naked mutants who rule, without punishments or statutes, their own golden earth. For I was as an envoy to another planet, conscious every moment of the racial superiority of my hosts. At forty-one, I needed time to grow back into myself and my people. Those close to me understood and attempted to aid me in my recuperation.

I left Windfall Last. Fresh winds blew across the waters of Pretty Coal Sack, and ruffles of white lace spilled over the coral barrier in the bay. The sky shimmered with the bluish white of noon.

I rode horseback along the beach, spurring my horse with incredible ferocity towards our destination. Soon –

even had I reined in the horse and turned him about – I could not have seen the cancer shape of globes and turrets and aluminium minarets that is the skyline with as much finality as if a fission bomb had fallen on the administrative sanctuary of Fearing Serenos himself. Galloping on horseback, the wind in my mouth, I rode free of mankind and its madnesses.

The horse belonged to Dr Yves Prendick. I spurred him along the water's edge, now and again forcing the good doctor's docile beast away from the stretches of sand and broken shells and up into the moist varnished-green foliage that lay inland. I rode to keep a rendezvous with Prendick's twenty-six-year-old daughter. It was my fourth day back, Christmas Eve Day, and Prendick had give me the horse and suggested that I go mind Marina at the gutted sailing vessel that a hurricane had long ago swept up and deposited several hundred metres from the edge of the sea. The vessel was a unique landmark.

'Marina's camping there,' he had told me, 'studying the vegetation, the migratory water fowl.'

'My God, Prendick, is she out there all alone?' Our centuries-old Navarchy had decreed no one could leave Windfall Last but the duly licensed and authorised (among whom Prendick and I and other counsellors to Fearing Serenos counted ourselves), but enforcing such a decree among two million imperfect subjects presents special problems. I feared for Marina.

'She's all right, Mark. She has a pistol, and she knows how to use it. Take Paris, go down the beach and find her. Stay out there a while if you like. You need quiet company, a woman's voice.'

And so I urged Paris, Prendick's dappled gelding, to aid me in seeking out Marina. In the glory of the white afternoon Paris' mane undulated like silken grass.

I found Marina when the sun had begun to fall a little towards the west. (Perhaps our first meeting after my return was a metaphor, who can say?) The old ship, the Galleon of the Hesperides as Marina and I had called it, lay wracked and rotting on the side of a small rise; and the sea had managed to cut a channel – a narrow channel – through the sand and then through the clamouring vegetation so that water sloshed and echoed in the caved-in opening beneath the galleon's forecastle. This same channel was fed in part from a fresh water run-off from the interior.

The ship dated from the 5100s; it had been built by the Parfects as an experiment in restoration, most likely, and then abandoned with their characteristic whimsicality to the elements. Somehow, its wood had not wholly decayed, in spite of the vegetation and the wet. The upper decks suffered under the liquorish weight of this vegetation; as a consequence, the Galleon of the Hesperides resembled a great basket of flowers: amazing varieties of cineraria grew there, as did acanthus, melilot, mallow and fenugreek, plants one would not have anticipated growing in the West Indian tropics.

And it was on the upper deck that I saw Marina, dark, lithe and inattentive to my approach, stooping over a bouquet of plush blue flowers. She was drawing in a sketchbook. She wore khaki shorts, a sort of sleeveless mesh-cloth hauberk, and, of course, a pistol. I halted Paris on the slope above the galleon and watched her with the eyes and heart of a man who knows himself too well. My eyes and heart ached. The wind was blowing from her to me, and it carried upon it the intimations of old perfumes.

Then Paris whinnied, drawing her attention. Paris danced sideways on the slope a little, and I had to pull him up with the reins.

Marina, below on the ship's deck, dropped her sketchbook, stood to her full height amid the blue flowers, and drew her pistol, all seemingly in a single motion. Her left arm came up to shield her eyes, and what I had forgotten during my ten months with the Parfects came back to me with heartbreaking cruelty.

Marina had been born with a left arm that terminated, just below the elbow, in a splayed paddle of flesh. It was a cruel and heartbreaking reminder of our ancestors' brinksmanship: the ash was always with us.

Whenever I remembered Marina, I remembered her without deformity. It was as if my mind unconsciously extrapolated from the tenderness of her nature and gave her the faultless physical beauty that she deserved. I *saw* the flat and slightly curved blade at the end of her arm, yes, but it had no genuine reality for me – only enough reality to make my eyes and heart ache in a way different from that provoked by simply beholding her face. Therefore, I suppose, that reality was enough.

Her father, a surgeon, might have softened the hard cruelty of her 'hand' when she had come of age. But when she came of age, she would have none of his reshaping and plastisculpting. 'I am as I am,' she told her father. 'I accept myself as I am. Besides, my seawing' – Fearing Serenos, our Navarch had been the first to call her deformed hand and forearm a *seawing* – 'serves to remind me of where we came from and what we've done to one another.' Moreover, Serenos himself, whose face and hands bristled with a covering of atavistic fur, frowned on surgical remedies.

The result was that Prendick obeyed his daughter; he refrained from angering his hirsute and bestially ruthless lord.

And the further result was that Marina now shielded her eyes with the stump of her seawing and in her good hand held a pistol that was aimed at my heart. At her back, the sea sparkled under the white sun of noonday, laving the distant beach with foam. The pistol glinted blue.

'Don't shoot,' I called. 'If you miss me, you might kill your father's horse. You know how your father is about his horses.'

'Markcrier!' She smiled and holstered the gun. 'Markcrier, come down here. Leave Paris on the hill.'

'To run away? A fine Christmas gift for your father.'

'Paris won't run away. If you get off his back and unbridle him, he'll graze and be happy for the chance.'

I did as Marina bade me and then descended to the galleon. Boarding the run-aground vessel, I felt like a pirate who has fought for doubloons but who discovers that his captive's sea chests all contain roses. But I am a bad pirate; I was not disappointed. Marina had more the odour of roses about her than the metallic tang of old coins, and I kissed her. She pressed her lips against mine with no little ardour. The sea laved the beach with foam.

I was a little surprised at the degree of Marina's ardour. We had known each other for almost her entire life, for I had met Yves Prendick in 5278 when he was elevated to the council and made the Navarch's personal surgeon. Marina had been five years old and I a precocious twenty. Even then, Serenos had trusted me more deeply than he did the fawning old magi twice and three times my age. I paid no attention to the children of fellow council members, however, and it was not until I returned from my first diplomatic excursion to the Parfects, eleven years later, that I became aware of Marina.

She was a self-possessed young lady, and our relationship developed into something subtle and significant – although it refused to acknowledge that it might be the prelude to marriage. The erotic aspect was not there, not even the first hints of a shy amorousness. Marina had other interests; so did I. When she turned twenty and I began to think about her as a possible wife, a political incident removed me from the council and the circle of my closest friends.

Fearing Serenos took umbrage at a semi-sardonic comment that I made in council session (a remark, I swear, which I cannot even recall) and ordered me to leave his chambers. I compounded this error by standing my ground and questioning the state of his mental health. How could so small a thing, I asked, provoke such a disproportionate response? Had the Navarch not loved me, I might have been killed.

Instead, I was exiled for almost fourteen months among the fishermen who live in the licensed colony of Barbos on Marigold Island, which lies to the south of Guardian's Loop. These men had been made fishermen and sent to Barbos because they were mutants, but, unlike most of us, mutants who offended either by their appearance or their mephitic odour, this last the result of unbalanced body chemistries. Many of them looked and smelled like rheumy-eyed beasts, but they treated me well; and I became one of them, working with boats and nets through the entirety of my exile. Serenos relented only when I had promised him, by messenger, to obey him in everything.

Upon my return I found that I had little time to think of Marina or of marriage. My duties, strangely enough, had multiplied. I handled countless administrative functions for the Navarch at the Palace of the Navarchy and spent many days at a time in the pressurised sacristies of the Sunken Library. At the bottom of Pretty Coal Sack, I worked with men who were carrying on the monastic tradition of preserving mankind's accumulated knowledge. Technically, regardless of professed affiliations, everyone on Guardian's Loop was either a monk or a nun under the supreme authority of our abbot, the Navarch. But the gradual – the miraculously gradual – crumbling of belief had turned Windfall Last into a secular community, rigidly stratified and stringently ruled. The monkish work in the Sunken Library went on only because the Parfects had built the library for us and demanded that we continue to transcribe and catalogue the intellectual achievements of man. Therefore, we did so. And Fearing Serenos kept me totally occupied supervising these labours and innumerable others in the city itself.

Marina and I saw each other very seldom.

Eventually I protested that I would collapse from fatigue if not given a respite, a chance to communicate with other people. The Navarch reminded me of my vow. I kept silence ever after, until one day Serenos dropped his heavy arm over my shoulder and told me that after my next sojourn to Azteca Nueva, under the dead volcano, he would permit me to retire on full pension from his service – provided that he might call upon me now and again for advice and comradeship.

I agreed.

But to the day of my departure, not one whit did my

work abate. I seldom saw anyone but those engaged in the same projects and activities as myself. I had no time for horsemanship, no time for poetry.

On the evening before I was to leave for the Parfects' homeland, however, Marina came secretly to my apartment/office and talked with me about other times. We talked for several hours, sipping rum from crystal glasses. When she was ready to go, Marina told me to take care and gave me a chaste girlish kiss on the nose: good-bye to her second father.

Now she was kissing me with the welcoming kiss of a woman for her lover, and I returned the compliment, having realised it for a compliment, more devoutly, tonguing the warmth between her lips. At last we stopped. She stepped back and looked at me.

'Hello,' I said. The sun raged small and white.

'Hello, Markcrier.'

'I'm not used to such welcomes. The Navarch merely shook my hand; then he turned me over to the council members for thirty hours of debriefing. And in three days not one of those bastards kissed me.'

'Not even Father?'

'No. When we were done, he loaned me a horse and told me to get lost.'

'And now you're lost?'

'Less so than I might have thought. Show me what you're doing, where you're camping. Does the old Galleon of the Hesperides still hold together well enough to provide a lady botanist shelter?' I pointed at the channel that the sea had cut beneath the ship. 'That looks ominous.'

'It's not,' she said. 'Come.'

We crossed the deck. Our legs brushed past and animated the umbels, stalks and gleaming leaves that grew from the accumulated soil on the deck's planking. The salt breeze re-animated this vegetation when we were by, and perfume was everywhere.

Down into the forecastle we went.

By the light that came through the planks overhead I could see that Marina had swept this area and made it her own. She had suspended a hammock across two corners of the room and stacked several books and sketch-pads beside the hammock. But a section of the tilted floor near the vessel's bow had fallen in, and through the ragged opening one could look down and see the dark water that had undercut the galleon. The light was stronger here, and a million flowers grew in the clumped dirt on both sides of the encroaching rivulet. The water here was only minutely saline because rain had apparently flushed the sea back upon itself several times during the recent rainy season. As we stood looking into the flower pit, the hollow sound of water lapping at wood made primordial echoes in our ears. At last we turned back to the rustic boudoir.

'Very good,' I said. 'But where's your transportation?'

'Oh, Hector. I gave him his head yesterday. He's up the beach most likely, nibbling at the green shoots that grow in one of the coastland swales.'

'Yes, Hector. Good old Hector. Will he come back on his own?'

'With wet fetlocks and a matted chest. Don't worry.'

'I'm not worried. I'm hungry.'

'Me too.'

We sat cross-legged on the askew planking, and Marina fed me. We ate biscuits and dried fruit and sucked on the stems of a cane-like plant that Marina assured me was not poisonous.

'Are you glad to be back?'

'Now I am.'

'Markcrier?' She let my name hang above the sound of echoing water.

'Yes?'

'What's it like living among the Parfects for so long?'

'Like being five years old again. Like being continuously embarrassed for wetting the bed. Like being caught in the act of liberating the legs from an all-too-alive grasshopper. I don't know, Marina. The experience has no corollaries.'

'How did they behave towards you? Were they contemptuous?'

'No, no, nothing like. They were kind but ... *aloof*. *Aloof* is a perfect word to characterise them because even when they engaged me in conversation, some part of their intellect remained ... disengaged, uncommitted. Simply because there was no need for them to commit this with-held part, I suppose. But they were always kind.'

'Were they always' – her voice became humorously in-sinuative – '*naked?*'

'Always. I'm surprised you're interested.'

'Why? Everyone has a prurient streak.' Marina handed me another biscuit and spat out a piece of fibre from the plant stem she had been sucking on. 'What I really want to know is, did they go naked all year? Even when it was cold?'

'Every day, rain or shine.'

'How could they?'

'No morals,' I said.

'No, I don't mean that. I mean, how could they tolerate the cold?'

'I don't know. It never seemed to bother them.'

'And you? Did you—?' She stopped.

'Go naked?'

'Yes.'

'You're asking that of me? A member of the Navarch's council?'

'Yes. Did you?'

'No,' I said. 'They never expected that of me. Besides, the disparity between my own physique and the Parfects' would have been painful to me. No pre-pubescent lad ever likes to shower with the big boys.'

'Oh, I see. The matter was not simply physical, but sexual as well.'

'No, no.'

'Well, then, what are they like?'

'I don't know. Like us, but more elegant.'

'*Elegant* is an equivocator's word, a weak word. Mark-crier, you're trying to put me off; you're trying to tease me.'

'I'm not. Besides, your curiosity is too much for me.

And the word *elegant* says it all; it encapsulates the essence of the Parfects. You're teetering on an abyss, young woman, when you correct a sometimes poet on his diction.'

'Very sorry, I'm sure. But I want to know what they're like.'

'They're prigs, if you want the truth. They make love openly, they refrain from sermonising, they speak whatever they feel – but somehow, don't ask me to explain it, they're still prigs. For nine months and two weeks of the time that I spent in the shadow of Popocatepetl, I was bored. My bones ached with ennui.'

'I don't believe you.'

'After the first two weeks they scarcely paid me any heed. And when they did, their kindness ran over me like cane sap.'

'Did you write poetry, then? In all that time you were alone?'

'No.'

'Why not? You used to complain of a lack of time.'

'Marina, poetry is a spiritual need. Many of us in Windfall Last turned to poetry when we lost faith in the mythologies of our still-dying church. But it's impossible to express the spirit when the spirit is submerged, and among the Parfects I had no more divinity in me than does a teredo, a wood-burrowing shipworm. I couldn't write a line.'

'Then you really believe they're creatures without original sin?'

'Marina, I deny original sin – but I acknowledge that man is carnivorous and cannibalistic, spiritually so.'

'But the Parfects are different; you've already said that.'

'Different, yes. They lack the more obvious human vices, the ones that are ours by way of evolutionary bequest. Doubtless, they have vices of their own.'

'Such as?'

'You ask painfully pointed questions, don't you?'

'Yes. What sort of vices?'

I had to pause. The ship seemed to creak with old tethers and old strains, the seawrack of yesterday. At last I suggested, 'How about the vice of being insupportably boring?'

Marina laughed, unconsciously rubbed her seawing with her good right hand, tapped her bare feet on the rough planking. I grinned at her. In a way, she had made me go through my second debriefing in four days, and I think she realised that I couldn't talk about the Parfects any longer without decorating the account with an uncontrolled and perhaps sub-hysterical flippancy. She must have sensed my precarious mental state. At any rate, she laughed at me without malice and asked no more questions about my mainland stay.

We finished our makeshift meal and went down to the beach.

*The whole of mankind on two islands in the Carib Sea.* That thought kept bubbling in my head even as I held Marina's hand and walked with her along the water's edge. Incongruous. Wasn't every man a piece of the continent, a part of the main? It seemed not – not any more – in spite of what the long-dead dean of St Paul's had once written.

Paris being content with his grazing, we were going up the beach to find Hector; as we walked, Marina did not permit me to dwell on the metaphysics of mankind's general exile.

She said, 'You're done with the council now, aren't you? Now that you're back from the mainland, you'll be given a pension and time to do what you want. Isn't that so, Markcrier?'

'So that accounts for my welcome. You're interested in my money.'

'It's true, then?'

'I don't know yet. Serenos hasn't mentioned the matter since my return. How did you happen to know about it?'

'Can't you guess?'

'Your father?'

She nodded. 'I ask only because I want it to be true.

21

For your sake, Markcrier – not because the matter might in some way concern me.'

I had nothing to say to that. The sea came up and covered our feet, then slid back down the wetted shingles as if unable to obtain purchase. I, too, was barefoot now, and I wondered how many bare feet and how many beaches this one same wave throughout the world had laved, this one same wave since Troy.

'My father and I have seen Fearing Serenos many times since your departure. We've been in his company often, Markcrier.'

I looked at her. 'Why?'

'Invitations. Always invitations.'

'But just for you and your father. Never for Melantha? Never for your mother also?'

'Never.'

I halted her and held her shoulders. 'A transparent arrangement.'

'Yes,' she said. 'But in the last two months I've been able to put him off. He's been busy, and I've spent a great deal of time sketching and collecting – with the Galleon of the Hesperides as my base.'

'Has the Navarch mentioned marriage to you or your father?'

'No. That would be a loss of face, I suppose. He wants the first word to come from us, from either Father or me.'

'Thank God for vainglorious scruple.'

We looked at each other but said nothing. There was no need. We resumed walking, holding hands.

Finally we left the beach and clambered into the green underbrush. Marina ran ahead. I followed. We found Hector, a huge brown beast just as matted as Marina had said he would be, in a clearing beside a pond. His lips worked methodically on the greenness in his mouth, and his eyes unconcernedly blinked. Marina scratched him on the plane of his forehead and behind his ears. After drinking from the pond ourselves, we rode Hector back to the Galleon of the Hesperides. Although he wore no bridle,

Hector responded to the pressure of Marina's knees and carried us surely home.

We arrived at four or five in the afternoon. The white blister of the sun had fallen further towards the westward sea, and the light had thinned to a frightening paleness.

We released Hestor at the foot of the rise upon which Paris still grazed, and the heavy mud-and-salt-encrusted creature plodded up the hillside to join his stablemate. Paris, glad for the company, tossed his mane, stomped, whinnied. Two convivial geldings at the top of the world, they murmured anecdotes to each other out of tirelessly working lips.

'Come on,' I said to Marina.

'Where? We're home.'

'Into the broken section of hull – where the flowers are.'

She did not protest. She followed me. We waded into the long narrow channel that snaked up the beach from the sea; we splashed through this ankle-deep water towards the ship. At the hull's sea-ripped portal we had to duck our heads, but we passed through it without scraping flesh, without having to crawl. Inside, the smell of rotting wood, tempered by the smell of mallow and tropic rose, was not unpleasant. Though even paler here, the afternoon light ceased to frighten me; instead it cast a warm white haze over the groined interior walls, over the clover that sprang from the mud embankments on both sides of the rivulet. Marina and I faced each other. We might have been in a ballroom, so spacious and warm seemed the foreward bilge of the Galleon of the Hesperides.

'We could have stayed outside,' Marina said, not rebuking me. 'I've seen no one on the beaches in all the time I've been camping and working here.'

'I didn't want it that way. I wanted shelter and just you with me in the closeness of that shelter.'

'Those things are yours, Markcrier.'

I took her face in my hands and kissed her. We moved out of the rivulet, still kissing, and went down on our knees on one of the clovered embankments, went down together with infinite mansuetude and care. The sea exhorted us.

23

Kneeling face to face, we unclothed each other. I removed the sleeveless hauberk from her shoulders and let the garment crumple to the ground behind her. She unlaced my tunic, she slipped it away from me, she pressed one perfect hand against my chest. Her eyes would not remove from mine.

'A child, Markcrier, are you afraid of a child?'

'No,' I said. I had no time to say anything else.

'I'm not afraid of a child, even if we never married. But if it would displease you, the thought of my deformity being passed on; if you were to think me immoral for taking that chance—'

'There'll be no child,' I said.

She looked at me expectantly, curiously, awaiting an explanation.

'There'll be no child because it isn't given to me to create one, Marina. We have both been visited by the ash, but my punishment is in some ways the crueller: sterility. Invisible but insidious.'

After a moment she said, 'Are you certain?'

'I'm forty-one years old.' And I had some understanding of the medusa of man's heart. 'Does it make a difference to you?'

She leaned forward. She kissed me briefly. 'No. I would have borne your children gladly, but had they been ... *wrong*, somehow like me ... I would have hated myself for making them suffer.'

I covered her mouth with my own. Then we broke apart and clumsily finished removing our clothes. Although we were both adults and forgave each other for being human, our clumsiness embarrassed us. Marina turned aside and smoothed out her wrinkled hauberk for a resting place. This delay also confused us, but we embraced again and eased our naked bodies together – eased ourselves backwards on to Marina's garment until our slow passion had deafened us to both our own breathing and the easy lapping of water against wood.

Without even thinking to be so, I was slow and easefully rhythmic; Marina ran a silken hand over the small

24

of my back while her seawing – her ash-given seawing – clasped my flank. When I came, we were not together; but Marina held me as if I were part of her, and we lay without uncoupling for the duration of the afternoon's pale light.

The vulva smell of the sea intensified as the light failed, and soon we slept in each other's arms in a bed partaking of (as it necessarily must) the smells of the sea's basins.

The next day was Christmas. We saw white otters cavorting on the sand.

# Two

*There is no life which does not violate the injunction 'Be not anxious.' That is the tragedy of human sin. It is the tragedy of man who is dependent upon God, but seeks to make himself independent and self-sufficing.*

*– Reinhold Niebuhr*

We were married on the first day of the new century.

The ceremony took place on the bay of Pretty Coal Sack, and the sky pulsed with the blue-white urgency of an adder's eyes. The breezes blew soft; the sails of the vessels in the harbour puffed out with their airy pregnancies.

And although the Navarch was present among the guests, he did not preside over our brief nuptials as we had asked him to do. Instead, after the recitation of vows, he spoke with me in an abstracted manner for a few minutes and then kissed Marina on the cheek and wished her happiness. Marina tried to draw him out; she told him of the white otters we had seen and teased him about his over-done wedding-day solemnity. 'This isn't a wake,' she said. 'You're permitted to smile.' 'Oh, I smile, Marina, I smile in my own inward way.' Then he bowed and left us. For the next twenty minutes he conferred with two elderly council members who happened to be standing on the periphery of the circle of our guests.

Between sips of rum and perfunctory exchanges of banter, I could not help glancing at him. His presence compelled attention. Moreover, Serenos had made a point of not speaking to Yves Prendick at all; that fact, along with his conspiratorial conference with my two former colleagues, cast a shadow over everything. I could not convince myself that these three venerable men were discussing only Windfall Last's innumerable social problems.

As a consequence, the seven riflemen who had come for the purpose of protecting the Navarch began to look like hired assassins. Positioned on two sections of the stone wall that partially enclosed the bayside altar, these men guarded all of us from assault with hunched, seemingly stupid backs. One or two of them stared down with set mouths. For that year had been notable for the number of bloody confrontations between the Navarch's Gendarmerie and the disorganised but sometimes murderous packs of prol-fauves that had taken to roaming the harbour area. When Serenos left, however, he designated only two of these riflemen to remain behind as our protection against the prol-fauves. I did not greatly fear these debased human creatures, but the Navarch's parsimonious allotment of gendarmes amounted to a not-to-be-ignored expression of displeasure. And the displeasure of Fearing Serenos frightened me more than any rampant horde of prol-fauves.

I had not expected such curtness from the Navarch. On the day after Christmas I had gone to him and reminded him of his promise of releasing me from formal government service. He had acknowledged both his promise and his unaltered intent to honour that promise.

'When, m'Lord?' I had asked.

'Immediately. But for a single lapse, Markcrier, you have served me well for more than twenty years – twice among the mongrel Parfects. You deserve whatever I can grant you: pension, comfort, access to my person, permanent status as a member of the Navarchy.'

'And marriage if I wish?'

'Marriage,' he said slowly, the hair on his cheek planes rippling with an involuntary grimace, 'if you wish.' He looked at me. 'I can tell that you've settled on someone, that you're asking my permission. Isn't that so, Markcrier?'

'Yes, m'Lord.'

'And the woman is Marina Prendick. That's so, too, isn't it?'

I admitted what he had already guessed.

27

Serenos paced the chamber, his brutal hands clasped in front of him. I realised that the delicate brindle fur on the man's face, the fur concealing everything but his hard rat's eyes, made it impossible to determine his age. How old was he? How long had he ruled in Windfall Last before I became a member of his privileged council?

Serenos stopped pacing. He made an unhappy gesture with one of those brutal hands. 'You have my permission, Markcrier – but only because it is you who have asked. I set one condition. Will you hear it?'

No alternative existed. 'I will hear it, Navarch.'

'You are still a young man. One day I will call upon you to perform an additional service to Windfall Last. When that day comes, you will do as I ask.'

'A legitimate service to the people, Navarch?' My question very nearly violated propriety, the distance between servant and lord. But I did not wish to be trapped by a man whose motives I did not trust.

'I would ask you no other kind,' he said sharply. 'A legitimate service to your people. Agreed?'

'Yes, Navarch.'

And at that, Fearing Serenos had smiled like a water spaniel lolling its tongue. My fears were put to rest, for the Navarch smiled only when genuinely pleased, never as a means of expressing contempt or sarcasm. Therefore, I believed that no stigma would attach to my marriage with Marina, that the dangers we had imagined were indeed wholly imaginary ones. It is true that Serenos declined my invitation to preside at the wedding, but he had done so with self-effacing charm, pleading that he had long since forgotten the sequence of the rites and arguing that he did not choose to embarrass us with his clumsiness. I had expected this explanation and departed from his chambers a happy man.

Then, on the day of the wedding, the first day of the new century, I stood on the harbour flagstones and watched Serenos climb the stone steps that would lead him to the administrative cluster of Windfall Last and the hilltop battlements of the Palace of the Navarchy. Five brightly uniformed riflemen accompanied him; two remained behind.

Although no one but Marina's father and I seemed to realise it, we had been reprimanded. I knew that a reckoning would come. I walked among our many guests, sipped rum, ate orange slices, talked – but all the while I tried to anticipate the outward form that the Navarch's displeasure would take. No man, I supposed, deserved to live out his life in complete freedom from anxiety (nature did not ordain man for insouciance), but neither should a man have to contend daily with arbitrary and featureless threats to his sanity. The two riflemen on the harbour parapet became symbols of a doom over which neither Yves Prendick nor I had any control. At that moment, an attack by the prol-fauves would have been preferable to the uncertainty that Serenos had bred in us – even with only two members of the Gendarmerie on the wall as our defenders.

In my distraction I began staring out to sea, wondering in which waters the rapacious sharks had attempted to slake their eternal hunger. I must have appeared forbidding company, for no one disturbed me.

That afternoon Marina and I returned to the Galleon of the Hesperides. We remained there a week. We did not see the white otters again, but no one came out from Windfall Last to summon us back. Still, I expected a messenger from the Navarch to arrive at any moment (sometimes I imagined an entire contingent of armed guards) to escort us, under arrest, back to the city. The white Carib sun could not burn away these fears, and Marina became aware of my uneasiness. I had to tell her what I feared. She accepted my account with a sort of facetious stoicism and kissed me. Our week drew to an end. Much to my surprise, no one murdered us in our sleep.

We returned to Windfall Last and took up residence in a climbing free-form structure on Dr Prendick's estate, The Orchard. Grass and trees surrounded us, and our white dwelling, shaped from a plastic foam that had dried to the graininess of stucco, surrounded the bole of a giant magnolia palm. The Parfects had created both tree and house long before mankind's enforced removal to the island, just as they had built almost everything else on Guardian's Loop.

Like the tentacled devil-fish that take over the shelters of other departed sea creatures, Marina and I moved into this sinuously magnificent dwelling. Her father called it Python's Keep. In our first years there, we seldom used that name, but the house did sheathe us as comfortably as its latest unshedded skin contains a serpent.

I continued to wait. We were left alone. Marina sketched, painted water-colours, worked at planting a vegetable garden in a sunlit section of the lawn. I made excursions to the Sunken Library. There I gathered material for a comparative literary history of the most interesting periods prior to Holocaust A. In the evenings we sometimes visited with Marina's parents. Yves told me a little of what was going on in the council sessions; Melantha gossiped with her daughter as if there were no difference in age at all. I also wrote poetry, much of it as good as any I had ever written. And, of course, Marina and I fell into the not entirely unpleasant routines of people who are married. No children came from our love, but we had expected none.

Nevertheless, I continued to wait. Not for children, but for the reckoning I was sure must come.

Occasionally I saw the Navarch. He inquired about my work, gave his best to Marina, scrupulously avoided mentioning the affairs of Windfall Last. Although I continued to wait for the inevitable reckoning, my memory fogged. I could not explain to myself the source of my nagging, subliminal anxiety. Where had it come from?

The years went by. Nothing occurred to suggest that Fearing Serenos had worked out his delayed wrath against us. Had Marina and I been spared? Did the Navarch possess both a conscience and a forgiving nature?

Other occurrences led me to discard these hopes as vain ones.

In 5306 the Gendarmerie went into the streets on administrative command. On the first day they slaughtered a pack of prol-fauves; the fighting (riflemen against rock throwers, bottle wielders and slingshot artists) lasted three hours and resulted in the deaths of eighty-two illiterate, shambling yahoos, not one of whom died understanding his predicament. There was blood from this engagement on the harbour flagstones for nearly a year, red-brown stains that gradually faded under the natural corrosives of sea water and pigeon crap. On the following days the Gendarmerie killed at a less spectacular rate; but riding horseback along the waterfront and shooting any adult male who had the twin credentials of raggedness and glassy-eyed idiocy, they managed to bag thirty or forty more. Eventually, even the most cretinous of the prol-fauves learned to stay away from the areas of patrol; and the once-vicious packs, never truly cohesive except in situations of unthinking rampage, disintegrated into a scattering of frightened, pitiable half-men. Taking pity, the Gendarmerie apprehended these stragglers instead of shooting them.

Public executions took place. In order to conserve rifle and small-arms ammunition (which the government manufactured on a limited scale for its own use), Serenos decreed that the captured prol-fauves would suffer decapitation. On several scaffolds erected at bayside, the blade fell more times than anyone but the sadists on the Navarch's council desired to count. Crowds oohed at each new delicious dramatisation, while the resultant gore drew another sort of devotee – carrion flies that iridesced in blue-green clusters over the damp scaffolds.

The majority of the population of Windfall Last accepted these tactics with delight and approval. Had not the Navarch dealt decisively with a troublesome social menace? This delight and approval continued unabated even when the Gendarmerie began mounting the severed heads on spikes and positioning the spikes at four-metre intervals along the harbour wall.

I recalled that I had once mentioned to Serenos the Elizabethan practice of ornamenting London Bridge in a like manner. How often I discovered that I had indirectly abetted the man's barbarism. This knowledge made me suffer uncannily.

Marina and I spent almost all our time at The Orchard. Python's Keep was secure, removed, isolated. Neither of us wished to go into Windfall Last and witness the grotesque reality of men's heads impaled on iron stakes, staring inland with hideous incomprehension. Too, I did not care to be reminded of my own failure to intervene in some way – or of the possible consequences of any such intervention. After all, the Navarch no doubt continued to believe that I had a debt outstanding, a debt he had consciously deferred the collection of. My anxiety was already too great to risk incurring another debt. In these ways I rationalised my refusals to act.

In 5307 the only word I had of the Navarch came to me through Yves Prendick, who had maintained his status both as Serenos' physician and as a member of the council of the Navarchy. Prendick said that Serenos never mentioned either Marina or me and that the old head-chopper's health could be characterised by the single word *excellent*. Like me, Prendick did not know how old the Navarch was: it seemed that he had ruled Windfall Last forever and that we would be foolish to count on his dying very soon.

About this time Marina and I noted a strange thing about her father. Though he frequently marvelled at the physical condition of his principal patient, he began to spend an untoward amount of time either tending to him or working in the theatre of surgery where he (Prendick) had trained as a young man. Prendick did not talk about these long sessions away from The Orchard, except to deny that Serenos was ill. 'I'm engaged in some difficult experimentation which I've undertaken upon the Navarch's order. I can't say any more. I won't.' Having said this, he would invariably fall into silence or stride out of the room. In three months' time he grew irritable, whey-faced and abstracted. And I, in turn, grew as suspicious of Marina's father as a man may be of someone he still respects and loves. What had happened to Prendick? What was he about? What did he mean by 'difficult experimentation'?

Obsessed with these questions and a nebulous fear almost eight years old, I concluded that Prendick would be the Navarch's instrument of revenge. Fearing Serenos had forced Marina's father to an insidious betrayal. By what means he had done so, I could not even guess.

But I was wrong. The Navarch required no helpmates beyond his own cunning and faithlessness. Although I did not then understand this fact, the day of reckoning was fast approaching.

On the anniversary of my wedding, New Year's Day, 5308, I received word at Python's Keep that His Excellency Fearing Serenos desired my presence in the chambers of the Navarchy in the newly renovated administrative palace. At once. Without delay. This rococo complex of turrets and arches overlooked the entire city of Windfall Last from a hill that the Parfects had raised inland from the bay, and I knew that it would take me almost twenty minutes to reach the palace from Dr Prendick's outlying estate. By then it would be noon, the precise hour that Marina and I had exchanged our vows.

Now that the anticipated moment had actually come, I found myself oddly composed: numbness and resignation, resignation and numbness. Not even Marina's tears could penetrate the shell of plastic indifference into which I withdrew. We had had seven complete years together, Marina and I. How much more could two ephemeral, parasitic creatures expect? The earth was not made for man, but we had fooled it for seven fruitful years.

I should have taken Prendick's autocart, but I did not. Knowing that my journey would take nearly an hour longer, I saddled Hector, now a tired, plodding beast, and left The Orchard on horseback. The white sun shimmered overhead, and in my numbness I almost forgot that I carried neither pistol nor rifle. What for? To be torn apart by renegade prol-fauves before reaching the Navarch's chambers would have been an exquisite irony.

And Serenos did not appreciate irony.

*Then let it befall,* I prayed to no one in particular.

The Navarch's private chambers breathed with the vegetable moistness of a garden. Ushered into this closed hothouse over a thick scarlet carpet, I was made giddy with the richness of the air. Vines tumbled down the walls, rough stone showed behind the vines, the upper portion of a tree grew through the floor in one leafy corner. I saw tapestries hanging free from two interior doorways. I saw also a large glass aquarium occupying a third of the wall opposite me. Golden fish swam through the fern-crowded waters there – golden fish, all of them golden. (*But where were the silver-grey sharks: the stupid dogfish with their evil porcine eyes?*) And then I saw the gleaming mahogany-red surface of the Navarch's desk and, behind it, the illustrious person of Fearing Serenos himself. I had not seen him face to face in over two years.

'You're late, Markcrier,' he said. 'Approach.'

I approached. There was not a chair other than the Navarch's in the room. I stood before the man and waited for some word from him. In no hurry to satisfy my numb curiosity, he leaned back and extended his arms inside the loose sleeves of the silken, canary-yellow robe that bore the emblem of his office – a stylised ship in scarlet thread – over his left breast. Then he interlaced his fingers, dropped his hands to his lap, and examined me as if I were an exotic artifact washed ashore from Azteca Nueva. The image of a mischievous baboon who has just raided the wardrobe of a prince played before my eyes. I had to fight the image down.

'It's good to see you, Markcrier. It's good to know that you're a man who honours his commitments – even if he does so tardily.'

'I obey my Navarch, m'Lord.'

'In everything?'

'In everything that a man can reasonably be expected to obey.'

His voice took on a husky resonance. 'You equivocate.'

I held my tongue.

'You do remember, don't you, M. Rains, the commitment that you made to me seven years ago? The promise that you gave me virtually on the eve of your wedding?'

'I've been unable to forget.'

'Yes, I know. The strain has aged you, Markcrier.'

I told him what his appearance told me. 'You, m'Lord, have not changed. You've borne the troubles of these last several years without alteration.'

The Navarch nodded. 'Quite true.' He looked directly at me. 'But even though you've aged, Markcrier, you've not suffered. Your existence on Guardian's Loop has been an idyllic one. Leisure in which to write. A home well removed from two million citizens less fortunate than yourself. And' – he paused for a moment – 'a beautiful wife.'

I wanted to sit down. My hands had begun to sweat, and this allusion to Marina chipped a little of the enamel off my shell of indifference. I said, 'No, I've not suffered.'

'Indeed you haven't. But, M. Rains, you have earned all the things I've just mentioned, and no one begrudges you.'

'That pleases me, Navarch.'

'However, one cannot expect to live out his entire lifetime on exhausted past earnings. Don't you agree?'

'I'm afraid I don't understand,' I said, not understanding.

'Just as I told you to expect. I now want you to perform another service for Windfall Last.'

'I want to sit down,' I said. It took three or four awkward minutes, during which time Serenos studied me with arrogant dispassion, but someone finally brought in a chair. I sat down. The fish in the aquarium hovered seemingly just out of reach; I felt that I was swimming among them.

'What is it you want me to do?' I asked when we were again alone.

'Go among the Parfects again. They no longer wish to

35

wait a decade between visits from our envoys. Some urgency compels them.'

I gripped the sides of my chair, digging my nails into the wood.

'I ask you,' Fearing Serenos continued, 'because you are still not an old man and because your knowledge of the Parfects is so much more complete than that possessed by any of the rest of us.' The voice was insultingly oily, as if the Navarch already knew what my answer would be.

'No,' I said. 'You have no right to ask that of me.'

'I may ask of you anything I like. Further, I may compel you to perform whatever I ask. Do you understand that, M. Rains?'

I spoke out of a profound numbness, a numbness entirely independent of the words that fell from my mouth. 'No, m'Lord. You may not compel me in this.'

'Indeed?'

'No, m'Lord.'

'But I could, Markcrier. I could do so quite easily.' His jowls reminded me of those of a large brindle dog. 'Do you know how?'

'I have seen the heads on the spikes.'

'Prol-fauves, every one. They have nothing to do with you, Markcrier.'

'Nevertheless, I have something to do with them. Even should you threaten me with tortures, Navarch, I will not go among the Parfects again. You yourself pledged to spare me from that possibility seven years ago.'

'*No* is your final answer, then?'

'I have no hesitation in rejecting to perform a service that you have no right to ask of me.'

'You insist on an extremely limited construction of what my rights consist of, M. Rains. In reality, no limits exist. At this very moment I could kill you without qualm or compunction, simply for refusing me. But I won't. You've already failed the major test of your loyalty to me — when I have given you everything that a man requires for his comfort.'

Fearing Serenos stood up and walked in his sweeping

yellow robes over the scarlet carpet to the tree that grew up through the floor. His hand touched something on the wall, and the ceiling opened like a giant Venetian blind – a blind with invisible louvres. White light sifted down through the skylight and paled the climbing foliage.

Serenos said, 'I will give you the opportunity of performing a humbler mission so that you may both keep your word and repay me for maintaining you in your present comfort. Will you undertake this second mission, as humble as it is, without asking me another question?'

'Will it benefit Windfall Last?'

*'Not another question!'* he roared, shaking a fist. He paced for a full minute, enraged. Then he calmed and stared at me again. 'Answer me, Markcrier: Will you do what I ask of you or not? Be quick.'

I stood up. I no longer had the bravado to deny one of the Navarch's commands. Even if the trap were about to snap shut on me, the trap I had anticipated for so long, I could say nothing but what he expected. 'Yes, I'll accomplish your *humble* mission for you. What is it?'

'A visit to some old friends.'

Once again, the spectre of exile. I had an instantaneous understanding of who my 'old friends' were. My hands trembled.

'The fishermen on Marigold,' Serenos said by way of needless explanation. 'The ones you lived with for fourteen months.'

'How long will I visit them this time?'

Serenos laughed. 'Don't fear me, Markcrier. As I said, this is a humble mission and it will require you to be away from your home and wife only a very brief time. A humble mission. You earn it by your forfeiture of the more important one.' He laughed again, darkly.

'Who, then, will you send to the Parfects?'

'Now, now, M. Rains, don't begin to worry about the opportunity you've rejected. I imagine I can put the Parfects off a bit.'

'Well, then, what am I to accomplish on Marigold Island?'

'There is an old man there whom you know quite well, I should think. An old fisherman. His name is Huerta.' Serenos paused for my response.

'I know him,' I said.

'Very good. Greet this man for me, tell him that I am lifting the interdict on his colony so that those who wish to return to Windfall Last may do so. Then bring him back with you. If it's possible, I will speak to him as one ruler to another.' The Navarch crossed the carpet and stood directly in front of me. I had forgotten how tall the man was. He was of a height with the Parfects of smaller stature. 'Can you accomplish this humble task for me, Markcrier?'

'Yes, m'Lord.'

'Then do so. A ship will be waiting for you in the morning. Go to the Navarch's quay at sunrise.' He turned his back on me and looked at the monstrously magnified fish in his aquarium.

'Yes, m'Lord.'

And with his back still to me he said, 'I'll never ask anything of you again, Markcrier.'

On that cryptic note I went out.

In the morning I sailed to the fishermen's colony of Barbos on Marigold Island. Mankind still owned ships, still went out on the waters in slim vessels whose narrow bodies imaged the form of woman. Marina was such a vessel, bearing the burdens of our shared nights and loving with me against death. A ship was love, a woman was love. And it may be that the Parfects' knowledge of this fact had persuaded them to grant us movement on the seas, for they had denied us land vehicles and flying machines (with the exception of small balsa wood gliders and battery-powered carts). In the early days of the Navarchy on Guardian's Loop, many sailors had hoped to use their ships as means of escaping the power of men such as Fearing Serenos. But there was no place to go. The Parfects would not permit these ships to make harbour anywhere in the world but at Windfall Last. Therefore, every vessel that departed port either returned home again or died the pelagic death of creatures infinitely older than man. Still, the sea continued to exist for our love, and ships moved over it, ships that imaged the form of woman.

Huerto greeted me warmly. He remembered my fourteen-months' exile on Marigold Island. And I remembered him.

He was an incredibly ugly old man with bandy legs and a chin that was joined by both bone and flesh to his sternum. He had virtually no neck and walked with his shoulders thrown exaggeratedly back in order to compensate for the earth-locked angle of his head and eyes. His rib cage jutted. His heavy mouth had been pressed into an obligatory pout. Fortunately, he smelled only of salt water and fish oil, not of the bile and sulphur of an imbalanced body chemistry.

Standing on the beach with Huerta triggered a series of remarkable memories, pictures of Huerta's people fifteen years ago and of a bewildered young council member dirtying his hands with physical labour, suffering the stench and closeness of a variety of man he had not entirely believed in. Now I was back. But this time for only three days.

After entertaining me with clumsy feasts and sentimental trips to other encampments, Huerta at last delegated his authority to a one-eyed man of twenty or so (where there should have been another eye, there was not even a socket – only smooth umblemished flesh); and we departed Marigold Island on the afternoon of the third day.

At dusk on the homeward voyage I looked over the starboard railing and thought I saw the triangular caudal fins of four or five small sharks. But the turquoise glinting of the sea made perception difficult, and no one stood beside me to corroborate what I had seen. The last time I had sighted sharks (which was also the first and only time they had performed their cruel ballet for me), Huerta and I had been out together in his wooden skiff. Fifteen years ago. Could it be that these sleek fishes were returning to the waters of man? For no reason at all I thought of Fearing Serenos. When the sun finally set, bloodying the sea with its last light, I suffered a profound depression and went below decks to seek company.

We reached Windfall Last between midnight and dawn – I had no notion of the exact time. Huerta was taken from me by three uniformed men in cloaks. They had been waiting since the previous noon, they said, and assured me that Huerta would reach the Palace of the Navarchy safely. A bed awaited him, and the old man would have an audience with Serenos in the morning. I said goodbye to my old friend and declined the gendarmes' invitation to go with them to the Palace. I had decided to sleep in my own bed, beside Marina.

Since we had arrived at such an awkward hour, however, I had no transportation back to Python's Keep. Nevertheless, I did not go aboard again, but paced beside the ship's black, impassive hull. The stars scoured fuzzy haloes into the face of the night, and my feet, as I walked, made echoing *tlaks* on the flagstones.

Grotesque in the starlight, the impaled heads of the latest batch of slaughtered prol-fauves stretched away from me down both directions of the harbour wall. I tried not to look at them.

I had almost resolved to wake somebody up (perhaps even the Navarch himself, although that would have required a long walk and I had already declined one invitation to stay in the Palace) when a horse-drawn wagon came rattling down the street. This wagon, as it happened, belonged to the shipmaster, a taciturn man who had refused to say more than four words to me on our entire voyage. He came down the plank from his vessel at almost the same moment that the wagon ceased its wooden moanings; and I asked, then importuned, and then reluctantly ordered the man to give me passage home. Python's Keep was some distance out of his way, and he refused to behave as if he were not annoyed. He disapproved of the Navarch's lifting of the interdict, he resented me, and he thought Huerta (if I correctly interpreted his avoidance of the fisherman aboard ship) the vilest and most stomach-souring creature he had ever encountered. Strangely enough, the shipmaster's own wagoner looked himself to be a kind of living abortion – he had no arms and no tongue and smelled of dried excrement. He drove the wagon by manipulating the reins with his bare feet.

When Dr Prendick's estate, The Orchard, at last came into view, green-black trees tangled against a lightening sky, I got down with relish and left my two charming comrades without a word.

Python's Keep was not dark. A light burned behind the stained-glass port in the sculptured module at the base of the palm. A light for the returning voyager? My heart quickened; I did not think so. The stillness on the lawn was not the stillness of the tender hours before sunrise. It was another kind of stillness entirely.

I ran to Python's Keep, the taste of copper, like the grease from old coins, poisonous in my mouth.

Seated on the driftwood chair in the receiving chamber, Yves Prendick stared up at me with scoured eyes when I came in. His thinning grey hair stuck out comically on all sides as if he had just risen from bed. But because his head was tilted back a little, I could see his exposed throat and the angry lip of a long cut just above his Adam's apple. For a moment – so still did Marina's father seem – I thought he was dead. But the cut was a shallow one, and Prendick blinked at me, pulled himself erect, and raised an unsteady hand.

His voice seemed almost to come out of the wound in his throat. 'Markcrier, Markcrier.' He looked at me imploringly. 'Don't go upstairs, she won't know you for a while anyway, so don't go up there, please, Markcrier.'

'Prendick!' I grabbed his shoulders. 'What do you mean "won't know me"? Why the hell won't she know me?'

I turned to go up the stairs, but Prendick leaned forward, clutched the bottom of my tunic, and pulled me down to my knees with surprising strength. His eyes shimmered behind a wild provocative film. 'No,' he said,

'Don't do that. Her mother's with her now, Melantha's up there with her, and she'll be all right if you control yourself.'

'Prendick! Prendick, tell me what's happened!'

And restraining me with both hands, holding me on my knees before him like a supplicant before a priest, Marina's father told me what had happened. I continued to stare at the wound in his throat, the crimson lip that wrinkled as he talked. I thought: *The story you're telling me is an unpleasant story, I don't like it, it must be coming out of the angry half-developed mouth under your chin, a small malicious mouth, a story that has nothing to do with the sea and ships, a murderous narrative from an evil mouth, like the ravening undercut mouth of a shark, even though the sea has nothing to do, I don't think, with the malicious words that wrinkle under your chin.* On my knees before Prendick, I listened.

'Early yesterday afternoon Fearing Serenos raped your wife, Markcrier,' my wife's father said.

'He came to The Orchard with three soldiers of the Gendarmerie, found me in the main house, and invited me to accompany him to Python's Keep. He was extremely cordial, he talked of the work I've been doing for him, he said Marina deserved some word of explanation in regard to his disruption of your anniversary. He wanted to apologise, to explain. He thought highly of Marina. He said, "You know how much I think of your daughter, Yves. You've always known, I think. You both deserve some evidence of my esteem for you," or something very much like that. We went together to Python's Keep; the cloaked gendarmes followed, laughing with each other as soldiers do, as if they shared a joke. I thought that Serenos would order them to wait for us on the lawn. He did not; he asked them to enter Python's Keep with their dirty boots and their smelly rifles.

'Marina came down the stairs from the third-level module. The Navarch continued to chat amiably with me, the soldiers to whisper. I suspected nothing – even though the presence of the gendarmes bothered me.

42

'When Marina reached him and extended her arm in greeting, Serenos pulled her to him, kissed her violently, and then slapped her, once with each hand. "This is for your father," he said. "And this is for your husband." The soldiers laughed.

'I lurched forward, but one of the gendarmes slammed the butt of his rifle on my instep. Another pushed me into the wall and leaned against me with his forearm, choking off my breath. Marina screamed, but Serenos covered her mouth with his hand and raked her cheek with his nails. I could see blood, Markcrier, in the openings between his fingers, and the sight of it made me lurch forward again. Again, the rifle butt. Again, the gendarme shoving me to the wall. This time he put the blade of a long crescent-shaped knife under my chin and held it so that I could not move my head.

'"Make a sound," he said, "and I will slice your jugular."

'The third soldier ripped Marina's gown away from her, tore it straight down her body, uncovered her for their greedy eyes. Then the Navarch grabbed the hem and tore it up to her waist. He put his knee between her legs. When she screamed, her mouth uncovered again, he struck her with the flat of his hand. I strained forward, but the gendarme who held me lifted the blade of his knife against my throat; I felt its edge slice into me.

'I was helpless, Markcrier. I could have died, I suppose, but I didn't have the courage to die. They made me watch as Serenos beat my daughter insensible; they made me watch him rape her, viciously rape her as the soldiers laughed. He lifted her like a puppet, again and again with his hands and body, biting her on the lips until they bled. I shut my eyes, Markcrier, I couldn't stand it. But by the laughter and the noise I know that Serenos raped her twice, once for her father, once for her husband.

'I wished that I could force my head forward, slice open my throat on the gendarme's knife. But I couldn't, I just couldn't, my body wouldn't move, and after a while it was over.'

43

The story was over, the shark's undercut mouth ceased its wrinklings, the evil mouth resolved into a wound, and I found my strength coming back into me – just as if a soul-tormented priest had granted me absolution for the sin of doubting him. I stood up. Prendick's hands fell away from me.

'What about the gendarmes?' I said.

'No. He wouldn't let them touch her. They wanted to, but he wouldn't let them. They were afraid of him.'

'Everyone's afraid of him.'

Prendick sobbed.

'I'm going upstairs to my wife,' I said.

As the stained-glass windows began to colour with the translucent coming of dawn, I climbed the winding stairs to the room where Marina lay.

# Three

*Thou talkest of harvest when the corn is green:*
*The end is crown of every work well done;*
*The sickle comes not, till the corn be ripe.*

— *Thomas Kyd*

*... Strange as it may seem to the unscientific reader, there*
*can be no denying that, whatever amount of credibility*
*attaches to this story, the manufacture of monsters ... is*
*within the possibility of vivisection.*

— *H. G. Wells*

I contemplated revenge, even if it meant the abrogation of many things that I believed in and perhaps even my own death. I discussed revenge with Prendick, but his work in the theatre of surgery kept him occupied seemingly day and night now, and he was too weary upon returning to The Orchard each evening to listen to the ignorant schemes I had concocted during his absences. His mysterious work – the work he would not talk about – drained him; it continued with more urgency than before Marina's rape. When he was home, however, I badgered him.

Once he told me pointedly that I should shut up. 'If we fail,' he said, 'I'm afraid of what will happen to our family, to Marina and Melantha. You haven't thought about that, have you?' Still, the idea nagged. Only when Marina began to recover and became aware of what I was contemplating did the idea finally die. Marina helped it to its death.

'Markcrier,' she said, 'think about the way you've conducted your life. You're a genuinely good man – one of the few who live in Windfall Last.'

'That's a rankly sentimental judgment.'

'But a fair one. Now you wish to comport yourself in a way wholly out of keeping with the way you've lived.'

'I want what's right.'

'It isn't right to take a life when one hasn't been lost. I'm alive, Markcrier, I'm with you at this very moment.'

And so I did nothing. Having been given a lesson in the morality of post-Holocaust B (a morality that Serenos did not subscribe to), I kissed Marina, tended to her during the long days of her recuperation, achieved a strange inner peacefulness, and wrote two sections of a long poem which I called *Archipelagoes*. My doing nothing about Serenos, Marina convinced me, was in reality an active reaffirmation of the ethos that made us who we were. Three weeks lapsed.

We discovered that Marina was pregnant.

My own sterility mocked me, the fierce chagrin of the seedless. But too much philosophy ruled me, and I fought down both my chagrin and my incipient rage – with self-administered doses of temperance. I could see that Marina wanted the child. I did not tell her that I would never be able to love it. How could I tell her? We had resolved to live as intelligent human beings, we had determined not to seek revenge, we had committed ourselves to affirmation and love. My inner peacefulness dissolved, but I would dissimulate if Marina's happiness depended on thinking me happy. Unfortunately, it did. It always had. However, a diplomat learns how to role-play early in his career, and for the first time in our married lives I role-played for Marina. But God! how my own sterility mocked me, how my cancerous chagrin gnawed!

I acted my role well. The only clue I gave Marina to my real feelings was the fact that I did not resume work on *Archipelagoes*. This failure of discipline I attributed to excitement; there were too many other things to do. The mother in her aroused, the wife in her less perceptive, Marina believed me.

And for the final six months of her pregnancy I kept up the deception. I very nearly convinced myself that nothing was wrong, that we were indeed happy. But at night in bed I lay awake, knowing the truth. Before it became uncomfortable for her, I often turned to Marina in the early morning and kissed her half-awake and entered her with inarticulate desperation. She responded as best she could. She imagined that I had grown amorous with the psychological aphrodisiac of a new image of her – the image of her as a fertile, child-carrying woman. My amorousness derived instead from my intense need to believe that the child she carried had sprung from my own flesh: there was no love inside me on these mornings, only the sickness of my need and the mechanical impulse to fuck away the nightmares that pursued me through every waking moment. But in our shared waking hours I kept up the deception. I am certain that she never knew. And she had either forgotten or forced herself not to think of the possibility of the child's being deformed.

Her time came upon her early. An hour before midnight.

We had expected her father to deliver the baby, but Prendick was busy in Windfall Last, occupied as always in the performance of his duty. Fearing Serenos ruled him, but Serenos ruled us all. Even when locked behind his own bedchamber doors, the Navarch manipulated the strings of our lives. Sometimes he could not have known in what pernicious ways.

Marina's contractions were frequent and long in duration; they caused intense pain in her lower back. We had made no provisions for the child's coming so early, and I did not know what to do. My wife's pain frightened me. After making Marina as comfortable as I could on our dishevelled bed, I told her that I was going to the main house to fetch her mother. She understood, she told me that she would be all right, she winced involuntarily, piteously, at the onset of a new contraction. I left her and went to the main house.

When Melantha and I returned, Marina was screaming. She lay with her good arm and hand behind her head, clutching a rail in the headboard. Her seawing was twisted at a level with her shoulder, flattened awkwardly

47

against the grey sheet. The linen under her hips was wet, her knees up and apart. Melantha straightened Marina's deformed arm, smoothed back the hair plastered against her brow, and helped her remove the underclothes that her amniotic fluid had soaked in breaking.

'I think this is going too fast,' Marina's mother said. She was a tall woman with thin lips and eyes the colour of bleached shells. 'Much too fast.'

'What can I do?'

'Get some fresh linen, Markcrier.'

'Shouldn't I try to reach Yves? Can't we get him here somehow?'

'I don't see how. Just bring fresh linen, Mark. If you try to reach Yves, you'll only leave me alone for the delivery, everything's happening so quickly.' Her thin mouth was Marina's mouth. She said, 'You should be beside her – not on your way to Windfall Last.'

Marina cried out, turned her head, stared with filmed-over eyes at the ceiling. Something was wrong. Something other than simple prematurity. I went out of the room and crossed an enclosed section of scaffolding to the utility module. Through the window of clear glass I could see the moon-projected shadow of Python's Keep on the lawn, an entanglement as tortuous as death itself. I found clean fragrant linen and returned to the bedroom.

Melantha had eased Marina forward along the bed so that she could squat between her daughter's legs and receive the infant as it was born. Marina lay on the fluid-drenched bedding that I had been sent to replace. Like a serving man at one of the Navarch's dinner parties, I stood with the sheets draped over my forearm.

'Put those down. There isn't time. Hold your wife's arms.'

I obeyed. I smelled blood and salt. Leaning over Marina, I could tell that she did not see me; she squinted into a limbo somewhere beyond my head, her face was purpled with the agony of labour. 'It's going to be all right,' I said, knowing that it wouldn't. Something was wrong. Something other than early parturition.

48

Marina's mother spoke to her over the glistening mound of her belly, told her to concentrate, to push as if she were having a bowel movement. And I held Marina's shoulders and kissed away the salt on her furrowed forehead, saying, 'It's going to be all right, it's going to be all right.'

The first thing that came out of her womb came within five minutes of my return to the bedroom, so quickly did her labour progress. It was a sluggish, slowly flailing thing with a down of amber hair all over its body and tiny flippers where its hands should have been. I looked at Melantha. Her thin mouth was set. She refused to acknowledge me. She placed the whelp, umbilical cord still trailing, on the bed beside Marina and told me to wrap it in the clean linen. The thing was alive. And very small. It did not cry. Perhaps twenty minutes had passed since my summoning of Mrs Prendick from the main house – but Marina's contractions continued. She did not open her eyes; she still had not seen the product of her agony.

'There's another child, darling,' Melantha said. 'I want you to do what you did before, push when the contractions come.'

'No,' Marina said. 'Oh, please, not another one, no, no.'

'What the hell is this? What's going on? What is it?' The smell of blood and salt turned the room into a nightmarish slaughterhouse. I was powerless to control or influence events. Mrs Prendick ignored me.

'Oh, lord,' Melantha said after a while, talking in a whisper to herself. 'This one has presented me its buttocks.'

'What does that mean?' I demanded.

'A breech delivery,' she said, finally showing a fissure in her apparent invincibility. Her voice broke. She held up her bloodied hands. 'I don't know, I just don't know.'

And she didn't know, for Marina's labour went into its second hour, then its third, with no progress. Melantha had no instruments; she would not have known how to use them if she had.

When the second thing at last permitted itself to be

49

born, we had both exhausted our repertoire of hysterics. Marina was dead, the tiny creature out of her womb was dead, and Mrs Prendick, her tall body twisted around upon itself, sat slumped on the floor where she had tried to play midwife. She was not asleep, she was not awake. I covered Marina. Then I picked up Melantha, carried her to another module and placed her on a long brocaded divan. The night smelled of distant azaleas.

With that odour in my nostrils, I climbed back through the dark labyrinth of Python's Keep. As if hypnotised, I found my wife's deathbed. It had about it the ancient stillness of an archaeological dig. The corpses were remarkably well preserved, one small mummified form feigning life with shallow breaths. I picked it up and covered its mouth and nostrils with the heel and palm of my hand. It scarcely struggled. Then I lifted the other small corpse from its resting place and withdrew from the ancient tranquillity in which Marina slept. She was too far removed from me to elicit my grief.

Not grieving, merely sleep-walking, I carried the animal things from her womb downstairs to the lawn. I walked through the entangled shadow of Python's Keep.

In Marina's garden I dug shallow depressions with my bare hands and buried the things she had grown. For a long while I continued to dig; I tore at the soil with my bruised nails. At last I stopped and sat on my haunches in the dirt – almost comprehending how little free will a free man has.

For I was indeed free.

I resolved, as the tree-entangled dawn came back, to make Fearing Serenos regret the day of his own birthing. I resolved this with all the ruthlessness of incorruptible natural phenomena, the ruthlessness of sunlight and tide. Serenos would burn in a candle of gas; he would drown in the waters of a malignant moon. I resolved these things freely and knew that the Navarch would not escape my vengeance.

On the day of Marina's cremation, Prendick and I went down to the quay to scatter her ashes on the water.

We had just come from the official crematory of the Navarchy, several rows of terra-cotta houses away from Prendick's waterfront hospital. We were alone. Marina's mother had remained in the main house at The Orchard, fatigued, uncommunicative, ill.

I carried an amphora – a narrow-mouthed jar – tenderly before me. This contained the final, soot-flavoured residue of a human being, and I had to make a concerted mental and physical effort not to raise the jar to my lips and drink of my wife's ashes. Unlike the ashes, the jar was cool.

Together Yves and I descended the stone stairs to the flagstones on the quay. No ship was docked in the place we had chosen, and no sinister trunkless heads adorned the spikes along the harbour wall. The sky was the colour of milk.

I began the ritual. I poured the ashes into my hand, waited for the wind to blow away from me, and scattered the ashes over the water on this gentle wind. Silently, Prendick followed my example. As we scattered Marina's ashes on the bay, I realised that her ashes, metaphorically, were those of Holocaust C, the fallout of a miniature Armageddon. On the rainbowed water she floated like sentient dust.

God no longer prophesied doom, he was through with us, nor did the Parfects truly concern themselves with our petty murders. Dust on the water Marina was, ash on the sea.

'Yves?'

He looked at me – not with a great deal of responsiveness, his hand feebly emptying its contents on the wind. In seven months he had grown slow and morosely sullen. How often he had been forced to change.

'Yves, we're going to do something about Marina's death.'

'What?' He stared. 'What will we do?'

'Kill Serenos. Or cripple him. Make him experience, in a similar species of coin, some part of the pain he's caused others.'

'With what chance of success?' the doctor said. 'And how?'

'You have a head, you have a heart, you once had a daughter. Whatever you decide or fail to decide, I'm going to do something, something to unburden my soul.' I paused. 'As the Navarch's personal physician, you have access to him.'

Prendick stared. 'What do you mean? What're you implying?'

'That you should use your head to determine how your access to Serenos will most benefit us. A very simple thing, Yves, very simple.'

He stared at me for a long moment. Then he turned back to the water and cast a last meagre handful of ash into the sea. Our conversation was over, but Prendick had begun to think. I saw inside his head, I saw his emotions running into little wells of intellection, I saw his mind turned into a bleached brain coral and from the brain coral into an ambiguous living thing, confined but free. Soon the wind blew across the empty mouth of the amphora, and the low bass notes of emptiness arose.

We left the quay.

Three days later Prendick invited me to visit him at the theatre of surgery for an entire afternoon. Never before had he extended to me or anyone else in his immediate family such an invitation. I knew that the significance of this invitation lay in its following so obviously on our brief exchange on the quay.

Ordinarily, Prendick spent two hours every morning in the Palace of the Navarchy, whether Serenos demanded his attention or not. Then he went by carriage down the cobbled streets, past dwellings of rose-red terra cotta, to the waterfront and the only major building that the Parfects had erected among the salt-drenched quays. The theatre of surgery was located in this structure, which everyone called Hospitaler House.

A monument of aluminium and glass, its windows polarised against the sun, Hospitaler House rose fifteen storeys over the bay of Pretty Coal Sack on an immense round platform that seemed to float on the waters of the bay. Deep in the great cylindrical column upon which the Parfects had long ago erected this symbol of mercy, one might find the submerged, echoing, antiseptic chambers of the theatre of surgery – if one were lucky enough to receive an invitation. Once inside the central chamber, the visitor encountered a window of gargantuan proportions facing towards the open sea. A window on a submerged world. When the waters of the Carib lay unruffled under the refracted sky, one could almost swear that the rippling dome of the Sunken Library, further out in the bay, was visible.

A man in a frock escorted me into the central chamber of the column and departed.

I stood alone in the copper-bright vastness, the smells of alcohol and of something oddly zoo-like preeminent among the odours that clamoured there. Looking up, I saw that a kind of tier went around half the cylinder and that Prendick was standing on this level, his hands on the railing, looking down at me. He said nothing.

I navigated a path through the surgical equipment on the main floor until I was almost directly below him. His face sang with the madness of one who communes with the sea and with sea anemones, one who eats the hallucinogens of shipwreck and death. In fact, he looked like a poet – the way Markcrier Rains ought to have looked so soon after 'personal tragedy'. But he said nothing. Finally, to provoke some sort of response, I spat on my hands and did a mocking toe-tap dance on the sleek floor.

'Stop that,' Prendick said, 'and come up here. The stairs are over there.'

I found the stairs and climbed up to him. Doors with metal sliding panels for windows made a circuit around the inside of the tier – ten or twelve such doors in all. They were all closed and tightly sealed, but on this level the zoo-like smell overrode that of the alcohol: I knew that behind the closed doors was the distinctly animal source of this smell. But the thought did not disturb me. Outwardly, I was loose and cheerful. Prendick, after all, was coming round and we would soon have a plan.

'What is this?' I said. 'A cell-block for the dogs that the prol-fauves haven't eaten yet?'

'Let's not waste any time, Markcrier. I'll show you what it is.'

He selected one of the doors and slid back its window panel as if he were a medieval gaoler in the dungeon of his lord, which, to some extent, he in fact was. The copper panel slid smoothly aside. Unctuous as dead fish, the stench assailed me anew. Immediately upon the panel's opening, it coated the membranes of my mouth and nose like a rancid oil. I stepped back from the window.

'My God, Yves!'

'Look, damn you, turn about and look!'

My mood declined from cheerfulness into apprehension. I examined Prendick's face, then forced myself to stare into the gleaming cell. The cell was clean, the walls gleaming, the floor an immaculate grey – so that the stench had to originate with the hoary creature that sat in the cell's far right-hand corner. An absurdly squat animal.

Propped in the angle of two walls, it appeared to be asleep, its paws draped decorously over its middle. A mangle of white fur, somewhat mangy and sparse, gave the beast the look of a worldly gentleman fallen on difficult times. Although fairly long through the torso, the animal had short deformed hind legs that canted outwards from its body so that its sex lay exposed in a thin lawn of pubic white. Turgid and intricately veined, the organ had no apparent relevance to the body structure of the creature possessing it. But in spite of the piscine stench that had nearly overwhelmed me a moment before, I judged the animal to be anything but a predator.

I turned away from the window again. 'It looks a little like a sea otter.' *The memorable scent of hard flesh, intimate and pelagic, on Christmas day.* 'Except for the size of its limbs and head. And the primate-like genitals. You've been carving on him pretty viciously, Yves, from what I can see.'

'You don't see very much. Look again.'

'Please,' I said with some exasperation. 'What for?'

'Look again, Markcrier. This time I'll wake him up so that you can make a more accurate judgment – although I'm glad that you think it looks like a sea otter, that being what I was striving for.' He slid the copper panel back and forth across the window, causing it to clank against its frame. 'Now look again!' he commanded me.

Exasperated, uncertain, afraid of what I was being shown, I looked. The animal had not moved, but now its eyes were open and luminous with fear. It remembered Prendick's knife, no doubt, the eventide eternities when the anaesthetic had not taken hold.

Then the anomaly of its posture there in the corner struck me – the languidly hanging paws and the tight uncertain eyes. What was it in the creature's lineaments that so unsettled and mocked us? Since its head remained down, only its eyes – looking up under a shaggy mis-shapen brow – could be responsible for the shame I felt in spying on it: its eyes were the eyes of a human being, trapped but intelligent. The creature seemed unable to lift its head from its breast, but its frightened eyes flickered over our prying faces and showed us, beneath each upward-straining eyeball, a thin crescent of eloquent white. The whites spoke of unspoken horrors.

I turned again to Prendick. Horrified, I shrugged non-committally.

'That otter used to be a man, Mark. And the man he used to be was your friend from Marigold Island, I've forgotten his name. Do you understand what I'm saying?'

'Huerta?' I said incredulously.

'That's right. Huerta. I'd forgotten the name, it's been so long that Serenos has had me doing this one.'

'Doing this one,' I echoed. I stared at Prendick. The madness singing in his tortured face had softened into an expression of professional distance; he had no concept of the awesome disparity between his words 'doing this one' and the gut-rending fact of converting a human being into an animal. His face registered an hysterical calm, his puffy eyes a smug aloofness from reality. Prendick, I realised, was grown into the archetypal mad scientist – with the telling qualification that his madness had seeped into him from the ubiquitous distillation of the Navarch's evil. I was touched by that madness myself. How could I upbraid a madman for the enormities his madness had perpetrated? How could I condemn Marina's father for succumbing to the evil that had begun to drive me? I turned back to the cell window, I ignored the stench, I shouted at the incomplete thing slouched against the wall, 'Huerta! Huerta, it's Markcrier, I'm going to let you out, I'm going to try to help you!'

Huerta did not move, but the eyes – the eyes fixed on me reproachfully.

'I've decerebrated it,' Prendick said. 'It doesn't understand.'

'Why? Why have you done this to him?'

'Because Serenos wanted me to. He said I could restore creatures like this one – and specimens of the prol-fauves – to a condition more suited to their natures or I could condemn my family to death by refusing to do so. Do you understand me, Markcrier? I'm not supposed to be telling you this.'

'I understand,' I said, going to the railing and looking across the operating hall at the huge window there. The sea pressed against the glass like a woman embracing her lover: crystalline ambiguity.

'At the turn of this century Serenos ordered me to perform experimental work on cadavers, simple work that never required me to be away from home. But about two years ago, perhaps more, he demanded that I "create" things for him out of living human beings – things that would be demonstrably less than human. I was to use animals for models, both living animals and extinct ones.' Prendick pointed at a door several metres down the tier. 'There's a kind of protoman in there. A dawn creature, aeons before either of the Holocausts: the books sometimes call it Zinjanthropus. I did it very well, I think – at least in regard to its outward anatomy.'

Prendick joined me at the railing. 'Of course, after the cadavers the work was more difficult. The Navarch set deadlines. I had to be away from The Orchard for longer periods. After Marina's rape, he provided me with the old man who was your friend, the old man who became the raw material for the sea otter you've just looked at. Serenos said he wanted a sea otter this time. A white one, he specified a white one. But the old man was so old that he almost died while I was working on him . . .'

I folded my hands on the railing and put my head down.

Consolingly, Prendick put his arm around my shoulders; he whispered in my ear so that I could feel his breath. 'Don't be upset, Mark. It wasn't a personal thing, what I did to your friend.' He tapped my shoulder. 'Besides, I have a plan.'

I looked into the mutely singing eyes of my dead wife's father.

'You see,' he said, 'I can do the same thing to Fearing Serenos; I can do the *same thing* to the Navarch.'

Long ago, in a very old book, I had read about a man who had attempted to turn animals into men through vivisection. What Marina's father was doing embodied the opposite notion; and although innately more repugnant than 'humanising' dumb beasts, it was a simpler task than the other. After all, the insidiously rational Dr Moreau had failed because he could not instill a lasting human intelligence in his brutish subjects: the nebulous quality of human-kind's 'soul' invariably faded with time. But insofar as Prendick had succeeded in carrying out the Navarch's will, he had succeeded precisely because it is easier to destroy than to build, to demolish than to create.

Huerta (if one could forget his eyes) was an animal in every respect. The human being in him had departed with each successive incision of Prendick's scalpel, with each expert deletion of brain tissue, with each cruel alteration of his hands and feet. My rage grew. My heart pounded with the syncopation of *ven-geance, ven-geance*. I knew that I did in fact wish to do the same thing to Serenos, to reduce him completely to the animal he already was.

Understanding that Prendick approached the world from the perspective of a madman enabled me to work with him. We were madmen together. I drew energy from his insanity as surely as if I were a psychic vampire. Prendick's plan had no more brilliance than the recommendation of a bactericide for a sore throat, but we sought to effect his remedy with all the insane zeal we could muster and our very zealousness made the plan work.

It was two months after Marina's death in childbirth that we put this awkward strategy to the test, two months to the day. The first torrential rainfall of October scoured the streets outside the Palace of the Navarchy, scoured the stained terra-cotta dwellings, caused the rabid sea to foam against the quaystones under the force of the October deluge. We had waited, Prendick and I, for just such a morning.

We left The Orchard in Prendick's battery-powered autocart and arrived together at the Palace perhaps an hour before the breaking of a thin winterish light. We had informed not a single other person of our intentions; and because Serenos would have suspected some sort of underhandedness if he had seen me, I remained in the hot, breath-fogged cockpit of Prendick's autocart while he ran up the seemingly varnished steps of the main administrative building. I looked around, prepared to hide if a gendarme in a poncho should approach. Since not a single member of the Gendarmerie came forward to check Prendick's vehicle and since it would be better for us if his autocart were not so brazenly conspicuous at the beginning of our ruse, I dared to expose myself for a moment and drove the autocart out of the way. I drove it into a high-walled shelter between the Palace itself and the eastern wall of the 'imperial' stables. Because of the rain, no one challenged me.

Bitter cleansing rains of incredible ferocity conspired with us against the Navarch. It was fitting. Had not one of my ancestors washed his sullied body in such torrents and taken their name for his own?

All I had to do was wait. Prendick knew where I would be. I crawled into the autocart's back seat – in reality, a storage well – and covered myself with a heavy tarpaulin. Immediately drenched in my own sweat, I listened to the roar of the world.

In time, Prendick would emerge into the rain with Serenos and the Navarch's inevitable uniformed riflemen – Molinier, his favourite, among them. The pretext for getting the Navarch to take a jaunt in the rain would be Prendick's avowal of a genuine miracle of vivisection at Hospitaler House. For several weeks Serenos had been pressuring my mad friend about his progress with Huerta, but Yves had put him off with clumsy excuses – so that we might take advantage of the beginning of the rainy season.

Now it had come. At no other time would the Navarch have even considered riding from the Palace to any other part of Windfall Last in a vehicle other than his ornate open carriage, a conveyance drawn by four identical Percherons. But like many men who place no value on the lives of human beings, he did not choose to let valuable animals suffer; therefore, we had assumed that Serenos would not require his beautifully groomed horses to brave this inclement October morning. And we assumed correctly.

I heard footfalls on the flagstones. The door of the autocart opened, turning up the volume on the rain and allowing a gust of muggy wind to lift a corner of my tarpaulin. Then the slamming of the door and a return of the storage well's stifling humidity. Crouched under the tarp, I waited for some word from Prendick.

Finally he said, 'He's going to ride with us, Markcrier – or with me, that is, so far as he knows. I'm driving over to the entrance to pick him up.'

I said nothing. Moving through the rain, the autocart whined softly.

'Did you hear me?' Prendick said. 'And it may be that his personal gendarmes will follow in another vehicle. Perhaps even on horseback, since their horses aren't his own coddled Percherons. Do you hear me?'

'Yes,' I said. 'I was just wondering what Serenos smells like when he's wet. Have you ever wondered about that?'

'No. Why would I wonder about something like that?'

'Your unique perspective on the human condition,' I said, at once regretting the condescension of my tone. But Marina's father had not heard me. The tyres of the autocart sloughed through the runoff from the Palace's rain gutters, and the gentle whine of the batteries ceased altogether.

We were at rest.

There were voices and footfalls. The door opposite Prendick roared open, then kicked shut with a violent *thwump*! We rocked a little. Even from beneath my concealing canvas I could feel another body adjusting to the narrow confines of our autocart, a body of no small proportions.

Then again the amplified crackling of the rain and Prendick shouting out his window at someone: 'Hell, no, I won't carry you in here! You're already sopping wet, your capes and jodhpurs all sopping! And this thing wasn't made to transport armies, it wasn't made to—'

A voice shouted back an indistinct response, '. . . . . .'

Then I heard the Navarch's voice (it was the first time I had heard it since he had told me, *I'll never ask anything of you again, Markcrier*). Now he was leaning over Prendick and shouting at the undoubtedly miserable gendarme in the rain, in a voice that sounded both annoyed and authoritative, 'Just follow us, Molinier, you and the others! Get in another goddamn vehicle and follow us closely. Dr Prendick can be counted on to see me safely to Hospitaler House!'

'. . . . . .' Molinier or someone responded. The window went up again, but I thought for a moment about Molinier. He was a handsome man in his late forties, with vestigial gill slits – unfunctioning, of course – just behind his jawbones on the upper part of his neck. I had known him relatively well in the final period of my service to Windfall Last. For a murderer, he was an amiable enough fellow. We had once worked together with a complete absence of either recrimination or jealousy.

60

Then the tyres began whirring through water once more and the engine whining like a swarm of summer mosquitoes. The rain pounded the fibre-glass hull of the autocart with barbaric tattoos, the patterns of which altered in intensity and rhythm every few minutes. I waited. I suffered the oppressive humidity of my closed-in hiding-place.

But when Prendick said, 'Your gatemen weren't very conscientious today, Navarch,' I uncovered and stuck a pistol in the intimate depression at the base of Fearing Serenos' skull. The pistol had belonged to Marina.

'If you move,' I said, 'I won't hesitate to let this nasty little machine take a core sample of your grey matter.'

There was a momentary silence. Then, 'Quite poetically phrased, Markcrier, quite poetic indeed.'

'Shut up,' I said. I pushed the mouth of the barrel deeper into the intimate depression at the back of his head. I was enjoying myself: the tough language, the gun butt cradled in my palm, this conspiracy of dark rains and lofty madness. Moreover, Serenos shut up.

Because Prendick allowed the autocart to career down the cobbled streets, rocking back and forth over its wheels, it took us very little time to reach Hospitaler House. Several unmasted boats pitched in their moorings beside the quays. A few fishermen huddled together on various decks, pointing and gesturing with heads and hands as if they were demigods attempting to calm the sea. But except for some children we had passed beneath the Palace of the Navarchy, no other people had ventured outdoors.

We halted on the perimeter of the great platform on which the hospital seemed to float.

As soon as Prendick got out and went around to the Navarch's door, Serenos slammed it open, knocked Prendick down, and hurtled his lithe muscular body into the downpour. I pursued. Bruising my upper thighs in the process, I lurched out of the autocart's back seat.

With rain slashing out of the sky into my face, I took aim on the Navarch and shot him in the calf in his right leg. I shot him again in the buttocks. His royal vestments fluttering about him like the wings of a manta ray, he toppled heavily and rolled on to his belly on the running concrete. The rain, like so many fluid needles, pinioned him there.

In a moment Prendick was up from his back, and the two of us lifted our wounded despot, held him erect between us, and stumbled with him towards the nearest entrance to the building.

We went in.

Prendick found his keys and admitted us to the elevator that would drop us into the submerged operating hall of the theatre of surgery. Down we went. But in the closed quarters of the elevator, supporting Serenos as he bled, I realised that the man smelled exactly like a wet dog. The reek of mildewed fur came off him as a nearly visible steam.

I grew angry. Why were we taking Serenos to the cloistered vivisection area to which only Prendick had access? We could end things quickly if we wished: I could shoot the bastard in the head at point-blank range, shoot him and conclude eight years of needless suffering with that same penetrating bullet-head. But we were down. We were on the floor of the operating hall.

Molinier and the other gendarmes were not long in arriving. In our submerged haven we watched them enter Hospitaler House via a closed-circuit television unit. Prendick went upstairs and told them the remarkable – absurdly remarkable – story that he had devised over two weeks ago especially for this critical confrontation. He told them (and I shivered in the submerged hall, imagining the words he chose) that the Navarch had had a sudden and acute attack of stigmata in his hands and side, an unpredictable infirmity to which men in high positions had been mysteriously subject throughout all recorded history. We hoped that the utter irrationality of our story would appeal to the superstitions of men as narrow as most of the gendarmes. Because of this attack of stigmata, Prendick went on, he had placed the Navarch in a private room in one of the lower levels of Hospitaler House, where Serenos was now resting comfortably.

Meticulously observant, Molinier had seen evidence of blood on the streaming pavement outside Hospitaler House and in the upper hallway as well. He did not choose to take Marina's father at his word. Therefore, Prendick came back down to me and prepared to give Molinier the assurance that he wanted. Only when I forced the Navarch, at gun point, to announce over the hospital's intercom system the nature of his injuries, the extent of his loss of blood, and the fact that he would be staying with us for three or four more days, only then did the gendarmes accept the lies we had fed them. Molinier and the others left.

We drugged the Navarch. He lay unconscious on his stomach on one of the metallic operating tables, and we sat on stools and talked like two medical students above his inert form. We had stripped him, and the finely haired body of the man fascinated us. Ageless and heretofore invincible, Fearing Serenos had the animal vibrancy of a jaguar – a jaguar with a muted sorrel pelt, a jaguar whose body was stiffened with bad dreams. The bullet holes in Serenos' calf and buttock actually hurt my heart; they were crimson insults to an otherwise perfect physique. But seeing him naked, I hated Fearing Serenos even more than I had hated him after Marina's rape, or after her pregnancy, or after her preter-natural labour. Beast creatures slept in the seed of the Navarch's loins.

'Well, what shall we do with him?' Prendick asked. 'What sort of thing shall we turn him into? After I've removed the bullets?'

Turning towards the hall's immense window, I looked at the surprisingly calm waters beyond. Faint undulations swept against the glass, a stirring of unknown powers and unwritten poems.

'Well, Mark, what do you want to do?' Prendick came back into line of vision; his mad eyes were upon me, opaque with dull expectancy.

'I want you to turn Serenos into a shark,' I said. 'I want

63

you to give him the shape and the hairlessness and the blunt stupid nose of a shark. That's what I want you to do with him.'

The mad eyes stared, they glinted. And without a single flicker of outrage, these same eyes acquiesced in the irrationality of my long-sought revenge.

*Yes, Prendick's eyes were saying, I may be able to make a shark of him, or something very like, no matter, the challenge compels me to attempt it, how did you settle so quickly on such a miraculous fashioning, a shark, a shark, even though I've never ventured away from homoiothermal creation before, always having begun with men, but this . . . this truly compels.*

So the eyes spoke to me, altogether consenting

And so we began.

No one truly knew what had befallen the Navarch, although Molinier demanded that Dr Prendick provide him with tangible evidence that Serenos still lived. This ultimatum came on the second day of the Navarch's captivity, and Prendick, acting upon no stratagem but the intuition of his madness, simply replied that he could offer no such evidence because in a paroxysm of nocturnal spiritual ecstasy the Navarch had cast his eyes up to heaven and died! For some reason, Prendick filigreed this unlikely 'official report' with the observation that the Navarch's ecstasy had followed closely upon his viewing a new marvel of vivisection, the Otter Man.

Although no word of Serenos' 'death' reached the general public, Prendick's report went out to every member and past member of the Council of the Navarchy, including myself. Everyone believed. Inherent in this bizarre account of our leader's dying was a drama that no one could ignore. Had the multitudinous sins of Fearing Serenos at last run him to ground and figuratively torn away the flesh at his throat? If so, the punishment was just.

I had to laugh – at my coconspirator's inventive fantasy and at the sanctimonious reaction of the council members.

Because no one had seen me on the morning of the

Navarch's journey to Hospitaler House, I was above suspicion. Therefore, on the fourth day of Serenos' confinement (the third day after the announcement of his death), I joined my former colleagues in the Palace of the Navarchy. They treated me with deference and respect. As the only man in Guardian's Loop's history ever to have lived twice in Azteca Nueva among the enigmatic Parfects, I had an enigmatic position all my own. Eight years in retirement had heightened for these men the illusion of my venerableness. And, finally, their quietly held knowledge that my wife had died as a result of Serenos' cruelty secured for me the status of a living martyr.

Desperate for direction, they turned to me. Even Molinier, who had expressed serious doubts about the complete accuracy of Prendick's report, accepted my assurances that no foul play had occurred. After all, I knew the doctor. He had suffered more than most of us at Serenos' hands (quietly knowledgeable looks passed between the council members when I said this), but no man had been so diligent as my father-in-law in the impartial execution of his duty. Swarthy, keen-eyed, gill-scarred Molinier listened to my words and believed me.

Without seeking the office, I had become the interregnal Navarch. I had not anticipated this outcome, had not been prescient enough to understand the impact of my own reputation. How could I have hoped to understand? My reputation and I shared nothing in common but those two amazingly complex words, Markcrier Rains.

Nevertheless, I assumed the pilot's role almost without thinking.

Although Molinier supported me in this capacity and rallied more than three quarters of the Gendarmerie in my behalf, a small segment of our official police force chose to support an aging bureaucrat who had never quite acceded to the prefecture of the organisation. Even while Serenos had ruled, this man – Duvalier – had openly criticised the policies and methods of his immediate superior, Molinier (perhaps with some justification, considering our relatively effortless capture of the Navarch);

but Duvalier had not been removed from his position, primarily because he understood the delicate business of bodyguarding as no one else and because he had made fast friends with several of the more elderly council members. On the second day of my 'reign', it became apparent that the faction supporting this man would not go quietly away of its own volition. Molinier approached me; he asked for permission to deal with these reprehensible few. I listened. Not yet aware of the power that resided in my simplest word, I told Molinier to do what had to be done.

The following day I discovered that twenty freshly severed heads decorated the spikes along the harbour wall. The faces were masks of hard black blood, and the sea-gulls dived upon them with the impunity of falling sunlight.

Once again I had indirectly precipitated an atrocity. How many times would I be responsible for other people's deaths?

Although this question genuinely pained me, tortured me in the long midnights, I sublimated its painfulness and tried to glory in the newfound security of my position. I had become the Navarch. I hoped that I had not become Fearing Serenos. The title was enough; I did not want the man's name.

A rumour started that the sea-gulls near the harbour had gone mad and that they copulated in the air as they fell in screaming torrents on the impaled heads of the slaughtered gendarmes. I half believed the rumour and expected the heads to have been devoured the next time I ventured to the quays. The appetites of animals, sexual and otherwise, haunted my thoughts.

Seagulls copulating in the air?

# Four

*May no one die till he has loved!*

— St-John Perse

Nevertheless, the disembodied heads of the rebel gendarmes greeted me when I finally found the time to visit Prendick at Hospitaler House. The libidinous gulls had not completely ravished them or themselves.

Trembling, I sought out Marina's father and came upon him in the sunken chamber of surgery. In the last several days he had taken the first strides towards effecting the metamorphosis of our drugged former leader. I wanted to halt this madness, but I could not. I convinced myself that the process had already gone beyond the point of legitimate reversal. If we stopped now, I argued to myself, Serenos would be a thing, a grotesque parody of his former self. Since we could not restore him, it was best to proceed. Moreover, I realised that under no circumstances would Prendick be likely to permit an interruption of his first tender modifications of our patient's anatomy. He pursued the animalisation of Fearing Serenos with too much innocent enthusiasm to be put off by my sober moral concern. He had worked too hard already. Therefore, inertia ruled me – inertia and my own persistent desire to see the Navarch suffer. I delighted in Prendick's malicious skill.

'Markcrier,' he said when I came into the hall. 'Have you come to see how our experiment progresses?'

I ignored the question; I had other matters on my mind. 'We must give the council a body, Yves. Molinier demands a body. Before we can announce Serenos' death to the populace of Windfall Last, there must be some evidence that he is, in fact, dead. Everyone wants a funeral.'

'Give them a sealed casket and a cremation ceremony,'

Prendick said curtly. 'Tell them that will suffice.'

'And if Molinier should wish to examine the body?'

'I have *already* examined the body! I am the physician to the Navarch, and no one has the right to question my competence or loyalty.' As if I had questioned both, he looked at me accusingly. 'All you need do, Markcrier, is tell them that no one views the Navarch's body once it has been prepared for cremation. Tradition dictates this procedure. You're the new Navarch. Who'll not believe you?'

'What tradition, Yves, what tradition dictates this procedure?'

'None. But say it anyway. No one remembers the occasion of the previous Navarch's death; consequently, no one will challenge you about the funeral procedures. The history of Windfall Last,' Prendick said in a far-away voice, 'is not so well documented as that of several pre-Holocaust civilisations. How very odd that is.'

'Yes. Odd.' I was not amused.

'Come with me and see how your shark progresses, Markcrier. It's slow, it's very slow – but you'll be proud of me.' In his eyes: the image of tangled seaweed and the minute tentacles of an old obsession, one we shared.

I followed him on to the tier above the chamber's main floor, the tier where I had come face to face with Emmanuel Huerta in his new incarnation. This thought I put in a far corner of my mind, but the odour of fish and fur recalled it to me with a punishing vividness at brief unpredictable moments in my conversation with Prendick. The tier still reeked. I refused, however, to let these moments rule me.

We looked down on a large round tank that had not been in the theatre of surgery on the day of Serenos' capture. A thin milk-coloured solution swirled in the tank – a solution that apparently flowed through an assemblage of swan-necked glass tubing into the adjacent cleansing unit and then back into the barbarously foaming tank, endlessly recirculating, like pale blood. So evil did this apparatus look that I had the ridiculous idea that Prendick had created it solely for its appearance. Ancient horror stories paraded their seriocomic plots through my mind. But Prendick was intoxicated with the very hatred and passions that had driven me; and madness oftentimes mocks itself.

Despite these somewhat calming observations, I could not overlook the fact that Fearing Serenos lay at full length in this milky whirlpool, his head held out of the water by means of a metal brace that forced his chin to point at the ceiling. And his face was naked. I would not have recognized the Navarch had I not already known what to expect – primal nudity, the hairlessness of reptiles, flesh the colour of burnt rubber.

Looking down at the open tank, at the milky solution laving Serenos's body, I asked, 'Does he know what's going on? Have you . . . decerebrated him?'

'No. I'm not going to. We decided not to, didn't we?'

'Then he *does* know what's going on?'

'No, he doesn't. Look at him, Markcrier. He's on a heavy dose of slightly modified pentobarbital sodium. The drug serves two purposes. It keeps him anaesthetised against the maceration process of the whirlpool, which is more frightening than painful, I should imagine; and it produced in his own metabolism the first evidences of a condition approaching that of poikilothermal animals: cold-bloodedness. Once we remove him from the tank, a partial severing of his spinal cord will ensure that he continues in this cold-blooded state, just like all good mantas and sharks.'

'And what does the whirlpool do?'

Prendick stared not at the tank, but at the gently heaving waters of Pretty Coal Sack. 'It also does two things. The solution in the tank consists in part of a depilatory agent to remove the Navarch's hair by inactivating the follicles themselves. I removed his facial hair by shaving and electrolysis. What's especially interesting, though, is that the solution contains another agent to soften his skeletal system and then reverse the ossification process altogether so that his bones turn back into pliant cartilage, the cartilage of the womb. At this very moment calcium and phosphorus are being leached from his bones, Mark-crier. When his skeleton consists entirely of cartilage and when the poikilothermal condition has been firmly established, I can begin to use the knife.' Prendick looked at me with a weary innocence. 'Two or three months' work will remain even after I've removed him from the whirlpool. Perhaps for a Christmas gift I can deliver into your hands this predatory thing which we have both fathered. A shark will be born.'

· 'Perhaps,' I said.

And I left Yves Prendick to his work and returned, under guard, to the Palace of the Navarchy. I did not go back to Hospitaler House for nearly two weeks – although Yves came to the Palace almost every morning to see me. I made use of this time away from the sunken surgical hall to strengthen my grip on the levers of power and to woo a population that could remember no Navarch but Fearing Serenos. Most of this courting took place during the public cremation ceremony, over which I presided from beginning to end.

I delivered an impassioned address about the right of men to govern their own lives within the limitations of the law; I read to the clustering crowd, flamboyant in their yellow and scarlet mourning dress, a small section of my uncompleted poem *Archipelagoes*.

And the casket remained closed throughout the ceremonies, even when on brief display in the outer courtyard of the crematorium. When the casket was burned, consumed at incredible temperatures, it yielded royal ashes – though they were not those of Serenos at all, but instead the charred dust of a misbegotten sea otter that had been Emmanuel Huerta.

I had ordered Prendick to kill Huerta in the least painful way he could devise; and on the morning before the requiem rites for Serenos, Yves had injected a minuscule air bubble into the old fisherman's bloodstream. His body we had later concealed in the Navarch's casket for the purpose of the state funeral. No one doubted our story; no one wept for a last look at the late ruler's corpse.

All went well in the weeks immediately following the funeral. The people accepted me, the council supported my every recommendation, Molinier and his gendarmes dogged my footsteps with an assiduousness beyond reproach.

I did not go back to Python's Keep. I did not leave the city. Prendick returned to The Orchard every night to walk among the trees with Melantha, to keep her company, to calm her fears about his long sessions at Hospitaler House. But I would not return to Python's Keep. Too many mementos of another time crowded upon me when I stepped over the threshold, a fragrance as of ancient perfumes and constantly rejuvenating seas. I experienced again the powerful intercourse of two hearts, and the experience always hurt me.

Nevertheless, I saw Prendick often. I visited him in the submerged operating hall where he continued to mould Serenos into the ichthyoid form of something resembling a shark. He cut. He performed skin grafts. He removed the former Navarch's genitals and sculptured his bifurcated lower body into the smooth, resilient fuselage of a fish. Working with the macerated bones of Serenos's skull, Prendick shaped a neckless head; he flattened the strong human nose; he moved the brutal eyes out of their forward-looking sockets and placed them on opposite sides of the streamlined sharkish snout.

Where a man had once existed, Marina's father saw to it that a knife-born member of the order *Selachii* came into being. I began to believe that no such man as Fearing Serenos had ever lived in Windfall Last, for the creature on Prendick's operating table bore no resemblance to any human being I had ever encountered. Its moist grey flesh was marbled with intimations of blue, its face grinned with the livid sewn-up grin of a museum horror. Things progressed nicely. But even though it was by then the middle of November, a great deal of delicate vivisecting and grafting remained to be done.

And by the middle of November I had begun to make enemies.

Molinier could not understand my refusal to permit bodyguards to descend with me into the sunken chamber of surgery. I argued that the intricacy of my friend's experiments demanded a silent surgical environment.

Why, then, did the Navarch go so frequently to the operating area? Was his interest in vivisection so profound?

I argued that Prendick was engaged in activity that might one day free the population of Windfall Last from its biological heritage. One day the Parfects might choose to readmit us to the world we had twice repudiated, and they would do so because of my friend's work. I went to him so frequently because my presence steadied his hand, my encouragement made him aware of our trust in his skill. These lies I told Molinier on several occasions, but he held his scepticism in check and continued as my friend.

He did not become my enemy until I had made a severe tactical error by attempting to formulate policy on the basis of moral conviction. The poet ruled where the bureaucrat ought to have prevailed.

I decided that the Gendarmerie (even after Molinier's October purge) was at a strength incommensurate with its duties – that too many of its members were callous self-seeking men who used their position as a carte-blanche to insult, intimidate, bludgeon, and kill. I ordered Molinier to discover the identities of these men and to remove them from the police force.

At that moment, Molinier became my enemy.

Perfunctorily, he did what I asked – but the men whom he removed went down to the quays and destroyed the vessels, the nets, and the cargoes of a council member's private fishing fleet. None of the remaining gendarmes would make an arrest, not a single marauder came to justice.

While Prendick's knife made careful incisions in the flesh of the former Navarch, my idealism gouged jagged rents in my own, the current Navarch's, credibility. But now I had power. I persisted. I refused to toady to the old men and the fiery youths who encircled me with their own peculiar brands of avarice and who gave me immoral advice. Because of what Prendick and I had done, the position of Navarch belonged to me.

*Let its use be worthy*, I prayed. For I intended to use it.

Then one night as I lay in my canopied bed, the ghost of Emmanuel Huerta came to me in the form of a white otter and sang to me in my dream. On the next day I took action to lift the interdict on the fishermen of Marigold Island, just as Fearing Serenos had once falsely told me he had done. I decreed that all who wished to do so could return to Guardian's Loop; the day of enforced exile was done.

I sent a vessel to Barbos to deliver this happy news, but few of the fishermen there believed. They knew that Huerta had never returned to them.

The vessel I had dispatched eventually came home – gliding over the waters of Pretty Coal Sack, its sails as lewd as soiled linen, its prow dull and stupid-looking above the spitlike froth through which it cut. I waited on the quay. Not one of the members of the colony of exiles disembarked, however, and the shipmaster insisted that my lifting of the interdict had meant nothing to the people at Barbos, so wanting in discernment and gratitude were they all.

Several nights later a crewman from this vessel, whom I had granted a clandestine audience, told me that three fishermen from the colony had come aboard ship, but that they had been murdered and cast into the sea not more than an hour out from Marigold. I believed this sailor, but I could do nothing.

The heavy rains continued to fall, drowning us with their vehemence and their unremitting noise. A biblical deluge for the world's last men, a deluge of tall rains striding over the earth.

As the rains fell, Prendick brought Serenos further along. He amputated his arms, smoothed the shoulders into his tough symmetrical body, began shaping dorsal fins from the skin he had cut away from the amputated arms – skin he had also treated in a chemical brine. Now

73

when I visited Prendick, the smell of the surgical chamber drove me on to the tier above the main floor; I watched everything from a distance, literally and metaphorically aloof.

Exercising my power as Navarch, however, I tried to remain aloof from the evil that existed in Windfall Last. I proceeded with my catch-as-catch-can programme of reform. Strangers and aliens seemed to surround me; they looked on as I ordered that all the iron spikes jutting skyward from the harbour wall be pried from their sockets and scrapped, never again to receive upon their cold lance-tips the heads of dismembered human beings. Even in this, unthinking men opposed me.

A work force of impressed prol-fauves removed the spikes from the wall, but the gendarmes whom I had sent to supervise this labour made bets among themselves and instigated bloody little combats among the individual work crews – so that prol-fauves used the dislodged spikes to maim and disembowel one another while their supervisors sat horse on the streets above them and cheered them on. Only the sudden onset of great winds and torrential rains prevented this casually provoked slaughter from developing into a small insurrection. Before the coming of the streaming torrents, the gendarmes had had to shoot several of the workmen for turning away from the quays and threatening to mob into the city with their crude weapons. On this same afternoon two horses with ripped bellies, having thrown their riders, bolted through the rain towards the Palace; slime-coated intestines gleamed with crimson intensity on the cobbles. Just as in Prendick's theatre of surgery, I watched everything from a distance.

Again I had failed. Eight years of isolation from the ways of men had not prepared me for the frustrations of thwarted authority. How had my Marina come to me from such a milieu of contradictory impulses? What sort of animal inhabited Guardian's Loop? Indeed, what sort of ambiguous animal ravened in my own breast, devouring both the bitter and the sweet?

74

At the beginning of December an unexpected thing happened.

Seemingly materialising from nowhere, a tall silver-eyed Parfect presented himself at the gate of the Palace of the Navarchy and told the gendarmes on duty that he would see the new ruler of our island. As a concession to our sensibilities, he wore a white linen robe with Grecian fretwork at the sleeves and hem. The guards fell back at once and found a council member to usher the Parfect into my chambers on the topmost floor.

When the Parfect entered, I was sitting beneath the open skylight looking at the fish in my aquarium and trying to decide if I should attempt sleep. Dusk had sifted down on me; my head ached. But startled by the twilight apparition of the Parfect, I stood up and discovered with shame that I was weeping. Inexplicably. I did not recognise this alien brother from either of my two stays in Azteca Nueva, but I embraced him as a friend.

We conversed in the fading light. He ignored the salt tears on the tilted planes of my cheeks and moved about the room as he spoke, gracefully gesturing with his hands. His voice dealt with our human words – our pragmatic Franglais – with a precision born of unfamiliarity. My own voice faltered, faltered in attempting to reach his heart; but neither of us, in reality, said a great deal. The message of this visitor from Azteca Nueva consisted not so much of words as of a perfectly communicated *tone*.

Disappointment.

The Parfects felt disappointment. For centuries they had waited for us, delaying an inevitable decision. It was not enough that we merely struggled. His voice smoothed out this last suggestion and played with another tone – although that of disappointment continued to undulate gently beneath the surface. The inevitable decision would be delayed again, this time for the purpose of receiving a final representative of mankind in Azteca Nueva. Serenos had put them off. Very well, then, the beginning of the new decade (still more than a year away) would suffice, and they desired that Markcrier Rains once again be that emissary—

—Markcrier Rains, he who no longer slept beside a woman sharing the sea-smell of her womb; he who held the poison-tipped sceptre of a mysteriously fallen prince; he who on past occasions had walked haltingly among the Parfects of the luxuriantly flowered mainland, in the shadow of Popocatepetl.

No other could come in my stead, they had settled upon me. Windfall Last would find a ruler more suited to her disposition during my absence, and upon my return that new ruler would step aside for me. Then the decision would be withheld no longer; it would come down to us, out of either disappointment or forgiveness. And the world would be changed.

'Do not think us unfeeling, Markcrier,' the Parfect said before leaving me. 'It may be that we feel too deeply.'

When he had gone, the twilight departing on the trailing hem of his Grecian robe, the room still contained something of his presence. Even in the resultant dark this intangible balm hung in the air, like the fragrance of foreign evergreens. The idea of living again in Azteca Nueva did not seem completely unpleasant.

Only in the morning, when sunlight cascaded in like harp music, did I realise that going once more among the Parferts would signal for me a private doom, a living suicide. I refused to see anyone that morning; I failed to visit Hospitaler House. Nearly thirteen months remained to me before the advent of the new decade, and in that time I might be able to devise an alternative acceptable to the Parfects. But I would not go, I would not. Still, it was almost a week before the lingering suggestion of the messenger's presence disappeared utterly from my council room.

On the ninth day of the month I went to Prendick again and found that his work was nearly done. He had given Serenos (*could this wicked-looking product of the vat and knife truly be Serenos?*) the crescentic underslung mouth of a shark. He had also given him an armouring of artificially cultivated placoid scales and teeth to occupy the predatory mouth.

As I watched from the tier of copper cages, Prendick went about the one task that he had purposely postponed until every other procedure of the metamorphosis lay behind him. Once again the tank came into play, but this time without all the paraphernalia of recirculation and cleansing. Marina's father had submerged himself in the tank, which now murmured with stinging salt water; and he was working on the snout of the creature that hung in traction over the water's surface, perhaps an inch or so of this brine lapping its underbelly. *Ah, Serenos, have we brought you to this?*

I watched for almost three hours. During all this time Prendick and I exchanged not a single word; of late we had had less and less to say to each other, as if the surgeon's scalpel had split our tongues. We communed in other ways, knowing that only the two of us – in all the world – knew of this ultimate degradation of Fearing Serenos. Prendick was mad, of course, and I ... It was too late to concern myself.

The last step was taking place, the creation of the shark's louvrelike system of gills: the fluttering, blood-blue branchiae through which Serenos would breath. Prendick had preserved this moment in order not to have to work in the water until he absolutely must. But the moment was upon him; and occasionally lowering his suspended patient into the tank and then raising him out again, he cut and cauterized, severed and tied. Sometimes he worked through the monster's cruel mouth.

At the end of the third hour, Prendick collapsed Serenos' useless lungs, administered a stimulant, and dropped him out of traction into the water – where his new respiratory system began to function. Then Prendick climbed out of the tank and grinned up at me, his face more cadaverous and his trunk and limbs more wanly etiolated than I had ever seen them. He looked ill.

But I grinned, too, and marvelled at the drugged pseudo-shark that stirred its body and tail with lethargic

77

gracelessness. We had done what we had set out to accomplish. If our specimen was not a perfect representative of the order *Selachii*, it approached that ideal and nevertheless did us honour. I could not help grinning.

Still, we knew it would be impossible to release Serenos into the bay before he had recovered from the gill operation and gained the necessary stamina to compete with the sea creatures who would challenge him for prey. Prendick said, 'Give him until Christmas, Markcrier,' and those were the first words either of us had spoken since my arrival in the early morning. I had no doubt that even in the body of a lower animal Serenos would compete quite well. As a man, he had possessed a gift for tenacious survival; and although his brain had been cut into separate lobes and flattened into the narrow brain casing of a shark, Prendick believed that Serenos still had at least a portion of his former intelligence. He would not be ready for the open sea, however, for well over two weeks. An eternity.

In Windfall Last I received word of a plot against my life. Informers came to my gates nightly with fantastic stories of treason and rebellion. All pled for my ear, all expected recompense.

A week before Christmas a man came to me with letters bearing the signatures of Molinier and a young lieutenant in the Gendarmerie. The contents of these letters pointed, without hope of any error, at the desire of these two men to kill me. The next day I ordered Molinier to send me the reports of the Gendarmerie's activities for the last two months. When they came, I compared the signatures on the reports with the handwriting and signatures of the assassination letters supposedly written by Molinier. No noticeable differences existed. I paid the informer, himself a member of the force, and told him to find at least five other gendarmes who shared his active loyalty to the Navarch. With less difficulty than I had expected, he did so.

These six men I dispatched at a predawn hour to Molinier's quarters in the lower courtyard; they took him from his bed and returned with him to a vacant section of the stable where I awaited their coming, two of the older council members at my side. We showed Molinier the documents, and I confronted him with the damning similarity of the signatures, studying his impassive face for those involuntary tics and crawls that of themselves confess the man. But he said simply, 'I would never have put my name to a letter so crassly seditious, Navarch,' and glared at me with unrepentant eyes.

My heart was torn. I did not believe him. I said, 'You will die as quickly and as painlessly as a man may die, Molinier, because until now you refused to lie to me – even when you disagreed with my executive mandates.'

He looked at me coldly. Soul sick, I waved my hand and left.

The informant and his five companions took Molinier to the ivied wall between the stables. There they shot him. The rifle reports echoed over the flagstone like polyps exploding in their shells; a sea dream died with each report.

The repercussions of these shots were felt from the Palace to the quays. Because the force might have deposed me if properly unified, I left the Gendarmerie directorless. As a result, I could not leave my own sleeping chamber and conference rooms for fear that a fanatic worse than Molinier would slay me in the streets. In the Palace, the younger council members treated me with borderline courtesy and whispered among themselves.

But Prendick, who was now free of our self-imposed labour, stayed with me during the afternoons and 'monitored my health'. While every other bureaucrat in the government engaged in intrigue, he kept me informed of our patient's progress. He seemed entirely unaware of the precariousness of my hold on the Navarchy. He thought only of Serenos, of our magnificent pseudo-shark.

'He doesn't eat,' Prendick said one afternoon in the administrative suite. 'I'm afraid he's losing strength rather than gaining it.'

'Why?' I meant, *Why are you afraid that's happening?*

But Prendick responded, 'To deny us our revenge,

Markcrier. Some part of his conscious mind is operating to bring all our efforts to naught. He's *willing* himself to death. But to combat his will I drug him and feed him intravenously.'

'He'll finally grow stronger, then?'

'I don't know, he's a preter-natural creature. Do you know what I heard a simple fisherman once say of him?'

'No. What?'

'That Serenos and the Adam of Genesis are the same person. The fisherman claimed that Adam never really died but wandered throughout the earth cursing his fall and his own meekness before God after the expulsion from Eden. Since no one can remember when Serenos was born, the old fisherman believed this story. He believed that Serenos was Adam.'

'A legend,' I said. 'The legend of the unregenerate Adam. It has great antiquity, Yves, but not a great deal of respectability.'

'Well, if it's true,' Yves said, 'we've finally ended it.'

'Yes, I suppose we have. Or else the unregenerate Adam is in the process of ending it himself. Forever. By foiling our plans for him. An extremely unregenerate Adam is Serenos.'

'I don't want to lose him, Mark, not after all the work I've done. If he dies, I'd have to create another like him — only more detailed and less flawed than this one. My hands know what to do now.'

To that I answered nothing. Marina's father had regained a little of his former colour with several successive nights of uninterrupted and heavy sleep, but he still spoke from a nightmarish, topsy-turvy point of view. Had he transferred his love for the memory of his daughter to another of his children? Locked inside the Palace of the dominion which I ostensibly ruled, I did not understand how one could develop an affection for sharks, even man-made ones. Pride in accomplishment, perhaps, but never abiding affection. Spontaneous awe, perhaps, but never love.

When Christmas came, the old residual festivities took

place and everyone silently acknowledged the existence of a general truce.

Men and women danced in the streets. The ships in the harbour flew brilliant handmade banners of gold and scarlet. The officers of the Gendarmerie wore their blue dress uniforms and organised a parade of horses and men from the Palace to the quays, a parade in which drums, flutes, and teakwood mandolins (these last played by the only Orientals on Guardian's Loop) provided a gay and stately accompaniment to the clatter of horses' hooves. Sea-gulls, screeching and wheeling, rode the updraughts above the Christmas festivities like animated diacritical marks on a parchment of pale blue.

At nine o'clock in the morning I went out on the balcony and told the gendarmes and the footmen in the courtyard that they too could join their merry-making companions. The truce was both general and genuine.

Then I put on a cape with a hood and Prendick and I left the Palace. We walked down the several levels of narrow rose-tinged houses to the hospital. There was a smell of rum on the morning breeze, and children ran down the cobbles and darted in and out of doorways, shouting. Most of them paid no heed at all to the deformities with which they had been born – unless of course their legs or feet had been affected, in which cases they sat on stoops and window sills where their parents had placed them and shouted as insistently as the others. The children with untouched bodies seemed to have the grimmest faces; they played with the quiet determination of soldiers.

Prendick and I said nothing to either the children or the adults.

At Hospitaler House we got immediately to business.

The day had come to release Serenos into the waters of Pretty Coal Sack. For five days Prendick had refrained from administering any sort of sedative or stimulant to his creation, and he believed that a further delay in this final test would serve no purpose but the continuation of our anxiety. I said, 'It's now very much a question of sink or swim, isn't it?' but Prendick was either too distracted or too well-bred to respond. In any case, we had no more opportunities for humour, however feeble or strained, for the duration of that protracted Christmas morning and afternoon.

The long experiment failed.

We placed the tank of sea water containing Serenos in a pressure chamber that was sometimes used by divers. We closed the weighted inner door and introduced enough water to fill the chamber completely – so that our pseudo-shark could swim effortlessly out of the tank, free of all artificial restraints but the iron-grey walls of the pressure chamber itself. Then we opened the outer door, commanded it to swim with measured slowness into the still, cathedral-solemn depths of Pretty Coal Sack. We felt our heartbeats echoing solemnly in the conches of our ears. We waited for our patchwork primeval icthyoid to float free of the shadow of the pressure chamber and into the boundless sun-warmed sea beyond the sunken surgical hall's giant portal. We waited by the cold glass. We waited for the appearance of the thing we loved and hated, our hands clammy with salt sweat.

At last, the narrow misbegotten body of Serenos dropped laterally through the shadowed waters towards us. It moved its tail and fins with no enthusiasm, no beauty, no apparent purpose. And then it turned its sleek grey-and-blue-marbled flank to the glass behind which we stood and slid down this nearly frictionless surface to a height exactly on a line with our eyes. Here the creature hung, flank pressed against the glass, one piggish unblinking eye staring without hope or love into our wide illuminated sanctuary. The seas of the world stretched away behind it, like so many disregarded suitors, but only the perfunctory movement of the raw pectoral fin betrayed that Serenos was still alive to rebuff these lovers more.

Then even that movement ceased, and Serenos died.

Created without an air bladder, as all sharks are necessarily created, the pseudo-shark canted to one side, suffered a spasm throughout the length of its trunk, and drifted away towards the bottom of Pretty Coal Sack, spiralling down in dreamy slow motion.

When Serenos had disappeared, Prendick and I looked at each other in silence and then turned away from the window. Three months of our lives we had spent in this enterprise, no inconsequential portion of the time a man has allotted to him. Prendick sat down and wept.

I thought, *And is it thus that we have finally avenged the death of a daughter and a wife? What manner of beast are we?*

It is the Year of Our Lost Lord 5309. Or so we believe. From the sea we came, and to the sea we eventually return. There is very little more to tell in this account of our exile in the terra-cotta city of Windfall Last.

On the day after our failure with Serenos I abdicated my position as Navarch and thereby forestalled the inevitable assassination attempt. I did not take this action out of cowardice. Too many other factors influenced me.

The first of these was the knowledge that no emissary to the Parfects, no matter who he was, would alter their ultimate judgment upon mankind. Under no circumstances would I go again to Azteca Nueva; under no circumstances would I offer myself up as the ritual scapegoat of a species doomed from the very moment of its prehistoric inception, particularly when my own sacrifice – just like that of another long before me – would signify nothing, would mark the waste of still another spirit yearning towards the unattainable. For that reason and others, I abdicated. How could I face the Parfects after my part in Serenos' mutilation and murder?

Instead, I have settled upon another course of action, one that appeals to the tenets of my aesthetic and moral feelings.

Tomorrow morning in the sunken theatre of surgery, I am to go under Prendick's knife. He has already agreed to my plan, and his insane dedication to the rationale behind it will see him through the disconcerting early stages of my

83

metamorphosis. Later, when my resemblance to a shark has grown more and more faithful, he will forget altogether that inside the tapered head resides the essence and the intellect of his own son-in-law. He will not fail with me as we failed with Serenos – from that failure Prendick learned too much, his hands derived too many unconscious skills.

And three months hence I will go with supple zeal into the waters of the Atlantic, no more a man.

I am convinced that we are the freaks of the universe; we were never meant to be. In our natures there is an improper balance of stardust and dross, too much of one, too little of the other – but not enough of either to give us the perfection of the extreme.

My entire life has been a struggle to achieve that which the universe long ago decreed we might not achieve. I have been living with the delusions of the evolutionary mistake of which I am a product. But no more. Tomorrow morning I am tacking about into the indifferent winds of the cosmos and altering my course. Though perfection is denied me in the direction of the westward seas, I will attain it by swinging towards the dawn. God! even now the salt is in my blood and the power of a shark's primordial lust surges through my heart and loins!

I will swim against the current.

I will seek out the channel that cuts beneath the Galleon of the Hesperides and beach myself among the flowers. There I will die, knowing that the white otters will observe my death and scramble into the sea – aghast at so much unprincipled might.

And my death will be more honest than any single instance of a good man's piety.

*Beneath the Shattered Moons*

*And strange at Ecbatan the trees*
*Take leaf by leaf the evening strange*

Archibald MacLeish

# PART ONE

# One

I went with the old man because Our Shathra Anna's
foremost minister had bade me watch his every move. For
ten days I had been at the old man's side, and uncom-
plainingly, though not very congenially (though this was
changing), he had accepted my presence. The old man's
name was Gabriel Elk. He was sixty-three years old. He
was universally acknowledged a genius, perhaps the only
bonafide one in all of Ongladred, indeed on all of our
ruthlessly harsh planet, Mansueceria.

And on the night with which this account begins Gabriel
Elk and I were going into Lunn, our capital, to buy a
dead masker.

The city lay before us as ominously quiescent as an
unstruck gong. I had been living – these past ten days –
with Gabriel Elk, his wife, Bethel, and his son, Gareth, at
Stonelore, the neuro-theatre he had built nearly seven
kilometres outside of Lunn. Now we were coming back
into the city under the cold light of the Shattered Moons,
and I was glad to see Lunn's majestic squalor again, the
unbroken rows of four-storey dwellings, the canyonlike
alleys, the ever-visible lemon sheen of the dome under
which Our Shathra Anna resides and towards which
nearly all the dirty alleys lead: the Atarite Palace. As an
aide to Chancellor Blaine, as a very minor doer of the sort
of work Our Shathra may not sully her hands with, I was
going home again – even though Gabriel Elk and I would
not set foot within several city squares of the domed
palace. We were going among the poor, 'the Mansuecerians themselves', Gabriel Elk would say, and our way was
through the torch-lit sidestreets.

We were walking our horses. Their hooves clacked on
the stones, their eyes were round with a mute claustro-
phobia, their nostrils quivered with the pungent smells of

packed-in humanity. But we met no one in the streets. It was the time of the Halcyon Panic (hence, my assignment to Elk, whom the Magi feared as a potential demagogue), and at night everyone stayed docilely indoors – everyone but those with state business and, of course, the maddeningly uncoercible Gabriel Elk who had come on business of his own.

'Do you know where we are?' I asked him, a bite in my voice.

He halted his shaggy animal and looked at me. The old man's eyes were a pale green, his face as heavy as carven marble, the jowls giving way only slightly to his sixty-three years. Great white sideburns framed his cheeks, and his hair fell in bearish curls over his forehead and neck. 'On Earth my sixty-three years would be seventy-five,' he had told me when I was first assigned to him, but he carried himself with an intractable agelessness. In this alleyway in Lunn he looked like a statue that has willed its limbs to move, that has broken out of stone into life.

'I know where we are, Ingram. This city was mine long before you entered the service of Our Shathra or the elitist gangs of Chancellor Blaine. Some say the Chancellor got his roan tooth by sucking blood up through it, and, from what I see, a bit of that blood is yours, Master Marley. You're as bumptious and ticky as a person of power.'

'I work for persons of power, Sayati Elk.' Against Blaine's wishes, Our Shathra Anna had given Gabriel Elk the title *sayati* in his fifty-sixth year, after the construction of Stonelore and the presentation of the first series of neuro-dramas. In the seven succeeding years Blaine and the Council of the Magi had agitated quietly for the revocation of Elk's royal dispensation to assemble the people and for the nationalisation of the formidable power complex he had built in the upland arena.

'So you do, Ingram, so you do. And in your own way you also are a person of power.'

'I do what I must – to ensure that the Halcyon Panic doesn't break out roaring in the throats of our within-doors maskers.'

'And I do what I must, Ingram, to ensure that when the "maskers" come out to Stonelore they perceive an order in things which the universe and the Magi of Ongladred don't always choose to grant them. The order is there, it inheres, and I'm the man who reveals it to them.'

The Shattered Moons moved in a yellow band beyond the in-leaning rooftops, a monochrome rainbow in the night sky. Only the brightest stars were visible behind it, and it was hard to imagine that Ongladred was an island besieged, that the culture we had twice before built up over six thousand years as colonists on Mansueceria was in danger of collapsing again, collapsing completely.

The street was silent; my voice echoed in it. 'And so to give the maskers order, you've come tonight to buy a dead man.'

'Not exactly, Ingram. I've come to buy a dead woman, a beautiful girl killed by reivers. And the order I try to give the Mansuecerians, the gentles, is a glimpse of the order inhering outside themselves – for inwardly they're disciplined, Ingram, they're more serene, more in control of the animal in themselves than you or I. Only artists have to rage, artists and rulers.'

'Our rulers don't rage, Sayati Elk.'

'No, they simmer, Ingram. The worse for them.' His horse, a woolly beast, lifted its head, whickeringly barked. The old man pulled the horse's head down and began walking again. The stones rang. Shadows wrapped themselves around us like voluted capes. 'My sense of direction never faileth,' he said after a while. 'Look there.'

We had come to a side-canyon, a narrow crevice between two rows of maskers'-houses perpendicular to the alley by which, on the city's southeastern outskirts, we had originally entered Lunn. There was no room for our horses here. But I looked where Elk was pointing and saw a green-gowned figure on a third-storey balcony on the left-hand side of the alley, a figure stooping beneath a pair of conical lanterns to see us. But for this solitary revenant and those two lanterns, the 'street' was unhaunted, dark, and coldly daunting.

The Halcyon Panic had begun to play in me; I wanted no part of Sayati Elk's sinister purchase of a dead girl.

'Come on, Ingram,' he said. 'We'll tie our horses here.' He wrapped the reins of his animal around a stone gutter-spout; I did likewise. Our footfalls reverberating in the night air, we walked through the alley between the maskers'-houses. There was a balcony across from the one on which the stooping figure stood, and it seemed to me that it would require very little effort to step from the left-hand balcony to the right-hand one, three storeys' worth of darkness gaping beneath that step.

'Who's up there?' I asked.

'Josu Lief, the father of the dead girl. Or so I'd guess.'

The man on the balcony called out. Before he called, I had not been certain that he was a man; the gown had confused me. It was mourning garb. Under him now I could see that the gown and his shaved head – he was newly bald – were his only concessions to 'grief'. The Mansuecerians are immune to it, genetically serene, philosophically spartan. 'Sayati Elk?' Gentleman Lief called out. Then: 'Please come up, both of you.' A serene, spartan voice.

We entered the bleak doorway. We climbed the cork-screwing stairs. We let Josu Lief usher us into a three-room apartment where the rest of his family, dressed in forest-green mourning gowns and sitting in the candlelit central chamber, awaited us. There were introductions. Lief's wife wore her hair cut short, as did the two female children. Josu and his young son were bald from the razor. They accepted the news that I was a minor official of Our Shathra Anna's oligarchy with utter blandness; they were maskers, and I was a nouveau Atarite, pro-grammed to rule. Gabriel Elk was of them, but different; a throwback in whom the primeval aggressions still roiled, still threatened eruption. The old man was the bridge between the Lief family and me.

'Where's Bronwen?' Gabriel Elk asked.

'Through here,' Gentleman Lief said, and led us out of the central chamber into a sleeping-room where there

94

were six pallets on the floor. The girl lay on the pallet on which she had undoubtedly slept while alive: Bronwen Lief, eldest daughter of these anonymous maskers. One family amid a city full of similar families, all of them debeasted, shaped in their genes towards a civilising harmony. On them had been founded the state of Ongladred; only rulers and artists raged, and we Atarites so seldom as to suggest an innate serenity akin to that of the maskers.

'Will you accept my price?' Elk asked Lief.

'I accept it, Sayati Elk.'

'Good. The money has already been credited to you. It's there for your use. Three days from now, bring your family to Stonelore.'

'And she will perform?'

'A special performance, for the Lief family and some privileged others. Not a neuro-drama, but a kind of reading.'

'Will she later act in the dramas?'

'Such is my hope.'

The three of us looked at the dead Bronwen Lief – her father with an expression predictably neutral, in which there was neither pride nor remorse nor pity nor anything paternal in a strictly Atarite sense; Gabriel Elk with quiet appreciation; and I, the outsider, with an awareness of terrible loss. For Bronwen Lief, arranged on her pallet in her white death-gown, was an image that called up evocative names: Helen, Guinevere, Ligeia. She was beautiful, but there was something in her young face hinting at the ability to betray; in a Mansuecerian, a masker, that look disconcerted, it slept in the corners of her mouth like an incongruous smirk, an anomaly of character. As a dirt-runner I had long ago learned to recognise such telltale glimmerings under men's false, placid exteriors. But Bronwen Lief was a masker girl, and a corpse, and the candlelight made her flesh resemble porcelain.

Gabriel Elk said: 'I'm very pleased, Gentleman Lief. She's beautiful; she's what I'd hoped for.'

'Our thanks, Sayati Elk.'

95

I said: 'How did she die, exactly?'

The two older men turned their faces towards me. Josu Lief, I saw, could not have been more than forty; even with a shaved head he was a handsome man, with full lips and dark eyes. 'I have told our friends, in a fall. But there's more, as Sayati Elk knows. Last night she went with a young man, the one selected for her, to see the bonfires by the eastern channel, the bonfires holding off the sloak—'

'You let them go?' I said. 'At this time?'

'Bronwen did as she wished. It wasn't for me to permit or hinder her, either one. She had a good life, Master Marley.'

'And a short one. What happened on the coast with her young man?

'Laird and she was walking in the rocks, looking towards the Angromain Archipelago where your renegade ancestors kill each other and catch fish, Master Marley. They was thinking on the cycle of the sloak and the barbarians way out to sea there. Bronwen's young man says they spoke of the bonfires on the beach and of living to oldsters in Lunn, such things as that. Then they saw an empty boat, just a pinnace, beached in a rocky place between two of the bonfires. No sooner had they seen it than they heard voices, men speaking in accents not of Ongladred. The men surprised them, a party of three or four thick-bearded Pelagans on a raid of some sort. The Pelagans ran at them, pushed Bronwen and young Laird from the rocks, and leapt to the sand. It was a short drop, Laird says, but Bronwen must have twisted her neck. Laird fell into a gravelly place and broke his leg. He shouted so the bonfire tenders on both sides come running, you know, but it was too late. Out to sea the Pelagans went, oaring it like madmen or fiends – and Bronwen was dead. And so she came home to us, and we dressed her like you see her. In her death-gown.'

'And Laird!' Gabriel Elk asked.

'He's on the mend, I'll wager.'

# Two

We went back into the apartment's central chamber. The women sat on straight-backed chairs, doing something to the patterned quilts in their laps. Lief's son, his bald head shining, was on the floor marking a piece of paper with a stylus; he was about six.

'At least your boy won't be called up,' Elk said. When the Halcyon Panic broke, military service for men between the ages of fifteen and fifty would be obligatory. Unless one were an Atarite (and in many cases, even then). I knew that inductions had already begun. Josu Lief confirmed me in my knowledge.

'They tapped me two days ago,' he said. 'I go in five days.' And he would too. Docilely, he would take off his mourning-gown, don a warrior's breeches, and cover his shaved head with a leather cap. Then off to the Lunn garrison for his assignment. The masker, the gentle, would become a soldier – pacific in his innermost soul, but ruthlessly obedient in war.

'Then Gareth will be touched soon, too,' Elk said, and genius or no he could not keep the regret out of his huge, corrugated brow. Unlike the serene Gentleman Lief's, his feelings towards his children – his child rather, now his only son – ran deeper than stoic affection. After all, Gabriel Elk was a mistake, an artist; in all things he raged, he harkened to a gong inaudible to maskers and Atarites alike.

We sat down. Gentlewoman Lief left her chair, went to a cabinet in the apartment's kitchen, and returned with three cups of *haoma*. This is a mildly intoxicating drink distilled from the bullcap fungus and banned at court; the maskers believe that it induces righteousness and piety rather than drunkenness. Curious, I sipped what was given me. Simultaneously sweet and tart, the haoma seemed to transfuse warmth through the lining of my stomach, into my veins and marrow, like a flow of heated blood. While Gabriel Elk and Gentleman Lief talked, I nodded and tried to heed their words.

'When will the Halcyon Panic break?' the old man asked.

'Not yet, Sayati Elk, not yet.'

'Your neighbours?'

'They continue calm. There's talk of the sloak, and of the Pelagans, and even of the rupturing of the sun – but no one screams in his sleep, no one's yammering of Ongladred's death. Our Shathra Anna watches over us. She's a wise-eyed lady, wise in her watching.'

Gentlewoman Lief smiled at her husband, the girls continued sewing, the boy coloured his scrap of paper without heeding his father's visitors at all. At court, a young official's death would have kept us from secular activity for at least a day or two; here, it required all my haoma-ridden powers to remember that Bronwen Lief lay dead in the next room. Haoma. No doubt Josu Lief had had the examining physician administer an undiluted extract of the principal drug in this beverage to his daughter's corpse, as a temporary preservative. And here I was, embalming myself in a maskers' drink. Bronwen's face, her ambiguously smiling face, floated into my mind, into my sight. I gripped my chair.

Unaffected, Gabriel Elk was standing. The other people in the room began rising, too. I heard Josu Lief say, 'Do you want me to bring her out to Stonelore tomorrow, Sayati Elk?'

'Have you a blanket you can spare?'

'I've finished this quilt,' Lief's wife said. 'You may take it, if you like. For Bronwen.'

'Good. I'll wrap her in it, and Marley and I will take her with us now. There's no need in your carrying her out there tomorrow, Josu.'

I was standing now. Someone took the cup out of my hands. Josu left the room. He came back with his daughter wrapped in the quilt. I noticed that the silken quilt, a series of cream-coloured squares, was embroidered around its hem with blue flowers, the kind that grow on the cliffs above the Angromain Channel. Bronwen's face was not covered; her black hair fell over Josu Lief's supporting forearm. I watched as the father gave her into the arms of Gabriel Elk, even though by rights I ought to have been the one to carry her.

'Remember,' the old man said. 'Come three days from now.' Then, turning to me: 'Ingram, let's go.' I managed to get to the door, and to open it for the burdened-down old codger. The stairwell yawned beneath us. The family, but for Lief's son, crowded into the opening. I stood with my back pressed against the open door, cold seeping up to me from the street.

'The Light stay with you,' Gentlewoman Lief told Elk, 'and the Lie die.' That was their religion, the whole of it, conveyed in two gently spoken imperatives. The woman said nothing at all to her dead child, though I half expected her to. The girl had gone to the Abode of Song – despite the fact that maskers never sing during their lifetimes. Singing is an activity that lies outside their stoic code; indeed, outside their very natures.

Gabriel Elk was on the stairs. I looked back into the Liefs' main sitting-room and saw the six-year-old boy standing there with a piece of paper dangling from his hand. He raised his blond, boyishly thin eyebrows a little.

'Goodbye, Bronwen,' he said.

I reeled towards the stairwell, grabbed the railing there, and clumped groggily down the steps behind the old man and the dead girl he carried. In the cold street we found our horses and rode towards Stonelore and Elk's rock-capped residence. Bronwen Lief, wrapped in a quilt embroidered with blue flowers, lay doubled over the old philosopher/playwright's saddle, wedged between the pommel and his paunch, deprived of dignity. Lunn faded behind us, and the Shattered Moons danced. Our horses climbed powerfully into the dark of the countryside. Immersed in wind, my head began to clear.

# Three

Even though Stonelore lay seven kilometres beyond Lunn, to the southeast, it was easily accessible by a road running from the capital to the fishing village of Mershead on the Angromain Channel. In the spring the maskers set up produce stalls and vanity booths along this road, and did a good business among the travellers and fishermen going between Lunn and Mershead. Since it was in the spring that Elk presented his three neurodramas of the year, he had no difficulty attracting maskers to fill his circular stone amphitheatre. But, on the night we rode back from Lunn with Bronwen Lief over Elk's saddle, the equinox was still a good Mansuecerian month away; consequently, the Mershead Road was deserted but for a company of lately inducted maskers, carrying antiquated Yorkley rifles, marching towards the beaches. (The Halcyon Panic had had its subtle grip on Ongladred for the whole of the winter.) A few of these men hailed us civilly as we rode by, then the darkness loomed up again, and abruptly Elk goaded his horse off the road and into unmarked country – a stony short-cut to his home in the rocks.

The ground, covered with short grass, seemed to swell up beneath us, the horizons to expand. I imagined that at any moment we would ride into peril; our horses would plunge from the sea-fronting cliffs, the withdrawing tides would carry us to the barren archipelagoes where our enemies lived out their hatred for us. – Instead, the horizons contracted again as chunks and blocks of stone began to rise up around us.

Finally we rode into the rock-walled upland arena in which the Stonelore amphitheatre had been built. The amphitheatre was white under the Shattered Moons, its broad plastic cap gleaming dully. To the left of the amphitheatre was the energy unit that provided the power for both Elk's house and the animation of the delicately programmed actors in his neuro-dramas; it squatted in the dark like an outsized toadstool.

In Lunn a similar but differently constituted unit powered the heating and cooling systems in Our Shathra Anna's palace, as well as the glass flambeaux in the corridors and bed-chambers. Solvent from his early literary activities, wealthy from his share of booty taken from the Pelagans during the mid-century skirmishes in which he had served as a commander, Elk had bought the components of the energy unit with his own funds; then he had engineered its design and construction, engaged in covert talks with a Pelagan minister, and acquired enough fissionable material to keep Stonelore running for three hundred years. Later he had admitted – openly – making a reciprocal arrangement with a representative of the barbarians that Ongladred had held successfully at bay during the undeclared, mid-century hostilities.

Those days were gone. Elk was past the age of conscription, and he lived and worked beyond the means or the capabilities of the citizens whom his work 'enlightened'. Only Our Shathra Anna and the wealthiest of Atarites could challenge his lifestyle. Several days before, I had asked him about this. 'How can you, one of the people, justify the way you live, Sayati Elk?'

'I don't have to *justify* anything, Ingram. Our Shathra Anna gave me the title by which you address me, and Stonelore grew up around me as the result of the efforts of my hands and mind. I dwell here, but I don't look upon a single pebble of this site as "property".'

I laughed. 'You're just a caretaker?'

'No, I'm a creator. Transient as they are, Stonelore and the neuro-dramas are my gift to the civilisation of Ongladred.'

'A civilisation now threatened,' I reminded him.

'Exactly, Ingram. So I create the harder. A social order promoting social order, and nothing more, isn't civilisation at all; it's a machine for maintaining the *status quo*. The Mansuecerians live as they must, the Atarite Court rules as it must – but I have to give shape to voices and forms lying outside your experience or muffled so close to you that you're blind to them.'

'Why? In these times, to what purpose?'

'So that you can experience them. And so that I can live.' He had started to say more, but bit his heavy lip and turned away.

Now we guided our horses to the right of the amphitheatre and dismounted in front of the house carven out of the rear wall of the upland arena: Grotto House. Gareth, Elk's son, came out to greet us; he took the horses and led them to shelter in a stable down from Grotto House. (The stable was an anomaly; it was made entirely of wood, and it could not be seen from the environs of the amphitheatre.) Holding Bronwen, I watched the boy go. He was sixteen, very nearly the child of his father's dotage – except that Gabriel Elk was a long way from senile garrulity; he struggled to contain his natural affection for the boy.

Gareth was his parents' last child. Two older sons had died in separate accidents, one drowning in the Angromain Channel, the other apparently the victim of a thief or Pelagan raiders, very like the dead girl in my arms. This was years ago. A daughter lived in Lunn, married to a masker with no more fire in him than any other of their kind. She did not like to come out to Stonelore. As for Gareth, he had his father's heavy face, and he was trying to grow a beard. It was coming out thin, red, and lugubrious-looking, but he persisted in a standing refusal to shave. Too, he had some of his father's spark: already he had shown himself skilful at hacking boulders into strange, sinuous shapes. Sculptures, he called them, although it wasn't always easy to tell of what. He said they were supposed to be trees, artwork designed to suggest the possibilities of growth.

'Come inside,' Gabriel Elk said. 'Before you drop her.'

My arms *had* begun to ache. We passed through a heavy wrought-iron gate that blocked the entrance to

Grotto House, a gate with old Spanish scrollwork in the iron; and then I followed the old man into the foyer of the rock house. Illuminated panels made every wall glow, and two rough corridors led out of the foyer to right and left. 'Where do you want her?' I asked.

'In the programming room.'

Bethel Elk came out of the right-hand corridor to greet us. She took her husband's hand and said hello to me. She was as tall as I; her arms were bare in a pale-yellow gown. Without self-consciousness she also wore a thin wire brace as additional support for her back, which she had long ago injured in a fall. She was a Mansuecerian, but it was rumoured that her father had been an Atarite. How else account for the saucy cast in her eye, a look heightened rather than dampened by her age?

'The girl's beautiful,' she said.

'Aye,' Gabriel Elk said. 'So I bought her. Now if Master Marley'll escort her down to the programming room—'

'Tonight?' the woman said. 'Let her lie in a bed-chamber.'

'I'm going to work tonight,' Gabriel Elk said. 'Haomycin doesn't hold forever, my lady, and we have company in three days. Go on, Ingram.'

I said: 'Surely you can begin in the morning and still get done.'

Elk grinned; his sideburns stood away from his smile like white wings. 'Ingram's on orders to watch me,' he said, 'and he's too tired to do it. Don't worry, Ingram, I'm not going to sneak off while you're sleeping and file for citizenship among the Pelagans. Take Bronwen down the hall. Then go to bed.'

'Fine,' I said. Alone, I went down the corridor to the left, all the way to its end, then halted in front of the elevator there. The door slid open. I stepped in. Humming, the elevator dropped us three or four metres to the programming room.

I carried Bronwen Lief into this chamber, placed her on a table, opened the silken quilt away from her, and stared at her gowned body and her non-committal lips. Still, the ability to betray was there even yet, in death as well as in life she could betray. In the programming room, amid support consoles, minicomputers, oscilloscopes, and Elk's privately engineered neural-surrogate equipment, I associated Bronwen Lief with everything that was then threatening Ongladred's civilisation: the barbarians of the Angromain Archipelago, the mythical sloak, Elk's own wayward genius, and, damn me for thinking it, maybe even the inflexibility of Atarite rule. Somehow Bronwen Lief was all of these things; somehow she embodied all the intangibles of the Halcyon Panic.

Weary, I left the programming room, found my own bedchamber on the upper level, and slept until the sun was high.

# Four

All the next day I saw nothing of Gabriel Elk. However, there was a tunnel running from the programming room to the comp-centre beneath the Stonelore amphitheatre, and I was certain that the old man, labouring alone, was preparing both the corpse of Bronwen Lief and the comp-troller room itself for the special performance two evenings hence. I was of Our Shathra Anna's intelligence service, the Eyes and Ears of the Court, but I'd begun to trust Gabriel Elk – more, to respect him. He was too busy, too unconcerned with our petty preoccupations to try to elude me.

At midday I threaded my way through the rocks to the stable. In the barren paddock I found Gareth and the Elk family ostler, a middle-aged masker named Robin Coigns. He had been sleeping when we arrived from Lunn the previous evening, and Gareth's father had chosen not to disturb him. Gareth, as usual, was chiselling at a block of stone on a split-rail table, and Robin was grooming Gabriel's horse, pulling out long strands of kinky sorrel hair. The other animal was beneath the wooden awning, eating.

I entered the paddock. 'Hello, horsesweat,' I said to Robin.

Blandly, the ostler grinned. Gareth was too busy to do anything more than nod. His chisel glinted in the anaemic sun; splinters flew away from his gloved hands. This statue, this 'tree', was going to be as convolute as any he had ever made. I shielded my eyes and looked into the sun, into feeble old Maz.

'Well, Robin,' I said. 'What do you think? Is Maz going to nova, blow up in Ongladred's skies? Everything else imaginable is supposed to happen when the Panic breaks.'

'Maz won't blow,' Robin said. 'I'll expect the sloak first.'

'Do you believe in the sloak?'

'It's been ver-i-fied, hasn't it, Master Marley?'

'Postulated, not verified.'

'Well, Our Shathra Anna says there's geo-logical ev-i-dence.'

'Some.' I was always amused by the gullibility of maskers, particularly uneducated ones like the ostler Robin Coigns.

Gareth looked up from his work. 'I believe in the sloak,' he said. His wide face glistened with sweat; his patchy beard oulined his jaw with a moist, plastered redness. 'And Father believes in it. As Robin says, there's evidence to support its existence – at least in theory.'

'In theory,' I said. I had heard all the arguments before. *Sloak* was the masker name for an apparently chimerical sea creature that no one had ever seen. No one had ever seen it because it dwelled kilometres off the coast of Ongladred, on the very bottom of the ocean floor: a millimicron-thin membrane of otherwise immense proportions cloaking the sea bottom all the way to Mansueceria's equator, where the planet's waters supposedly became too warm for so sensitive a monster. Legend had it that the sloak, which moved in slow, vaguely peristaltic undulations, thickened itself consciously every two thousand years and pulled its bulk over the entire surface of our island. Then, like a huge dappled eye, it lay basking, breathing for a year or more, in the dull sunlight of our world – after which it returned to the marbled green depths of the Suthward Trench.

An unhurried, rhythmical departure, no doubt.

'Two previous civilisations on Ongladred died,' Gareth said. 'Died seemingly at the height of their glory; died without suffering human conquest. And Father says that it wasn't so terribly long ago – during or after the creature's last cycle – that the Angromain Archipelagoes were settled by fleeing Atarites. Only enough people survived on Ongladred to begin again. Ours is the third civilisation of colonists so threatened, Master Marley.'

'The sloak is an explanation only if you have no other,'

I said. 'There's firmer evidence for two periods of mild glaciation. Why not accept these as the means of destruction you're looking for, Gareth?'

'Glaciation from the south!' the boy said heatedly. 'Why accept the illogical? I prefer the sloak, Robin's sloak.'

'The sloak it was,' Robin said. 'The sloak it was.'

'And if the cycle holds true,' Garth said, 'this is the year.' With his chisel, he made several chips of stone fly.

'The more immediate threat to Ongladred is human, Gareth – the Pelagans. They're real, they're avaricious, and they've finally begun to demonstrate the unity to undermine us. Before, their own divisiveness kept them manageable.'

'Ten thousand years ago, on Earth, the threat was always human,' the boy said, chiselling, his brow furious. Then he halted, looked over the block of stone on the table, fixed me with his blue-green eyes. 'And you, Master Marley, see a threat even in my father. That's why you've come to Stonelore. That's why we bed and feed you, one of the Eyes and Ears of Our Shathra.'

'I do what I must.' It seemed that I had used these same words a hundred times before. Ingram Marley, a dirt-runner, a spy with no cover. Robin Coigns finished grooming Gabriel Elk's horse and led it under the shelter; he began pulling the wire comb down the flank of the other animal, tactfully out of earshot. Aswim in a welter of ambiguous loyalties, I watched him.

'And so does my father,' Gareth said. 'He also does what he must, but you've placed him among the potential dangers to Ongladred. In reality he is in himself the culmination of what that civilisation ought to stand for. Does the Atarite Court know what it's doing, Master Marley?'

'Do you question Our Shathra Anna?' I was ashamed to frame this response, but I didn't know what else to say to the boy; therefore, subtle intimidation.

He would have none of it. 'Not Our Shathra Anna. She alone among you may understand what Gabriel Elk represents. It's Chancellor Blaine and the Magi of the Atarite

Court whose wisdom seems to me suspect, Master Marley.'

'How suspect, Gareth?' Then I asked him something else, before he could answer my first question. 'Will you disobey your conscription order when it comes, as it surely will?'

'If Ongladred requires men to defend her, I will aid in her defence.' The boy was indignant; his voice quavered. 'My father fought for this island, and so will I. I, too, am an Elk, Master Marley.'

'Your father's a man of influence. Will he let you go?'

'He would have to, wouldn't he? In everything, he obeys the laws of the island. Besides, he knows if he attempted to hinder me, I wouldn't be stopped; I would go without his consent.' The boy's stare fell away from me, a gratifying respite.

Robin Coigns came back, his currying unfinished. He sat on a bale of fodder between Gareth and me; I was leaning on the paddock rail. Robin said, 'They say all civi-li-sations die, Master Marley. It's the nature of things. En-tro-py, you know, all of it running down. But it seems to me, one way or the other, it can be fought, you know. So I'll fight it, too.'

Apparently he had heard the last part of our conversation. I asked, 'Are you of induction age, too, horse-sweat?'

'Forty-nine,' he said. 'I'll go with Master Gareth. The top and the bottom of their numbers, we'll be. Youth and sa-gassa-ty.'

Gareth laughed. I was grinning too.

'Oh, I'm not worried a' tall,' the ostler went on. 'My father always said that at the third coming of the sloak, the Parfects would return, too. To watch over us, you know. They dropped us here six thousand years ago, he said, and they'd come back if things went too swackers, like they're starting to do now. Why, it's my opinion, Master Marley, that the Parfects are cruising a ship out there among the Shattered Moons right now, orb-it-ing, you know – watching over us Mansuecerians, the People

Accustomed to the Hand. And maybe over you ruling Atarites, too, for governing us good like you have.'

'Those are comforting notions, horsesweat. But I'm afraid your sloak and the hoped-for return of the Parfects are cut from the same mythical cloth; they cancel each other out. We're left with the Pelagan threat, and no mitigating circumstances.'

'And don't forget the peril posed by my father,' Gareth said.

My grin faded; then I saw that Gabriel Elk's son was baiting me, prolonging the moment of uneasy jocularity that Robin Coigns had given us. In the same spirit I said, 'I won't. You keep reminding me. The children of geniuses ought to voluntarily slit their throats as soon as they're cognizant of their heritage – a gash in the Adam's apple. Otherwise, they begin to take themselves too seriously.'

'You don't like my stone work, Master Marley? My trees?'

'You'd be better off petrifying driftwood. Wouldn't take so long, and the results would be about the same.'

'That's a hit,' Robin Coigns said. 'That's a hit.'

We talked some more, then went back through the garden of rocks to Grotto House. Bethel gave us haoma, biscuits, and jerky for a midday meal, and sat down to eat with us herself. It was the first time since I had been there that she had served haoma. The old man did not appear; it was doubtful that he had even slept that night. I thought for a moment of Bronwen Lief, of her disquieting beauty. Then I put her out of my mind and enjoyed the company of the Elks and Robin Coigns, the company and the food. The haoma began to work in me as it had done the night before in Lunn.

Afterwards I excused myself and retired to my bedchamber for a nap. I didn't see Gabriel Elk at all for the remainder of that day. Nor did I see him the next. Nor the next – until late afternoon.

# Five

The Magi at the Atarite Court had determined that if we on Mansueceria converted our system of time-keeping into Earthly terms, it would be the year 12,500 AD. Of course, this was an approximation. We measured time not in this long-ago-discarded way, but in terms of how many Mansuecerian years had passed in the reign of our current shathra. The winter and spring of the Halcyon Panic were preternatural seasons in the Year 35 of Our Shathra Anna, and ensconced in Gabriel Elk's house at Stonelore I wondered how many more years she would reign. I hoped it would be many; she was an estimable woman.

As Robin Coigns had said on the morning after Elk's and my return from Lunn, there had been colonists on Mansueceria for six thousand of our years. We had been brought from Earth in starships conceived and constructed by a neo-human species whom our earliest records had always referred to as the Parfects – principally because Earth's last men had considered them free of all human vices, cleansed of the quasi-mythical taint of Original Sin. It was the Parfects who had saved mankind from ultimate extermination in the terra-cotta city of Windfall Last in the Carib Sea; who had redeemed us genetically, providing for two contrasting but complementary types of individual (the stoically disciplined Mansuecerians, or 'maskers', and the more aggressive, more emotional Atarites); and who had then delivered this population of half a million to the rugged heartland of Ongladred, on a planet more than eight hundred light-years from Earth. Another chance. Yet another chance, in an isolation even more splendid than that the ambient sea had ensured at Windfall Last. Then, the early records and later legends unanimously agreed, the Parfects themselves had left us, gone back to turn all of Earth into the gardens of Adam's first paradise. As for man, he had the rocks of Ongladred – and another chance.

And for six thousand years, despite two major collapses, we had maintained ourselves entire; more, we had managed, with very few exceptions, to maintain our genetic heritage as well, the People Accustomed to the Hand and the People Touched by Fire alike. Together, we had survived. Now Atarite barbarians from the sea-blasted, storm-scoured archipelagoes in the Angromain Sea threatened all we had built together, and there were rumours in the land of the coming of the slow, ravening sloak and the imminent explosion of woebeset Maz. It was the Year of the Halcyon Panic, as well as Year 35 of Our Shathra Anna; a self-conscious calm prevailed.

Late in the afternoon of the third day after our return from Lunn, Gabriel Elk emerged from his seclusion and greeted me in the open courtyard in the centre of his house. My ankles crossed, I had been sitting on a stone bench watching Maz drop mauvely down the sky. 'How have you been faring, Ingram?' the old man said. His green eyes looked tired; his great, winged sideburns were unkempt, and I could see the previously muted resemblance between him and Gareth. For the first time, I could see it clearly.

'Well,' I said. 'And you? Are you done?'

'Done. I had to be. Tonight the Liefs are coming, Ingram, and some others.'

'What others, Sayati Elk?'

'Be patient, and see.' He stood in front of me for a moment, casting his long shadow over both the flagstones and my legs, then turned and went back into the house. I had to pull myself up and follow. I felt uneasy. I could sense all the diverse strands of my anxiety preparing to knot themselves together.

There was no supper that evening, no haoma to share. Bethel met her husband in the foyer, took his hand, nodded vaguely at me. Then we left Grotto House and walked across the sandy arena which the Stonelore amphitheatre completely dominated. Instead of entering

Stonelore, however, we took up sentry positions in one of the natural doorways in the rock wall overlooking the Mershead Road. The wind blew balloons of sand out over the grass, Gabriel and Bethel talked in low voices, and I waited. Just waited.

At last the Liefs came, man and wife, distant figures walking on the low road; they had walked the seven kilometres from Lunn. Even after we saw them, it took a good while for them to reach us. Maz had set, and when they arrived the five of us stood in the twilight like liquid ghosts.

'Hello, Josu,' Gabriel Elk said. 'Welcome, Rhia. Tonight you'll see your daughter reanimated, given a kind of life again. Bethel will take you into Stonelore and show you your seats. I'll follow in a while. There are others whom I'm pledged to greet.'

The Liefs went off with Bethel in the liquid dusk, towards the amphitheatre. When I looked after them, I saw Stonelore's broad circular cap glowing a soft yellow-orange. In response to my questioning look, Gabriel said, 'Gareth's in the comptroller room. Tonight, he does my work.' We turned again to the Mershead Road. Overhead, the Shattered Moons were scarcely visible, as milky as a thousand clumsily shaped pearls floating between Ongladred's strong rock and the heavens' weak stars.

At last we saw the vehicles on the roadway, and I knew that our visitors were Our Shathra Anna, her Chancellor, and some Atarite retainers – guardsmen. Two chariots preceded Our Shathra's equipage, and torches burned in the hands of the men in the chariots. The sound of the horses' hooves grew steadily beneath the sound of the wind, and Gabriel Elk and I watched as the chariots separated from Our Shathra's carriage and circled off in different directions, one halting about fifty metres from the gate in the rocks, the other undoubtedly taking up guard on the other side of the upland arena. The equipage, however, proceeded on up to us, black and silent, its matched horses caparisoned and haughty.

Gabriel Elk, waving his arms, directed the vehicle to

the steps at the base of the amphitheatre. Robin Coigns had appeared from the darkness to help our eminent visitors get out and to show the coachman where he might shelter himself and his horses during the neuro-performance.

'Sayati Elk,' Our Shathra Anna said.

The old man bowed, as did I. The carriage drew away from us. Arngrim Blaine, a tall, ascetic-looking man in his sixtieth year, smiled at us. Even in the failing light his roan tooth was visible, a translucent reddish-black canine pointing upwards like a knife. Long ago he had had it scrimshawed with his initials (it was rumoured), but over the years these had either faded or worn away (if they ever existed). He was a well-meaning, narrow-principled man. 'Hello, Ingram,' he said. 'Sayati Elk. I'm happy enough to greet you, but not at all convinced that this trip was merited. Stonelore has always seemed a frivolous waste to me, and now more than ever.'

'Arngrim has no taste for the arts,' Our Shathra Anna said. She wore a black cloak that fastened at her neck; although she smiled, there were grey circles under her eyes.

'Neither did Cyaxares of Mede,' the Chancellor said. 'Nor Walpole of Augustan England. Besides, Ongladred wasn't made for art.'

Our Shathra Anna said, 'With which man do you compare yourself, Arngrim – the Median king or the English minister?'

'The minister, Lady. The other would be presumptuous.' He bowed.

'Art is an enrichment granted those cultures deserving it,' the creator of Stonelore said. 'Or inflicted on those attempting to repress it.'

Our Shathra Anna looked at Gabriel Elk. When she spoke, her tone was liltingly sharp, ironically humorous. 'Blaine is irritated because he can't rule in all things. Most of all, he can't rule me. I've come to see your entertainment, Gabriel, because I may not be able to come again.'

'The season's danger ought to have dissuaded us from

coming tonight,' Blaine said. 'Two chariots! An inadequate guard, Lady.'

'Then I love the lady for the dangers that she's passed,' Gabriel Elk said. 'And I welcome you both. Let's go inside.' He didn't bow; his gallantry derived from conviction. Taking Our Shathra Anna's arm, he escorted the lady up the stairs to the wide illuminated portal of the amphitheatre. Chancellor Blaine and I trailed them up the steps, two serving-men, each as much a dirt-runner as the other – a situation which I found satisfyingly amusing.

Two of Gareth Elk's tree-sculptures flanked the wide door.

Inside, Elk led us to a glass booth on the theatre's highest circular tier, a booth reserved for Ongladred's Atarites and Atarite retainers. The top of the booth was open, and even though we were on Stonelore's uppermost level, the ceiling arched over us like a miniature sky, utterly out of reach. Our chairs were velvet-upholstered wingbacks set so that we could look comfortably down into the neuropit. Across from us, in the preliminary dark, we could discern Bethel Elk and the Liefs sitting poised and expectant on the continuous stone tier. Otherwise, Stonelore was empty – but sentient, immense and brooding. Gabriel Elk had infused it with something of his own character.

'Those are my actress' parents,' he said. 'I felt that they should be here, too, if they wished to come.'

'Of course,' Our Shathra said.

'I hope,' Blaine said, 'that they're maskers in every sense, inured to feigned emotions and resigned to their daughter's death. This sort of thing can undermine even the stolidest personality, Sayati Elk.'

'It hasn't yet, Chancellor. Tonight, in any case, a reading only. The neuro-drama doesn't undermine anything; it offers release, purgation, for a people manufactured to think they don't require it, but subliminally craving it in any case. The neuro-drama illuminates our oneness, it strengthens the social order you represent.'

'When it's comprehensible, perhaps,' the Chancellor said. 'Mostly, at Stonelore, it criminally drains energy reserves.' It was not impossible to admire the roan-toothed old pragmatist; even genius left him unabashed, wittily clawing.

Gabriel Elk answered him angrily: 'The reserves are mine, not the state's! And the drain is far from criminal since the law refuses to permit human actors. Stonelore is a compromise with that law, Chancellor Blaine – a law of Atarite urging which you capably championed before the Magi. Perhaps you remember?'

'Very well, Sayati Elk, very well.'

Our Shathra Anna leaned forward in her engulfing chair. 'May we begin now, Worthies? These things are past argument and I've come for intelligent entertainment, not debate.'

'Certainly, Lady.' Gabriel Elk left the booth.

Chancellor Blaine turned to me. 'Well, Ingram, what can you say for yourself? It seems you've been enjoying a vacation from the Court, a holiday at Stonelore.'

'Shame,' Our Shathra said. 'You wanted him to come out here, Arngrim. Now you scold him for doing your bidding.'

I said, 'Anyway, I don't believe the old man is a threat to Ongladred; he'll precipitate no early break in the maskers' steadfastness, Chancellor – nor will the neurodramas planned for after the equinox.'

Blaine asked, 'What *does* Sayati Elk have planned, Ingram?'

'I don't know,' I had to admit. 'I'm not even sure what we'll see this evening, but Gabriel Elk's neither a fool nor an apostate.'

'Thirteen days out here, Ingram, and you don't know what the man's planning. You're arguing from faith.' Blaine's roan tooth seemed to slash at me. 'When the Halcyon Panic breaks, when the maskers give themselves over to fear and misdirected anger and other inutile emotions, you'll find Ongladred's biggest fool and darkest apostate co-existing in the same skin, Master Marley: *yours*!' The Chancellor's thin lips drew together firmly, hiding the red-black canine.

'Melodrama,' Our Shathra Anna said. 'Your own fears betray you into rhetoric, Arngrim.'

'I hope so, Lady,' Blaine said, immediately calm again. 'But I see no reason to court disaster. The neuro-drama is a folly, a corruption of masker and Atarite mores, that I can't comprehend your fondness for. In times like these, Lady, your protection of it – forgive me – seems almost perverse.' He looked at me again. 'In the meantime, Ingram, I think your mission at Stonelore is effectively at an end. Tonight you'll come back to Lunn with us.'

'Very well,' I said.

# Six

Suddenly the neuro-theatre was plunged into absolute, impenetrable darkness. There was music: a single, stringed instrument playing mournfully. The sound – not loud, but resonant and golden – seemed to issue from everywhere at once. 'At last,' I heard Our Shathra's voice say, 'the *folly* commences.' Then a battery of incredibly bright lights threw their stinging yellowness into the sunken arena of the neuro-pit, Sayati Elk's 'stage'. Even yet, however, the blackness obliterated everything else in the Stonelore amphitheatre; we could not see Elk's wife and Bronwen's parents on the tier opposite us.

Then Gabriel Elk stepped into the light. As he spoke, he turned so that all in the theatre could hear him, even the phantom maskers whom he apparently imagined to be in the tiers above him. His foreshortened body, his monstrous hands, his upturned, expressive face all had a sharpness of focus intensified out of the realm of nature. Ageless he was, ageless and transcendent. Turning slowly, he spoke; and, without amplification, his voice reached out to us like a wave breaking. 'My performer tonight is the corpse of Bronwen Lief, a girl killed by the Pelagans four days ago. I bow to her parents, for allowing me to buy her.' He bowed in their direction. 'What she will perform is not of my composition; indeed, it is not even of our tongue, and I have decided to let her speak it as its ancient poet, now forgotten, set it to paper. The strangeness of the language will be no stranger than the strangeness of our times. Ultimately, all languages are vehicles for the same remorseless, unending reaching out – even to the moment of man's extinction.'

On that word he walked out of the neuro-pit, into the ambient dark. But he didn't return to our booth.

We were left staring into the neuro-pit. Then a section of the floor about three metres in diameter withdrew into the bowels of the amphitheatre; when it returned on its pneumatic lift-shaft, Bronwen Lief was standing on it – her supple body clad in a white Etruscan stola, her eyes reflecting back at us the disquieting glaze of her deadness. The music began again, livelier than before but still mournful. Just as the girl had no soul, the music now had no body; the thin plucked notes slipped away into the air. Perhaps Gabriel Elk intended for the music and the girl to complete each other, to make a whole human being out of an empty shell and a disembodied noise. I didn't know. This was the first time I had ever seen any sort of performance at all at Stonelore; Arngrim Blaine enforced his own prejudices among the Eyes and Ears of Our Shathra Anna, and except for my assignment to Elk as a dirt-runner I might never have been permitted to receive the old sayati's special brand of 'enlightenment'.

The performance itself both bewildered and moved me. I saw a corpse behave as no living masker ever had, even under Atarite command in war.

Bronwen Lief, a dead girl, danced.

Maskers never danced – nor did Atarites, even though the range of emotions conducive to dancing lay well within our psychological compass. It was against the law. For the same reason that dancing was against the law, living human beings were forbidden to be actors.

As products of the Parfects' genetic engineering, the population of our planet reflected their unanimous verdict as to what qualities a reasoning creature ought to have. Out of the maskers the Parfects had bred avariciousness, aggressiveness, xenophobia, lust, and even a degree of the inclination to fear. At the same time the Parfects had recognized that survival in a new and hostile environment depended, at least in part, on these very 'vices'. Hence, they had engineered a second, smaller group of colonists to guide and administer to the first; these were the original Atarites, people in whom the dangerous dross of the animal, the primeval recourse to fang and claw, still had a bit of play – but subordinated now to the need to build, command, and protect.

The Parfects had even tried to programme into our ancestors' genes and blood the elementary knowledge that the two groups were dependent on each other; that the seemingly irresistible urge to interbreed would lead to ruin; that the similar tendency for the People Accustomed to the Hand and the People Touched by Fire to go their separate ways, to take their own evolutionary roads, would have to be subconsciously, intuitively, fought. In all of this, the Parfects had perhaps demonstrated the extent of their own limitations. Still, we had managed to survive. Renegade Atarites had established themselves long ago on the islands of the Angromain Archipelago, and for several generations on Ongladred there had been more liaisons between ruler and ruled than were wise (my own grandparents were an example); but even so threatened and picked at, our civilisation stood.

In Gabriel Elk's neuro-theatre I watched the dead Bronwen Lief go through the motions of a choreography programmed into her but seemingly motivated from within, from a *human* source. Of course, that source was Sayati Elk himself (and Gareth, too, for he directed some of the girl's movements from the comptroller room). The old man had turned technology into a kind of aesthetic, he had tried to infuse spirit into what was essentially a mechanical operation – not because he wanted to, but because he had to. The neuro-theatre was a compromise with the laws of Ongladred, a compromise that the old man could not have been entirely happy with. I was moved by Bronwen's dance because her programmer had come so close to accomplishing the impossible. She moved with genuine grace; her garment followed the flow of her limbs like a ghost counterpointing her motions. But, in reality, it was Gabriel Elk's vision, his need to communicate, that was flowing down there under the withering brightness of Stonelore's lamps.

Bronwen Lief was the vessel into which he had poured both vision and need. Because she was a corpse.

The law said that no human being could be an actor, no human being could take part in any sort of performance contrary to Mansuecerian nature. For uniformity's sake, the law included Atarites. The relatively high incidence of inter-breeding between the two groups during the last century had made the law seem reasonable to many. An actor, after all, is one who constantly assumes roles requiring him to abase or repudiate, if only momentarily, the genetic characteristics given to him by the Parfects. One becomes something other than himself. Drama derives from conflict and emotion – excessive and aberrant emotion, according to men like Chancellor Blaine. In a society like Ongladred's, these men felt, such 'artificial' emotions posed a very real danger to the persons acting them out; the audience for these spectacles was also in some danger of corruption, but a few of Our Shathra Anna's most influential Magi had deterred the closing of the neuro-theatre by arguing that it might be a healthy outlet for the subconscious turmoil of the ordinary Mansuecerian. Or maybe this was the rationalisation of Our Shathra herself, who was a sympathiser, who enjoyed a slightly illicit entertainment. And so the issue of Stone-lore balanced on the horns of the fuzzy moral ideologies of these two factions: One could attend Gabriel Elk's dramas, but one could not perform in them.

The dead, however, were exempt from the non-participation law. No stigma attached to the re-animation of corpses for actors; in Ongladred we had developed an almost callous disregard for death and the attendant luxuries of mourning, burial and lingering memory – or at least the maskers had, out of both necessity and the hope for survival. Therefore, Sayati Elk re-animated the dead. He poured his vision and need into the only vessels the state would allow him, striving always to touch and transfigure. This he did for an audience that almost invariably sat mute and subdued to the end. That his audience again and again came back to be silently worked upon was his incentive to continue – that, and his obsession with a dream, and occasionally Our Shathra Anna's reaction, whether approval or pique,

Tonight she approved. 'Beautiful,' she said.

Mansuecerian dancer, Atarite applause – except that Arngrim Blaine made a sighing noise. He shifted his thin body in its chair and his lacy clothes rustled. I ignored the Chancellor. Leaning forward, I tried to catch every nuance of Bronwen Lief's performance.

Then it was over, or at least this preliminary part of it was. She came out of her last graceful pas seul into an equally graceful walk. Then stopped. She turned her eyes up to her parents, then faced in the direction of our booth and looked up at us. They were still dead, those eyes, still empty and glass-like.

The lute continued to play.

When she finally spoke, her voice was deeper than seemed right – but melodious. The ancient language in which she spoke came naturally to her lips and mesmerised us with its accents; we forgot our inability to understand and simply listened. From somewhere in the dark, his voice coming rich and assured after each line Bronwen delivered, Sayati Elk translated the forgotten poet's words.

The poem dealt with time, and with the inevitable crumbling away of empires, and with the poet's awe in the face of their passing. It dealt, too, with the nearly inconsequential prospect of his own death. A fluid poem with few pauses, and a headlong surging towards its final lines.

In Elk's translation we heard them:

> *And here face downward in the sun*
> *To feel how swift how secretly*
> *The shadow of the night comes on . . .*

Bronwen Lief folded her hands and let her head fall to her breast. And that was all; the show was over. A dance and a reading, with very little room for the sort of *emoting* Chancellor Blaine took exception to. Sayati Elk had programmed the girl and cautioned Gareth to underplay the 'entertainment'; in everything but the subject matter of the reading he had aimed at conciliating my roan-toothed superior. Less than twenty minutes had gone by since the dimming of Stonelore's house-lights and the flaring of the great lamps around the neuro-pit.

Brevity had always impressed Arngrim Blaine.

# Seven

But afterwards, in the tapestry-hung dining chamber of Grotto House, we discovered that the poem's subject had not impressed him, except negatively. There were six of us around the great stone table there, and places for two more. Those two were for Gabriel and Gareth, acting now as our stewards, moving between dining chamber and kitchen with platters of food and decanters of vintage haoma. A silent masker woman, the cook and scullery maid Maria, helped them with these labours. Our Shathra Anna and Bethel Elk sat at opposite ends of the table, each as queenly as the other. To the right of Our Shathra, Chancellor Blaine voiced his objections to the reading while the Liefs remained humbly non-committal.

He was saying, 'I can only assume, Mistress Elk, that your husband chose the piece we've just heard for its elegant pessimism. He must have had to rummage long and hard through your library – until he found a microchip whose very shape and colour suggested the defeatism of its contents. A tasteless choice, considering the dangers besetting us now.' He sipped the haoma from his cup, a small illicit pleasure.

'Or an appropriate one,' Bethel Elk said.

'No. He might as well be a propagandist for the Pelagans. Suppose that this were given on the first night after the equinox. How would our maskers—' Blaine's lips tightened; he began again. 'Forgive me. How would our *Mansuecerian* citizens react?'

'Why not ask the Liefs, Chancellor?' I said.

Husband and wife continued silent, Rhia smiling and Josu bland under his leather mourning cap.

Blaine went on: 'You see, they can't yet formulate their reactions. But I believe the effect of a presentation like the one we saw tonight is bound to be insidious. And the neuro-dramas themselves are a thousand times more disquieting than Bronwen Lief's recital. Eventually, the people's faith in Our Shathra and the Atarite Court will be sabotaged.' In the glow of the dining chamber's candles, his roan tooth glinted with carnelian highlights.

Gabriel and Gareth came in with baskets of potato bread. They were enjoying themselves. The old man smiled at his wife.

Our Shathra Anna said, 'Arngrim is maligning your choice of material, Gabriel. Says you'll sabotage Ongladred and me with barbarian propaganda.'

It was the boy who answered her. 'Father will respond to that after we have eaten – if the Chancellor leaves anything for us.' He and the old man went out again, and surprisingly enough, Blaine smiled – wanly.

Then the Elks, father and son, returned and took up their places at table with us. Gabriel spoke to the Liefs: 'Well, what did you think? Tell me how you felt seeing Bronwen as you saw her.' Unlike Chancellor Blaine, he genuinely wanted their reactions; I could see him preparing to take mental notes.

'I don't know, Sayati Elk,' Rhia said. 'She wasn't our girl, that one down there.'

'Her voice, it was different,' Josu volunteered.

'Getting the voice right is very hard,' Gareth answered. 'Father has to co-ordinate the neural impulses from the electrodes in Broca's area of the brain with the programming of the lungs, vocal cords and lips.'

'Why don't you just use a recording?' Blaine asked. 'It seems to me you've made things unduly complicated for yourself, Sayati Elk.'

The old man glanced at the Chancellor. He said nothing. He returned his gaze to Rhia and Josu. 'Bronwen didn't sound like herself?' he asked.

Josu said, 'No, sir. Not exactly – but it could've been that old sort of talk she was speaking in.'

'Maybe it was the talk,' Rhia said. 'That different language.'

'Which supports my contention that your choice of

material left a good deal to be desired,' Blaine said. 'The language itself, Sayati Elk, alienated the Liefs from their re-animated daughter, whereas the moany business about every civilisation crumpling into shadow certainly wasn't designed to send either Our Shathra Anna or me away from Stonelore happily whistling your praises. A bad choice – from a diplomatic point of view if not an artistic one, Sayati Elk.'

'It's spoiled your digestion, not mine,' Our Shathra told Blaine.

Suddenly there was a silence; a stillness descended on the dining room of Grotto House. Eight people stared at one another over the baskets of potato bread, over the decanters of haoma, over the silver platter of roast mutton and the bowls of bread pudding. A silence and a tenseness. Then Arngrim Blaine raised his cup and sipped. By this simple movement he directed our attention to him. Looking over the rim of his cup, he spoke to Gabriel.

'Is Ongladred going to die, Sayati Elk?'

'Probably. One day.'

'Soon?'

'*Soon* is a relative term, Chancellor Blaine. On what scale do you wish me to apply it?'

'Bronwen Lief's performance in Stonelore suggested that collapse is inevitable. I'm supposing that you selected the piece out of some rational, therefore comprehensible motive? What motive? To frighten us? To warn us? To suggest that resistance to fate is foolhardy? What, Sayati Elk? As for my definition of *soon*, do you think Ongladred will die during our lifetimes?'

'It's conceivable.'

'Is it inevitable?'

'Even its death isn't inevitable, Chancellor Blaine. Societies fall when their leaders fail.'

A pause; a darker tension.

Blaine's mouth was open slightly; a thread of spittle lay across his discoloured tooth. He sipped more haoma. Then he said, 'Who do you see as failing first, Sayati Elk?

The Atarite Court in Lunn or the wolfish Pelagan captains across the Angromain Channel?'

Gareth Elk, the boy, said, 'Whoever is least flexible, Chancellor Blaine; whoever is least adaptable.' It was a thought I had had before, but never voiced. Blaine himself, though capable of a quick and witty range in conversation, was not otherwise known for his readiness to abandon old ways, old prejudices. The boy, I felt, had inadvertently given voice to our most basic fears about Ongladred's time of trials – the suspicion, even among Atarites, that our leaders had lost the quality of vision.

Then Our Shathra Anna said, 'We may have as much as a year before the Pelagans put us to the test, perhaps as little as three months. Right now they're content for reivers and fear-strikers to harass, to steal, and' – here she nodded at Rhia and Josu Lief – 'to murder when surprised in these pursuits. Invasion is not yet. We have a little time to mobilise. Even so, Gabriel, you ought to remember one thing in particular.'

'Yes, Lady?' he said.

'That you must include yourself among that group of leaders who may fail or not fail in the attempt to preserve Ongladred.'

'I, Lady?'

'Come, come, Gabriel. You're too old to play coy. Just as Arngrim and I are' – she inflected her next word self-consciously – '*political* leaders, you're an intellectual leader of our island.'

Chancellor Blaine almost smirked. 'In other words, Sayati Elk, you have a responsibility nearly as great as ours.'

'Sometimes,' Bethel Elk said, 'Gabriel views his efforts at Stonelore in a Promethean light; against a hostile array of gods and vultures, he labours alone for the redemption and advancement of humanity.'

'Oh, no,' the old man protested, grinning. 'Not alone. The gods and vultures I don't dispute, but I've always had help – you, Gareth, and lately even tight-lipped Master Marley there. The labour's almost always been *intellectual*, though,' he continued slyly. 'I wouldn't presume to put my foot in *politics*.'

The meal went better after that. I studied the ornate woollen tapestries on the walls; I enjoyed the haoma, the food, the less sensitive drift of our talk. It was difficult to believe Stonelore's relative isolation from the Atarite Court, the belligerence of the inhabitants of the windy archipelagoes, the nightmarish threat of a creature called the sloak. Candles flickered. The evening drew to a close, as did my own residence at Grotto House. Oddly, I regretted this fact; I didn't want to go back to Lunn.

Then Our Shathra Anna said, 'Arngrim, you'd better tell the Elks of Gareth's conscription.'

Talk ceased again.

Chancellor Blaine said, 'The gist of it is that Gareth and your ostler—'

'Robin Coigns,' Bethel said.

'Yes. Gareth and Gentleman Coigns must report to the Lunn garrison in two days. Our Shathra wished this message to come from me personally, Sayati Elk, not from an induction-runner.'

'Two days!' Bethel said.

'That's very little notice,' her husband added.

Our Shathra said, 'The message was to have come a day or two ago, Mistress Elk, but we hoped that hearing it from our own lips would make the news less distressing. I'm sorry the notice is not more, though. Sincerely sorry.'

Josu Lief put his arms on the table. 'You'll be reporting, Master Gareth, when I do, it seems.'

'That's fine with me,' Gareth said. 'The hardship's not mine, but Father's. He'll have to do all the work, virtually all the work, in the neuro-theatre by himself. Mother can't work in the comptroller room; her back won't let her.'

Gareth's comment seemed to be a serendipitous clue for Chancellor Blaine; quickly he interjected: 'Sayati Elk, we can offer you the command of a unit of recently inducted men – a naval unit – if you choose to accept now. You will hold it for a year, or until this crisis is past. Should you accept, spring performances at Stonelore will cease to be a problem for you. Gareth's absence won't be felt here.'

'Certainly it will be felt,' Bethel said.

Blaine qualified this comment: 'I meant that your husband's work in the neuro-theatre wouldn't be impeded by his absence.'

'Because there wouldn't be any work in the neuro-theatre,' Gabriel Elk said. 'I'd be captaining a contingent of young Mansuecerian seamen against the Pelagans – at sixty-three. Stonelore would close.'

'Regrettably,' Blaine said.

'I refuse.' Gabriel Elk turned to Our Shathra Anna. 'Lady, was this proposal of your own devising? Am I to understand that you wish me to close Stonelore and hobble off to war?'

'You are far from hobbling, Gabriel. But no. The proposal originated with the Chancellor himself.'

'Who believes,' Blaine said smugly, 'your intellectual leadership can be put to good military use, Sayati Elk. Since survival depends on leadership.'

'I refuse. I'm too old for conscription. I've served.'

'Our Shathra Anna,' Gareth said, rising, 'I'd like to go tell Robin.'

'Please. Go ahead.'

As the boy left, Gabriel Elk said, 'In any case, we've nearly finished. When you return to Lunn, Lady, I humbly request that you let Josu and Rhia share your coach. The roads are dangerous at night.'

Our Shathra agreed, and in another twenty minutes our entire company was outside, in the shadow of Grotto House, under the motionful brightness of the Shattered Moons. The Stonelore amphitheatre loomed up before us like an immense round starship, promising us Earth. It was cool. We saw Gareth and Robin Coigns walking towards us across the upland arena, Our Shathra Anna's equipage rattling along behind them like a circus cage of noisy blackbirds. Somehow, the equipage struck me as an evil thing. Above the caparisoned horses the driver snapped his long whip; apparently they had not been unbridled during the whole of the long evening. A second time the driver snapped his whip, and a third.

In front of Grotto House, Josu Lief crumpled to his knees in the dust and then pitched forward on his face.

If I hadn't seen the spark of uncanny red in the rock spires opposite us, I would have supposed the man had fainted – but the three successive crackings of the carriage driver's whip had concealed the report of a rifle. The second shot had no such fortuitous cover, however, and the burst of fire from the rifle muzzle seemed terrifyingly brighter than the first one. The report and the ricochet were deafening.

'Get down!' someone shouted. 'Get back inside!'

I fell to the ground and rolled. I saw the three women – who had come out last – duck back into the deep well of Grotto House's inset entrance. Gabriel Elk and Arngrim Blaine scrambled into the rock garden to the entrance's right. I rolled again. On my stomach once more, I looked up. Gareth and Robin Coigns, caught in the open, ran for the protecting curve of the amphitheatre; the carriage rattled after them, horses whinnying.

Another spitting of fire; another shot. Everything was noise and moving bodies.

At last I found some cover for myself, a crevice on the side of Grotto House leading down to the stable.

'Gareth!' Gabriel Elk shouted. 'Gareth!'

'Here, with Robin!' the boy answered from the portion of Stonelore's wall out of our concealed enemy's sight. 'We're all of us whole.'

# Eight

For the first time all evening I was alone with my thoughts, blood revving through my temples, roaring in my ears. The Shattered Moons buckled, flowed, shifted in their myriad orbits. I tilted my head back against the rough wall of my hiding place and watched them.

I, Ingram Marley, dirt-runner and spy.

For three hours I had been subsumed in the personalities of people more important, more powerful, than I. Now, through this violence, I had been given back to myself. The gift wasn't entirely appreciated. Involuntarily my shoulders pulled up against my neck, my palms flattened against cold stone.

I wondered how long the lot of us had to live. If the armed men in the rocks had got past Our Shathra Anna's chariot guard, who remained to save us? Only ourselves: Gabriel Elk and son, our effete Chancellor, Robin Coigns and the coachman, and one member of the Eyes and Ears of the Atarite Court. Stonelore and Grotto House lay too far away from either Lunn or the Mershead Road for us to count on accidental reinforcements – although if the court party were too long in returning, the Magi would dispatch a contingent of horsemen.

Two, three, four more shots sounded in Stonelore's arena. Could they be heard on the Mershead Road? Maybe. As dull, echoing *pings* over the sounds of wind and sea. It wasn't likely that anyone would follow them up.

Frozen in place, I felt my own impotence in the face of a reasonless, impersonal hostility.

Then the hostility took on a distinctly human character: there was laughter from the rocks opposite us. Gleeful, self-assertive laughter which even the wind couldn't drown with its gusting.

Then two more shots, ricocheting away.

Then still more laughter and a voice crying out, 'Ilk! Ilk! You surrender!' After which the old man, from his hiding place with Blaine, shouted an obscenity. There was disconcerting silence then; no shots, no braying laughter.

Several minutes passed.

Finally the voice in the rocks began taunting us in a dialect both lilting and guttural, a dialect which I knew as Pelagan but which I had never learned. Our attackers – how many murderers peered down on us? – were men from across the Angromain Channel, reivers, thieves, fear-strikers, danger-drinking barbarians. I thought of Josu Lief lying face down in front of Grotto House. In less than a week these randomly operating Pelagan agents had killed two members of the same family. And one of them, drawing down on us with a stolen rifle no doubt, was alternately laughing and spewing out streams of incomprehensible invective.

After a time I realised that the hidden reiver was declaiming poetry at us, venomous couplets in his own tongue. He wanted Gabriel Elk, Ongladred's only literary giant, to suffer these insults in a form that mocked the old man's genius. And so he railed away at us like an actor, disdainful both of Sayati Elk and of the Atarite law that had indirectly given rise to the neuro-theatre. More than likely, Chancellor Blaine was chewing his upper lip with chagrin, his roan tooth on the verge of breaking flesh. How must he feel, in a situation in which he was as powerless as I?

'Ilk! Ilk!' the reiver called out; then regaled us with brusque, barbarian couplets.

For answer the reiver got three bursts from a hand-gun and a bit of bravado from Arngrim Blaine. 'You'd better get out while you can!' his thin voice shouted. 'If you don't go now, you'll not make it!'

I couldn't see around the crevice containing me, I was afraid to look out – but apparently the old Chancellor had taken the hand-gun from beneath his cloak and fired in anger. Gabriel Elk, beside Blaine in the low rock garden, translated his message into the Pelagan dialect and added a severe-sounding message of his own. I realised then that my own fear was greater than Chancellor Blaine's, that it was my own weakness that had imagined *him* chewing *his* lip. I was afraid because we were pinned down in Stonelore's arena. Still, we were not automatically doomed to end up like Josu Lief, wavy pencils of blood outlining our chins and discolouring the ground.

In my belt was a knife, a dagger with an elaborate haft. Almost every Atarite or Atarite retainer carried one like it; mine, like most of the others, had never been used. I curled my fingers around the haft and edged away from the crevice's opening, my back still making contact with stone. Rock encased me. Then the crevice funnelled out and the night sky seemed to flood in on me. A tattering of wind slipped through a smooth-worn hole in the granite passageway, and later two separate, fancifully carven windows looked out on the narrow path leading down to the stable. I pulled myself up and crawled through the larger of these.

On the path, I ran.

Almost at once I came to the fenced-in paddock in front of the horses' shelter, a stable without walls. Despite the moons and the attenuated starlight, it was dark here; every shape appeared distorted, angular, unreal. Above me, in the Stonelore arena, I heard more rifle fire, echoings of deliberately hysterical laughter, and the mocking lilt and clack of the reiver's 'poetry' – all of this noise incredibly tinny with distance. It was a temptation to go on down the path, find my way to open country and tall grass, and circle back to Lunn. *To bring back help*, I said to myself more than once; *to bring back help*.

Instead, I opened the paddock gate and walked between bales of fodder that Robin Coigns had left out for his animals. Maybe he had come down here during our entertainments at Stonelore and Grotto House and carried a bale or two back to the arena for Our Shathra Anna's horses. If so, he hadn't returned to the paddock for a while.

One of the distorted shapes that I nearly stumbled over was not a bale of fodder; it was Gabriel Elk's round-eyed, woolly gelding. I knelt. A reiver had plunged his knife into the animal's breast and then ripped the blade upward towards the long, vitally muscled throat. The other animal, the one I had ridden to Lunn, had been dealt with similarly.

How many Pelagans had done this? What had happened to the chariot guard? Alone, I almost wished myself back with the others.

The smell of recently spilled blood, warm and salty, commingled with that of dry fodder and the horses' last, scarcely cold droppings. These things daunted me. I trembled with nausea and the night's chill. I heard Chancellor Blaine's hand-gun again; he could not have many shots left, unless he also wore ammunition under his lace cloak.

Why had the Pelagans not placed men on both sides of the Stonelore arena? Had they done so, those of us emerging from Grotto House would have had very little chance of getting either back inside or to cover. Maybe we had come out before they expected us to. Certainly they had been busy up until that moment. The chariot guard must have purchased a little time for us. After slaughtering the guards and our horses (our transportation down from Gabriel Elk's citadel), the reivers had crossed back to the other side to see what they could do with Coigns and the unsuspecting coachman. There could not be too many of them; otherwise they would have worked in several concerted, simultaneous assaults rather than in cautious stages. Like me, the Pelagans were amateurs – infinitely more daring and bloodthirsty maybe, but not inherently more competent.

I stopped wondering; I stopped thinking.

If I managed to get on to the roof of the stable shelter, I saw that I could pull myself from there to the top of the rock wall into which Elk had built Grotto House. The rock wall, though broken in one or two places, inscribed a rough circle around the Stonelore arena.

So I climbed. I stacked several bales of fodder, then attained the shelter's roof. Then I fought the wind and the dizzying sky and clambered on to a rectangular ledge projecting out over the roof. From there, up to the rugged dentition of the rock wall itself.

Using hands and feet alike, I edged my way between these granitic, Brobdingnagian teeth, through the sudden drops, and over a few treacherous flat surfaces – towards the chattering Pelagan who had murdered Coigns' defenceless horses and the masker Josu Lief.

Something very ancient had come awake in my blood.

At one point I realised that I was on the roof of Grotto House. A useless realisation. The rooms lay embedded in the stone under me like fossils buried in strata geologically unapproachable. The tapestries in the dining chamber; the electric wall panels in the foyer; the sound of women's voices. I wasn't a part of those things any more; I was alone, moving stealthily towards some indefinable but necessary end. The Shattered Moons accompanied me.

Halfway around the wall I did something stupid: I stood full up and looked down into the arena.

I saw Gareth and Coigns huddled beside the amphitheatre, Our Shathra Anna's equipage a tangle of reins and shadows and jittery horses in front of them. The ostler and Elk's son were gesticulating madly at the coachman; he was slumped down in front of his seat, warily keeping his head low. As I watched, they managed to attract his attention and communicate to him their wishes.

Then, in rapid succession, these things happened: The coachman nervously jumped down from the equipage. He threw open the door on the side away from me. Gareth and Coigns rushed out from the wall and hurdled into the coach, which began angrily rocking. The coachman, shielded by the amphitheatre, slapped at the flanks of the gaudily accoutred horses, shouted at them, tugged at bridles. First a lead animal, then one in the second rank, reared in their traces; then all four of them plunged forward together, yanking the carriage out of its angry rocking. The coachman jumped back out of the way and sidled to safety along the base of the amphitheatre's wall.

Rattling and churning, the equipage jounced towards the opening by which the Liefs and the Court Party had originally entered the arena. The two men inside had not a bit of control over where it went or at what speed, they simply kept their heads down.

One of the reivers fired at the departing carriage. I saw him silhouetted on the wall's rim, upright among the rocks. We were almost on eye level with each other, though fortunately he didn't look my way. Fascinated, I remained where I was. I thought I could see another Pelagan crouched beside the first, staying out of sight: the profile of a hawk-like head.

Because of the intervening bulk of the amphitheatre itself, the man with the rifle had only a moment to stop the carriage, that moment when it burst into view again on the other side. But by then the matter was out of the reiver's hands. Although not in full control of the situation, Gareth and Coigns had escaped. Our Shathra's horses, ears flattened and manes floating, hurtled towards the Mershead Road.

A shot from Arngrim Blaine's hand-gun reminded the armed Pelagan that he couldn't take aim with impunity. He slumped quickly out of sight, so quickly in fact that I thought he might be wounded.

I waited.

It was several minutes before the more articulate of the two Pelagans began taunting Gabriel Elk again. 'Ilk! Ilk! You surrender! That coach going off, it means nothing!' Then the mocking couplets, a singsong of scorn. Arngrim Blaine responded; the old man translated. The old man shouted words that carried a taunt of their own. Back and forth, this colloquy of deprecation – and I began moving again.

*No thinking*, I told myself; *deeds only*.

In another ten minutes I had worked my way over a broken stretch in the wall and back into the gnarled rock. The voices of the Pelagans came to me more and more clearly; when the poet wasn't shouting his insults, I could hear their exchanged whispers and even the irregular breathing of one of the men. At last I could see them. I hugged a spire of rock behind their natural blind and tried to still the revving of my heart. Looking out over the grassy highlands surrounding Stonelore, I saw no sign of the chariot guard who had supposedly taken up his watch there. The Pelagans had so thoroughly dealt with him that the landscape might have cracked open and swallowed him, chariot and all.

*No thinking!* With that, I leapt down into the reivers' blind. Blood pounded viciously behind my eyes, rudely insistent. A face turned towards me, a face unlike any I had seen in Ongladred.

The Shattered Moons poured light over the features of that face and over the whole of the shape squatting to its left. It was the shape to the left that had the rifle, I saw the barrel glinting too late. That figure I should have attacked first – not this unarmed one, not this odd, glowering mask rising up out of its own off-balance surprise to confront me.

I could feel my fingers gripping the haft of my knife – was dimly aware of the knife itself sweeping up in an arc to my ear, the blade quivering briefly a forearm's length from the face beyond it.

Then, not wanting it to be the way it was happening, wanting a less terrible portion of the Pelagan's anatomy for a target, I pulled my knife down into his face – stabbed once – then drew back as the reiver screamed, clutched his fearsome wound, and rolled away.

(An image of the dead horses flashed into my mind.)

My weapon clattered into the rocks.

As I had done a few minutes before, I stood there upright and exposed, stupid in my immobility. The other Pelagan, his odd face somehow managing an expression, utterly incredulous, began to rise. He brought his rifle up, a rifle that had been throwing off sparks and noise for over thirty minutes now, and all I could do was remark the clumsiness of his effort and the way the barrel shone so prettily. Would this thing kill me?

Then a shadow eclipsed the second reiver, knocked the rifle out of his hands, and bobbed nimbly out of harm's way. Old Robin Coigns, alias Horsesweat, had jumped into the blind and disarmed my would-be assassin.

A moment later Gareth Elk followed Coigns out of the darkness, and the three of us stood there looking down on the disarmed Pelagan. The one whom I had stabbed lay off to one side, dead or certainly dying, his face mercifully twisted away from us.

No one spoke. There was the almost peaceful sound of heavy breathing, together with a misleading glut of peaceful white moonlight. I was empty of whatever had moved me so violently to this place. A malarial dizziness still ran through my blood, but the infection itself was gone.

I looked at Robin Coigns, I looked at Gareth Elk, I looked at the disarmed Pelagan. They in turn looked at me.

# Nine

Back in the Stonelore arena we tried to piece the situation together.

Someone had wrapped poor Josu Lief in a blanket; the women were inside Grotto House, Our Shathra Anna and Bethel Elk senselessly comforting the dry-eyed, almost unperturbed Rhia.

In the arena, I had my first real opportunity to look at the man we had captured. He was bound. Too, since he had proven annoyingly voluble on our trip back to the arena in Our Shathra Anna's carriage, he was gagged as well. Gareth had used the man's shredded undertunic for both the binding and gagging. Now the Pelagan sat in the dirt beside the luminous amphitheatre while Coigns and the coachman tried to calm the horses, and the rest of us huddled together beside the dust-covered equipage, assessing and reassessing.

'Just look at him,' Arngrim Blaine was saying. 'He *isn't* a man. How can you argue that he's a man?'

'Despite his looks,' Gabriel Elk said, 'he's a man very much like you, Chancellor Blaine.' He paused, then added sardonically: 'Or me. But perhaps more like you since the people of the archipelagoes were all originally derived from Atarite stock, and I have to confess a background predominantly Mansuecerian. Nevertheless, Chancellor, the man's a human being, not an animal.'

'Look at him, Sayati Elk! Look at him!'

I looked at the Pelagan captive. The Chancellor was over-reacting, as I had over-reacted to my first glimpse of the face of the reiver I had killed. It was easy to see that our captive belonged to our species, although certain minor differences in physiognomy and anatomy made it possible to *pretend* an evolutionary breach had occurred.

Sitting in the dust, his knees drawn up to his chin, his

head balanced sullenly there, the reiver was demonstrably human. His dark eyes followed us with the same pupil-bright disdain with which a minor court official might regard a nouveau Atarite like Ingram Marley: I knew the look. It was made bearable now by the fact that he directed it against all of us – Gabriel, Gareth, Blaine, Coigns and the coachman, as well as me. In the Pelagan's eyes, we were the subhumans, the creatures not deserving the name *Man*. He lifted his head from his knees and threw it back against the amphitheatre's wall.

These physical distinctions existed: The captive was darker than any of us; his hair hung straight and black over his forehead and ears. His upper eyelids had a tuck in them, an epicanthic fold, Gabriel said. In fact, the old man told us that the Pelagan's appearance would have once been termed at least quasi-Mongoloid. Contradicting this assessment, however, was the reiver's abundant body hair, a sparse, raven-like down over hands, arms and face, though so thin on our captive's face that only the moonlight and my own proximity made this hair visible; on the man I had killed this facial down had seemed more horrifying, the sort of animalisation of human features that Blaine was now insisting upon. Earthly Mongoloids, Elk said, had very seldom had a great deal of hair on their faces and bodies.

Finally, our captive had a purplish patch of skin on his throat, distinctly visible now because his head was back.

'All the people of the Angromain Archipelagoes don't look like this one,' Chancellor Blaine said. 'I know they don't, I've had distasteful dealings with a few of them before.'

'The man I killed had similar features,' I said. 'Face, body hair, all of it.'

Gareth affirmed this. We had left the dead man in the rocks, not wanting to sully Our Shathra's carriage any more than was needful. 'He even had a mark on his throat like this one.'

'From what I've heard and seen,' Gabriel interjected, 'this type – this quasi-Mongoloid type of individual – isn't at all uncommon in the archipelagoes now. I've had dealings with the Pelagans many times, Chancellor – more often than even you have, I'd imagine – and I've seen men resembling this one more than once. The Pelagans esteem men like him,' nodding towards our captive, 'because they seem to be particularly daring and resourceful, Many like him are in positions of leadership.'

'Do they also esteem them murderous and cruel?'

'Life in the archipelagoes is not entirely like life in Ongladred, Chancellor; values differ.'

'Obviously.'

'There weren't many Asians among the final population of Windfall Last,' I said. 'Were there?'

'No,' Gabriel Elk said.

'Then why should a people who look like Asians – the tuck in the eye, the dark hair, the yellow-brown skin – suddenly appear out in the Angromain?'

'It hasn't been all that sudden; it's been incremental, Ingram – though what the precise origins of people like these are, I don't know. Maybe the Parfects *engineered* an Atarite heritage into the genes of some of those penultimate Asians in Windfall Last.' Gabriel Elk, something of an engineer himself, here pronounced the word with a deliberate nasality. 'The descendants of some of these individuals were undoubtedly among the Atarites who fled Ongladred a millennium ago. Ironic, yes?'

'How do you mean, ironic?' Blaine asked, visibly peeved.

'Many of the oldest Earth civilisations were Eastern. Now, out here, eight hundred light-years from our spawning place, Oriental physical characteristics are asserting themselves again.'

'But altered,' I said.

'Yes,' the old man agreed. 'Altered. As everything alters, as everything changes – except ourselves.' Nobody said anything to that; the comment had a self-consciously sagely ring to it that Elk usually avoided. Moreover, the Parfects' grand experiment on Mansueceria didn't altogether support the concept of an unchanging and unchangeable human condition. Long ago, for our own good, we had been 'engineered'. No one could dispute that.

We were all beginning to feel the length of the day, the late-evening cold, the after-numbness of fading shock. We moved around in the arena's dust; we watched Coigns and the coachman soothing the sweaty-flanked horses, currying them with rags, talking to them; we tried to shake ourselves back into reality with random gestures and banal resolutions.

The reivers had murdered the chariot guards, just as I had earlier assumed, and the chariots' horses had more than likely pulled the empty vehicles all the way back to Lunn. This was something none of us had come to grips with yet. As was the death of Josu Lief. Coigns put the dead masker, wrapped in a borrowed blanket, into the equipage – on the seat opposite to the one on which Chancellor Blaine and Our Shathra Anna would ride.

Blaine raised no protest.

Then we all came back to our captive, the Angromain barbarian who had taken part in, perhaps even masterminded, the night's surreal carnage. The women remained in Grotto House, waiting for us to do something, regal in their patience; and at last all our movements came to revolve around the sullen, insolently watchful Pelagan who had very nearly killed me up on the rock wall.

Out of this uncertain numbness Gabriel Elk said, 'Take the gag out of his mouth.'

The coachman did so, stepping away as soon as the cloth was free. A film seemed to pass over our captive's eyes, he shuddered, his body feebly radiated its weariness.

Then the man began to curse us. He cursed vehemently, moving his head from side to side against the wall.

Gabriel Elk grabbed my arm and raised his voice over the belligerent cursing, 'This is the other one, Ingram. No style, no subtlety. You killed the poet, the one with the flair. Did you know that?'

'Not until afterwards.'

'Are you glad?'

'No,' I said. I pulled by arm away. 'Why should I be glad? Why should I be glad either way?'

The Pelagan stopped cursing, drawn to our disagreement.

Gabriel Elk ignored him; the old man's eyes, amid leathery wrinkles, looked into mine with an intense and unsettling concentration. 'You shouldn't,' he said quietly. 'You shouldn't be glad, Ingram. Forgive me.'

'I don't know why I did what I did,' I said. 'I'd never killed a man before. Something happened to me.'

'Never mind that now, Ingram,' the old man said. He turned to his son. 'He's run out of curses for the moment, Gareth; while he's quiet, put something on his wound. Clean it out first.'

The boy moved to do his father's bidding. Arngrim Blaine said, 'We needn't let our humanitarianism run past the cup's lip, Sayati Elk,' but his voice carried no real rebuke and he didn't try to impede Gareth's bandaging of the captive.

The captive himself clenched his teeth while Gareth worked at his shoulder, but kept his eyes suspiciously on the boy, now and again letting them rove to our faces as well – where they seared their suspicion and disdain into our flesh. I tried to return the man's intermittent stares; in the attempt I noticed something utterly untoward and startling in his expression.

The barbarian's mouth reminded me of Bronwen Lief's. The dead girl shared with this archipelago dweller an almost imperceptible pout, a downtugging of one corner of the lower lip, that flawed an otherwise innocent and lovely face.

For the Pelagan was handsome. Despite the epicanthic fold, despite the darkness of his complexion, despite the hair on hands, arms and face, he was imposingly handsome – in a ruggedly exotic way that no Ongladredan ever could be. But the set of his mouth! The set of his mouth sabotaged this alien handsomeness. That he should share such a flaw with Bronwen Lief, who had danced and declaimed as Gabriel Elk had programmed her to, amazed me. In the upland cold, the wind moaning through the rocks, I stared at him.

Then his eyes caught mine, and I had to look away.

Gareth was finished with him. 'Are you going to take him back to Lunn in the coach?' the boy asked. He pulled the captive to his feet.

'No,' Blaine said. 'We have a dead man there already. The widow will ride with us, but I don't want Our Shathra Anna exposed to the Pelagan's presence any longer than is necessary; if possible, not at all. Ingram,' turning to me, 'I'd like you, young Elk here, and the ostler to walk the prisoner back to Lunn, if you would. We have no horses now but those on the carriage, and this man is too insolently disposed against us to bleed to death from his wounds on the trip back. I'm sorry to ask it, but I don't see any other immediate alternatives.'

'Very well,' I said. I didn't relish the walk, especially in the company of a man whose stare burned so piercingly.

Elk said, 'You could leave the prisoner here tonight, Chancellor Blaine, and send someone back for him in the morning.'

'No,' Blaine said. 'You may well have a secure place for him in Grotto House, but I want him back in Lunn as soon as possible. I intend to have him questioned quite thoroughly about the activities of Pelagan reivers and the likelihood of a concerted invasion by the entire Angromain. When? Where? How? I don't want there to be any chance at all that he might escape from your custody, Sayati Elk; the responsibility is too great.'

'I'm not sure I want Gareth and Coigns on the Mershead Road tonight,' the old man said. 'They've been conscripted, yes, but their service doesn't begin until the day after tomorrow. Why should I let them go? A night is a long time, and it may be an even longer time after Gareth enters the Lunn garrison before Bethel and I see him again.'

Blaine protested, 'Ingram can't take this man back alone!'

'No,' Gabriel Elk said. 'The responsibility's too great. I don't propose that Master Marley go alone.'

Arngrim Blaine pulled his cloak tight over his throat, crushing the lace there. His lips parted slightly; the carnelian tooth gleamed in the opening. He sensed some Elkian manoeuvre he would be powerless to avert. 'Please, Sayati Elk, don't toy with me tonight. What is it you want?'

'Isn't it true you intend to cut short Master Marley's scrutiny of me and Stonelore? You're returning him to the palace?'

'That was my intention.'

'I want him to stay.'

'It was my impression you considered him a barely tolerable nuisance, Sayati Elk. He's been out here thirteen days eating your food, sleeping in your beds, an acknowledged agent of Our Shathra's Eyes and Ears – and tonight you decide you want him to stay? Why? Please enlighten me.'

'The why is immaterial, Chancellor Blaine. My proposal is that I allow Gareth and Coigns to accompany Ingram and the prisoner *if* you send Ingram back to Stonelore on the day my son and the ostler report for duty – if not before.'

'For how long?'

'Until Gareth and Coigns return.'

Blaine looked at me with contempt. 'You want to keep this indolent dirt-runner until the Halcyon Panic breaks, the Pelagans invade, the sloak crawls up, and Ongladred sinks into the Nathlin Trench? He's been on an extended sabbatical already, Sayati Elk, idling, idling every minute.'

'I'll have work for him. Don't fear otherwise.'

And so it was decided.

Our Shathra Anna and Rhia Lief climbed into the equipage with Arngrim Blaine, and the coachman galloped the tired horses through the Stonelore arena and down to the Mershead Road. Since there was no help for it, they went unguarded – although both the coachman and the Chancellor carried rifles on their laps.

As soon as they were gone, Gareth, Coigns, and I set off

with our Pelagan captive, whose renewed curses required us to gag him again. Blood had welled up through the bandage on his shoulder, but the man seemed none the worse for it. 'See that he's treated humanely, Ingram,' Bethel Elk said to me as we were leaving.

'Aye,' her husband echoed her. 'See to it.'

Down from the upland arena we went on stiff legs. Wind rippled the tall grasses. The Shattered Moons passed their shadows through the wind and careened among themselves like drunken soldiers. We reached Lunn well before dawn. Robin Coigns and Gareth Elk returned at once to Stonelore, refusing beds and breakfast at the Atarite Palace. I refused only breakfast. I slept a long time, untroubled by any nightmares of the murder I had committed.

Later, I learned that representatives of the Magi had tortured the Pelagan captive for information. The man died on the second day after our trek back from Stonelore: he died without imparting a single nugget of intelligence – not his name, not his dead companion's name, not the Angromain island from which they had set out, not the purpose of their reiving. Not anything. Every torture he had endured, reviling his tormentors each time he could summon breath to do so. A remarkable performance, the representatives of the Magi said. I had slept through a good part of it, oblivious to his suffering. What would the Elks say to me when I returned?

Several days after the man's death, when I had firmly renewed my residence in Grotto House, three fishermen found a two-man boat nine kilometres north of Mershead. The boat had been concealed in a cave on the shoreline cliff faces; undoubtedly it had belonged to the men who had attacked us, killed our horses, and murdered Josu Lief and the chariot guards. A two-man reiving party. Together they had come at least thirty kilometres, mostly at night, in an open boat.

On the side of the boat, painted there in a thick indigo pigment, was a cryptic symbol. It looked like this:

# Ten

Gabriel Elk indeed had work for me. The state had taken Gareth away from him, and the spring equinox drew inexorably nearer. With the equinox's approach came also the beginning of the old man's annual series of neuro-dramas. In preparation for these, he forced me to undertake a strenuous apprenticeship. I was to serve as Gareth's replacement in the comptroller room beneath the Stonelore amphitheatre. That I had little aptitude for such work Gabriel Elk refused to concede. He had need of me.

So long as no more than three reanimated maskers were taking part in the action in the neuro-pit, the old man required no help. But when more actors moved into the sunken 'stage' from below, another comptroller had to assist him. I was to be the second comptroller. During the concentrated weeks of training, the old man permitted me very little time to myself. I learned everything about neuro-drama that Elk could impart and that I was capable of absorbing.

I learned that none of Gabriel Elk's compositions called for more than six performers. When operating with a full cast, he controlled three corpses and I controlled three. Neural programming prior to each performance took care only of facial expressions and speech; the majority of the actors' movements Elk and I had to direct from beneath the neuro-pit by remote control. Stamina was required of us because each drama adhered to rigid Aristotelian standards of unity, and we sometimes held our swivel chairs – amid console banks, sweat-inducing light and closed-circuit television screens – for more than two hours at a stretch. An additional burden devolved upon us because the plays also invariably made use of pantomimic elements from an Oriental form called the *Noh* drama; these posings and gestures demanded of us a kind of agonising, empathic monitoring. Moreover, we had to take care of Stonelore's lighting, the operation of the pneumatic lift in the centre of the working area, and the synchronisation of musical scores with the action going on overhead.

One of my most vivid memories of that time is of my introduction to the dead actors; this occurred on the second day after my return to Grotto House, when I was beginning my apprenticeship.

'Come, Ingram,' Grabriel Elk said. 'It's time you lost your innocence. We can't really begin work until you've seen them.'

Together we went by elevator from the main level of Grotto House down into the programming room. Into the rock, into the realm of cybernetic miracles. But we didn't stop here. Elk guided me through this first crowded vault to a massive door opening on the tunnel leading to the Stonelore comptroller room.

The tunnel, the entire underground complex, called up in me uncomfortable sensations of *déjà vu* – and not because I had once carried Bronwen Lief into the programming room; no, I felt as if in some indefinable past incarnation I had denied the light and entered a secret, subterranean mausoleum resembling this one, out of which I had emerged as pale as a dead man. The tunnel was lit by red lights; we stood for a moment in its mouth, looking towards the sealed comptroller room. Then we walked a few metres to a door on the corridor's right-hand wall; here the old man admitted us to the dormitory of our dead colleagues, cohorts in Gabriel Elk's singular repertoire company.

This room was cold, icily cold.

The corpses that Elk had purchased lay in hard white plastic coffins, or preservators, with crystalline lids. A rank of three preservators on each side of the room, a narrow aisle in between. Each unit had its own self-regulating cryostat; all shared linkage with a central system of storage tanks containing liquid oxygen, these ice-touched canisters being ranged like bright, upended cannon barrels against the far wall. Or like organ pipes.

*Yes,* I thought, *like organ pipes.* As if each sleeping actor were listening to cathedral music in the numb privacy of his own death, forevermore plugged into the storage tanks' silent anthems, the seethe of unendurable cold.

I looked down through the unfrosted glass of a preservator at Bronwen Lief's face. Unchanged, she slept.

I moved down the aisle.

Through the cystalline lids I looked at the faces of four men and another woman. The masker woman appeared haggish and diseased. The men offered almost a cross-section of the male Mansuecerian population, two being relatively young, one stout and middle-aged, the fourth cruelly wizened by six or seven decades of Ongladredan winters. These were Gabriel's players.

I looked back at my host. He began telling me the names of the five performers new to me. About each he recited a litany of biographical information: birthplaces, families, occupations, accomplishments, failures and, finally, manners of dying.

'Did you know any of them while they were alive?' I asked him.

'No.' He looked at me, then exhaled another puff of breath. 'But I found out as much as I could about them over the winter. I bought all of them this past winter – except for Bronwen. I had to wait for her.'

'You buy every winter?'

'I have to. I burn them out, Ingram. One season at Stonelore burns them out, as life never really has the chance to do.'

'Do you program every one of them before the season begins? Then re-program them before each new play?'

'The ones who have roles always require surgical adaptation, electrode implanting, cybernetic neural grafting – the last of which enables us to control our performers from beneath the amphitheatre, Ingram. I'll work extensively on the ones who carry the brunt of the dramatic situation, less thoroughly on the others. Sometimes a performer will be masked, easing the preparatory burden on me; sometimes an actor or two will not have a speaking part. But the work's there, it exists. Your own efforts at Stonelore, Ingram, will be confined to the mechanics of immediate control, as were Gareth's; I'm not even going to try to introduce you to the other. That's my speciality, my hands and mind are inured to its tediousness.'

'And when the season's over, Sayati Elk? What have you gained? And our burnt-out company of players,' sweeping my arm backwards over the sleek, insidiously still coffins, 'what becomes of them?'

'Cremation. The funeral of Atarites rather than Mansuecerians, since in their last days – their artificial, posthumous lives – they will have behaved like people touched with fire. A death they have – then a brief, violently intense second life here at Stonelore – then a second, incontrovertible death. After which we put their burnt-out bodies to the torch and let the smoke curl up to Maz from the autumn bonfires.'

I thought of the sloak, of the fires burning on every beach, inlet, and strip of coast around Ongladred. What must those tiny pyres look like from the air? If the Parfects were indeed orbiting our planet amid the concealing Shattered Moons, wouldn't they realise the bonfires were cries for help?

Standing in Elk's cryogenic locker, I shivered and shook the thought away. 'But you, Sayati Elk,' I said, returning to an old question, 'what do you gain?'

His pale green eyes, combining ice and fire, lifted to mine; then he turned and walked out of the chamber, forcing me to follow.

Materially he gained very little.

On the nights when Elk and I sat in our cramped control niches beneath Stonelore, the Mansuecerians who filed into the theatre and filled its concentric tiers always 'paid' for their seats, not so much from economic obligation as out of a ritualistic impulse to honour the old man. No one was forced to give anything, but nearly every masker made a token donation of three or four mithras when he entered, dropping the small coins into an open-mouthed urn beside the theatre's inner doors. Elk fed this money back to the state, which taxed him mercilessly. Or else, in the autumn and winter, he used the small surpluses remaining to him to buy new performers and to acquire materials unavailable to most Ongladredans. Genius and madman, he was neither fish nor fowl, masker nor Atarite; he bridged the social order.

He bought materials and equipment from Atarites whose wealth, station and access to the Old Knowledge had bestowed upon them the benefits of an incipient technology. In fact, throughout his life Gabriel Elk had striven to assemble as many pieces of the Old Knowledge as he could buy, extort, or cajole from those privileged enough to possess it. His library in Grotto House was a tribute to this effort: forty thousand microchips, meticulously catalogued, all of them facsimiles of those the Parfects had given to humankind when we were dropped off, like so many unwanted curs, on to the rocky, gong-tormented planet of Mansueceria. Twice the Old Knowledge had survived the dissolution of Ongladredan civilisation; twice it had been at least partially restored by foresighted men who had found one another in the ruins. Now Gabriel Elk had his share of it, and the neuro-dramas, I discovered, both drew upon the Old Knowledge and radically augmented it, made it new. So perhaps this was one of the things Gabriel Elk gained from Stonelore, the satisfaction of an omnivorous mind communing across time and interstellar distance with its intellectual forebears. But that wasn't the whole of it. After all, the process had begun with Elk long before Stonelore, and it would have gone on until the old man's death, in different manifestations, even if the amphitheatre had never been built.

Why, then, this kind of agonising labour, the re-animating of corpses, the sweat and the emotional stridency of control? I didn't really have an answer.

One night, during the first week of the dramas, while Elk – helmeted and wired – was directing the action in the neuro-pit, I leaned back in my swivel chair and stared with bleary eyes at my console's central television screen.

There the haggish old woman and the middle-aged man acted out their parts in Elk's drama *Agon*. Life-sized figures projected as electrons through a cathode-ray tube and reassembled on the sensitised face of my receiver as tiny parodies of themselves. They hitched and spasmed on the screen, seemingly kilometres away, even of another universe; thin and metallic, almost garbled, their voices came through my headset. The spectacle grew violent as the woman brandished a temple knife and shrilly cursed her adversary.

How was our audience reacting?

I had no controlling to do for at least another fifty or sixty lines. I turned in my chair. I saw Elk across the room from me, his shoulders pushing forward, his arms stretched like knotted cables over the console top, his fingers curled beneath eight different switches at once and ceaselessly shifting among these. The cord-trailing helmet he wore gave him the look of a stocky, bellicose medusa.

Facing my own console again, I directed one of the cameras in the amphitheatre to scan our audience. I watched the lefthand monitor above my comptroller unit. In Stonelore's darkness the camera scanned by means of infrared floodlighting and a quartz-lens relay. Tier after tier of masker faces, all rigid beneath the movement of a camera, and because of the ongoing conscription programme many of these faces belonged to women, the elderly, and the very young.

I halted the camera. I brought a section of the audience into startling close-up.

On my flickering monitor I studied the expressions on their faces. A revelation discouragingly grim, not because the maskers appeared either stern or disapproving but because their eyes and mouths betrayed no emotion at all; they sat, merely sat, gazing down upon our actors and partaking of Elk's surcharged dramaturgy as if it were no more real than an indifferent daydream.

Faces rigid with blandness; eyes too wide-awake and attentive to suggest apathy, but so non-committal as to be damn-near inhuman.

As I watched the faces on the monitor, I began to feel that our audience wanted re-animating even more than had our dead actors, the ones who now vigorously shadowed forth Gabriel Elk's vision. The dead vicariously living through the dead, our audience seemed.

Then I had to go to work again. My visor came down. The pneumatic lift carried another actor into the arena, this one a young man under my direction. My eyes turned from the lefthand monitor to the screen in the centre. Watching this, I let my hands direct the movements of my protégé's hands; I wandered into his mind, then activated Elk's neural programming of the speech centres, and withdrew. My presence was external then, a transferral of will conveyed by delicate mechanical means and the aching implementation of rote memory – mine. For twenty more minutes I sweated (eventually controlling Bronwen Lief as well as the young masker) while Elk deployed every one of his corpses and kept them all hitching and spasming about like the decrepit primitives they were supposed to be: a *tour de force* of comptrolling.

Then *Agon* was over.

Wearily I leaned back in my chair. I looked at my lefthand monitor and saw that the closed-circuit camera was still scanning our audience, relaying their images into the comptroller room as they sat unmoving and seemingly unmoved in the rising houselights. Again, that infuriating and universal expressionlessness!

Finally they stood and, talking desultorily with one another or saying nothing at all, filed out of Stonelore into the night, a regiment of automatons. When they were gone, the amphitheatre was no more quiet than it had been while they were there. I turned to Elk, who had unhelmeted himself and swivelled towards me.

'Three nights in a row, Sayati Elk. Are they always like that?'

'Yes. Usually.' His sideburns were matted, the lower portions curled moistly over his cheeks; his eyes redrimmed and narrow. He looked very old that night, every one of his sixty-three years.

'You mean we can expect a response no more lively than what we've had these last three nights?'

'Probably not a bit livelier than this, Ingram.'

'A regiment of automatons,' I said. 'Blaine's conscripted almost all the men of fighting age, but there's still a regiment of automatons – several regiments – in Lunn, Brechtlin and Mershead; they come out to Stonelore every night.'

'Different ones come on different nights, Ingram. And they're not, as you would style them, *automatons*.'

'How judge a masker except on the basis of his behaviour, Sayati Elk?'

'With the People Accustomed to the Hand one has to judge on the basis of *significant*, not just conspicuous, behaviour.'

I shook my head. 'I don't understand you, Sayati Elk; I've sweated through this with you three times now and still don't understand why you do it. The money is nothing to you, and the maskers file out every evening as if they've simply wanted a warm place to sit for an hour or two. It demoralises me, Sayati Elk, it guts me of purpose and initiative. Whereas you . . .' My unfinished sentence hung in the room between the two of us.

Then Elk said, 'Whereas I notice that they come back, Ingram. No one forces them to come, but they come back – performance after performance in the spring and summer, year after year.'

He stood up. 'They always come back,' he reiterated quietly.

Then we went about the task of securing the comptroller room and caring for our feverish performers. I worked without speaking, in a spirit of weary half-comprehension of what he had told me and of listless ignorance of what he had left out. We spent a good deal of time pushing the mobile preservators up and down the tunnel.

Afterwards I slept, slept dreamlessly. And woke on the next morning to anticipate another evening in the comptroller room – for, as usual, Stonelore would be full.

# Eleven

Away from Stonelore things were happening. During the fifteen successive presentations of *Agon* events in the outside world threatened to break in upon us, to force us out of our isolation.

The far northern coasts of Ongladred, four hundred kilometres from Lunn, had begun to suffer the first of a number of Pelagan naval assaults. From what we heard, these were not merely the hit-and-run tactics of foolhardy reivers operating singly and apparently at whim, but the tentative strikes of a nation testing its full-scale capacities for war. Usually one or two large Pelagan vessels slipped through the veils of night and wind-whipped spray to fire their cannons at a coastal village and the small ships in harbour there. The bonfires crackling jewel-like at intervals along the coast to hold off the sloak did nothing but illuminate the barbarians' targets, betray the simple people who had set the fires.

Prows like dragons, sails like reptilian wings, banners like streaming serpents' tongues, witnesses said. Then, having wrought their sudden destruction, the ships were gone back into the night and the mocking sea wind.

But the little fishing village of Nogos, we heard, had not escaped so easily; the Pelagans had come ashore, murdered most of the citizenry in their beds, abducted perhaps twenty more people, and then fled seaward. The following day several fishermen from south of Nogos found bodies floating in their fishing grounds; most of the corpses had been stricken at and mutilated by boarnoses (shark-like creatures infesting the iciest waters of the Angromain Run). On the second morning after the attack at Nogos, two or three more bodies were washed up by the tide near Thumbre.

Because of the latitude and their remove from the main

islands of the Angromain Archipelago, the people in the north of Ongladred had felt themselves safe from this kind of brutal harassment. The Atarite Court in Lunn had agreed; most of the state's forces were positioned along our island's southern and eastern coasts, and not only because Arngrim Blaine wished to preserve Lunn over any other Ongladredan city. No. Lunn was vulnerable, that was all. The greatest portion of our navy, therefore, lay just off the coasts where our troops were encamped, a defensive barrier against the Pelagan fleet. Reivers had penetrated the barrier at night, yes, but Blaine reasoned that our enemies would have a difficult time sneaking a hundred large warships past us. Now it appeared that the Pelagans would not even try; instead they would sail their dragon vessels east from their own islands, away from Ongladred, circle then towards the polar cap, and descend on us from the White Sea and the multi-coloured Angromain Run.

Two days after the devastation of Nogos, four after the first hit-and-run raids on other villages, Our Shathra Anna ordered a reprisal.

She ordered seven of our galleons to strike swiftly and heavily at Orland, the largest island of the Angromain group and the suspected seat of the newly centralised Pelagan government.

At Stonelore, Elk and I were preparing for the ninth performance of *Agon*. We were in complete ignorance of what was happening over seventy kilometres out to sea. Later we learned.

The reprisal strike had failed.

Several ships of the Pelagan fleet had intercepted our galleons more than an hour from the Orland coast. Firing without warning, they had sunk three Ongladredan raiders, captured one ship, crippled two more, and sent the cripples limping home in the wake of our only unscathed galleon. Our enemies, it seemed, were strong, resourceful and determined to establish themselves, eventually, as masters of Ongladred.

That much we learned; little more.

For the most part, Gabriel Elk ignored these developments, although on two or three occasions I managed to draw him into brief, unrevealing discussions. The only link he and Bethel recognised between themselves and the fortunes of the state was their son, Gareth. He and Coigns had been assigned away from the Lunn garrison to the infantry forces of Pavan Nils Barrow, now encamped outside the northern coastal city of Thumbre. Bethel Elk, from all external appearances, saw this link as much more significant than her husband did; she feared for her son, but she also feared for Field-Pavan Barrow and the people of Firthshir Province.

One day she asked me, 'Do you think the Pelagans will land up there, Ingram?' She faced me stiffly, her back held erect by the brace.

'I don't know. Except for a few reivers, they've shown a general reluctance to put us to the trial down here – if that tells us anything. The raids on Nogos and the other villages must mean something, too, Mistress Elk. A clue to their plans.'

'It's almost summer now,' she said. 'But it's still cold up there, isn't it, Ingram? Like winter?'

'Yes. Or very early spring.'

'Gareth and Coigns have blankets and woollen coats. I hope the others are as lucky.' Then she left me where I sat, in Grotto House's open courtyard, enjoying the warmth of pale Maz.

During the days, Gabriel Elk left me to myself.

He spent most of his time reworking the formal lyric passages of the dramas he had composed over the winter. A little time he spent in the programming room, forecasting the methods and the equipment he would use in preparing our actors for new roles. As soon as *Agon* was over, the mechanical work would begin. In the interval he concentrated on perfecting the odes and the rhymed variety of stichomythia in which he often had his characters speak, parrying epigram with epigram. All I could get from him was that the next two dramas completed a trilogy whose subject was 'human suffering and achieve-ment'. After which pronouncement, he grinned.

First, *Agon*. Then plays entitled *Anabasis in Spring* and *Omega Thwarted*. The titles meant nothing to me, but Elk gave me to understand that the trilogy represen-ted a new direction in his work. Again, I didn't know. I had neither seen nor read any of his previous neuro-dramas.

Now he was revising *Anabasis in Spring*. I had nothing to do but wander about Grotto House thinking on the frivolity of 'enlightening' the masker population of Lunn, Brechtlin, and Mershead while the villages of Firthshir Province burned. An enlightened masker, as far as I could see, behaved no differently from one who dwelt in dead-pan ignorance.

Then our fifteen performances of *Agon* were over. The island was growing into summer – real summer – with meadow flowers nodding yellow and blue heads among the dull upland grasses. Fifteen days we had; then Elk and I would be back in the rending, grey world of the comptroller room.

Our fifteen days out of the comptroller room were no vacation. Although we did get to see the anaita-roses flut-tering – and the little blue flowers whose name I never learned (but remembered from Rhia Lief's embroidery) – and to feel the southerly sea wind, the *maloob*, blow like invisible velvet over our skins, these respites were rare. While Elk prepared corpses, I prepared myself. That preparation consisted of reading *Anabasis in Spring* and studying as well its diagram-laden companion, a Manual of Control. This last was a bleak little booklet in Elk's own minute longhand. Like some of the flowers around Stone-lore, the ink (I remember) was violet.

As summer came on, so did the rumour and the fact of Pelagan hostility. On one of these days between dramas, during the period of preparation, I caught Elk in Grotto House's dining chamber and sat down beside him. 'I'm afraid I'm beginning to be of Chancellor Blaine's persuasion, Sayati Elk. What we're doing, how do we justify it? I can appreciate the aesthetic experience of the neurodramas, or at least I can before the tedium of comptrolling blunts my responses – but too many things are happening beyond Stonelore, things of genuine moment, for me to rest easy here any longer. I'd like to go back to Lunn, to the Atarite Palace.'

'Oh?' The old man leaned back in his chair, a heavy wooden chair with thick arms. 'What will you do when you get back there, volunteer for a seaman's position?'

'As a member of the court, even as a relatively obscure dirt-runner, I'm—'

'You're exempt from any such demeaning service. I know, Ingram. So what will you do while "things of genuine moment" confront your countrymen?'

'Whatever Our Shathra Anna and Chancellor Blaine require of me.'

'Ah, duty; a noble sentiment, Master Marley.' It had been a while since he had slapped me with 'Master Marley'. 'For now, because Gareth's been taken from me, they require you to serve Ongladred by aiding me.'

'The two are equivalent, I suppose?'

'No, no, Ingram. I don't suffer from that delusion. Besides, as you know, Arngrim Blaine doesn't equate the two. To keep you out here, I intimidated him.'

'Then we're back to my original question, Sayati Elk. If my service to you isn't really service to Ongladred, why do we nearly kill ourselves for an audience whose only response is to come back as listless as they left? What are we accomplishing?' I had to pin the old man down.

But he said, 'Service is of different types, Ingram, and some varieties of it lie outside the stagnant pale of nationalism and duty. This is one of those. What we're accomplishing, though, I won't try to tell you – won't even try to articulate yet for myself. I'm a selfish old man, Ingram. *Selfish* and *old*, those are the key words. And if I'm deluded at all, it may be in the assumption that my selfishness serves Ongladred better than would a dutiful renunciation of self. At least for now. This, like all things, may change . . .'

And so we ignored the continuing depredations in the north; we forgot the fragrance of the anaita-roses, the freshness of the maloob blowing inland across a summer ocean.

Here is a summary of that time: The Ongladredan fleet overextended itself attempting to establish a defensive line across the coasts of Firthshir, Vestacs and Eenlich provinces; Elk and I, towards the end of our fifteen-day preparation period, began giving up great chunks of sleep time, courting exhaustion. Galleons burned; my morale sank. Rumours of impending invasion reached us via the itinerant tinkers and tradesboys who sometimes stopped at Grotto House; in my sleep I saw the amphitheatre filling with maskers who wore under faces bitingly vacant, tunics emblazoned with this: ☯ Then, receiving only token resistance the Pelagans landed an army of almost eight thousand men in Eenlich; on the evening of that day Gabriel Elk opened Stonelore for the first performance of *Anabasis in Spring*. Just as the Angromain barbarians had committed themselves in the north, we too had gone past the point of abjuration. Two darkly improbable enterprises had been set in motion, the Pelagans' and ours.

'How do you like the title of my play now?' Gabriel Elk asked me. 'I'm a prophet in my own land, unhonoured and indifferent to my neglect. The Pelagans, your erstwhile brothers, Atarites under the skin, march upon us. And my play predicts it.'

'Pillars crumble. People die. And we—'

'—*fiddle*. Is that the word you're looking for? Remember one thing, Ingram: Gareth's up there in Firthshir, with Barrow's forces.'

I turned away from him. So he was aware, coldly aware of the situation. Why, then, our singlemindedness in putting on a neuro-drama, in running corpses through an intricate, *unreal* series of events? Apparently Elk had his own satisfactions; I had only the sweat. My back to Gabriel Elk, I looked at the left-hand monitor.

Our audience was filing in.

'People die,' the old man was saying, talking to the back of my head. 'But not these. These still live, Ingram.' I could feel his eyes fixed on my monitor. Together we watched the audience come in:

Women, children, old men, cripples of every conceivable sort:

The bent, the legless, the scarred, the humpbacked, even the blind. All of them People Accustomed to the Hand, maskers who had come to Stonelore for undivulged reasons of their own.

Then Elk swivelled away from me, faced his own control console, signalled to me that we were about to begin. I put on my helmet, shut out my thoughts, turned a dial, and plunged the amphitheatre into darkness. The sweat, the sweat of comptrolling.

And that night Elk and I, working together, working begrudgingly together, orchestrated a beautiful performance of *Anabasis in Spring*. The poetry came through my headset; the alternating grace and clumsiness of our actors poured into me like haoma. I was a part of Elk's poetry, I was a part of our actors' movement. The sweat of comptrolling turned into the sweat of participation.

In the neuro-pit above us two dead men are discussing the cycle of the sloak; I am both dead men, two young soldiers. Then enter the corpse of the haggish old woman, inhabited now by Gabriel Elk. She is masked like a demon, somehow enormous and dreadful in spite of her tiny bones and frail gestures. To the soldiers she is an apparition, a minion of hidden powers. In a long, image-crowded speech she tells them the sloak is real, that it does the bidding not of its own protoplasmic desires but of a watchful intelligence external to itself – an intelligence vastly more alive than Man's but different in kind. She dances while she speaks, and her huge, one-eyed mask seems to float between her upraised arms like a kite to which her thin, twisting body is the knotted tail. As the accompaniment of tabor and flute grows more insistent, her head – her leering mask – threatens to pull her aloft, lift her into soaring flight. But the music stops, her speech ends, and the hag disappears into the underworld. The two soldiers whom I inhabit stare after her in awe and consternation.

That scene, even in the observation of *Elk*'s comptrolling, wrung me of energy. There were other such scenes.

*Anabasis in Spring* dealt not only with the threat of the sloak, but also with the problems of command in an army relentlessly on the march. It was not prophecy, as Elk had said it was, because one could not help feeling that the sloak and the army in this neuro-drama existed in an altogether different realm of experience, another world; everything was distanced, set at a remove – in spite of which the actions and feelings of the characters had an uncanny immediacy.

Still, though overwhelmed by the poetry and the detail Elk had lavished on this spectacle, I knew that it wasn't real. What relation did it have to reality? To the sloak and to the Pelagan forces? The real sloak, the real invaders? So absolutely powerful in Stonelore's comptroller room, Elk and I were ironically powerless in the face of these threatening certainties. Was Elk withdrawing into prophecy, abandoning the real for the sake of artificial order and contrived significance? He had said no. He had said that I ought to remember the dilemma of his son, which he had not forgotten either – which he could not forget.

Wrung out at play's end, I pushed my visor back and remembered nothing, thought nothing. The sweat of comptrolling, the sweat of participation, was dry on my neck. Elk stood behind me, a hand on my shoulder. Together we watched the maskers file out: the women, the children, the old men, the crippled and the deformed. Their faces were as dull as the underside of a leaf, their eyes were the wicks of guttered candles. Only a few of them talked.

'Nothing,' I said. 'Nothing.'

We presented *Anabasis in Spring* on three more evenings. Then stopped – but not because of this lack of discernible response on our audience's part. No. Events intervened, events and Our Shathra Anna. Against history and royalty Gabriel Elk ultimately had no more resources than did the simplest masker. And on the following morning history and royalty came to Grotto House in the person of Chancellor Arngrim Blaine.

PART TWO

# Twelve

His roan tooth glistening, slashing like a miniature tusk, Arngrim Blaine said, 'The Halcyon Panic has broken, Sayati Elk. It's broken, and I believe your neuro-dramas have been instrumental in destroying our citizenry's calm.' Anger lay under the planes of his thin, expressive face like a ripening bruise.

'Obviously you haven't attended a neuro-drama this season,' I said. We were sitting in Gabriel Elk's quiet little study on the main level of Grotto House; the room contained leatherbound books – not microchips, but books. Both the Elks were present, in adjacent, meticulously carven chairs.

Bethel said, 'The people have been kept abreast of the events in Firthshir, haven't they?'

'They have, Mistress Elk.'

'Then how can you blame the people's distress – the breaking of the panic, as you call it, Chancellor – on my husband's dramas, not a one of which you have seen in its entirety? The Lief girl's performance doesn't count.'

'I can do so, Mistress Elk, because things have culminated much too soon; the misdirected rage the young women of Lunn have exhibited in the last two days comes well ahead of schedule, it defies the computations of the Magi.'

Gabriel Elk said, 'But then again, Chancellor Blaine, the Pelagan invasion has taken place sooner than the Magi expected.'

'And the rage of the young Mansuecerian women, the wives of our soldiers and seamen,' Bethel Elk said, 'has been growing for a long time. That rage has been building since well before the Magi decreed the existence of a "Halcyon Panic". It's the product of a long-ingrained and periodically aggravated sense of helplesssness, which I feel too, Chancellor Blaine.'

'I don't doubt that you do. However, Our Shathra Anna – who is, as I shouldn't have to remind you, a woman too – says that the "sense of helplessness" you speak of need not reveal itself in hysteria and acts of vandalism.'

Bethel Elk said, 'Our Shathra Anna's experience has hardly been typical.'

A chill descended upon Gabriel Elk's study, like a dust of invisible snow sifting out of the very air. We were all as separate as corpses put up in our own sealed, soundmuffling preservators. Who would resurrect us?

I looked at Blaine, sitting cross-legged opposite me. He had come to Grotto House that morning dressed not as the Chancellor of Ongladred, nor even as a member of the Atarite Court, but instead like a reasonably successful masker tradesman. Two young guards had accompanied him, posing as his sons. All these precautions had grown out of the wish to prevent a visit as disastrous as Our Shathra Anna's last one. And yet the Chancellor had come himself, he had not sent a representative.

Coolly he said, 'Listen to me. Two days ago – the day after your newest production had opened, Sayati Elk – a large group of young women left Lunn, marched out the Mershead Road, and began turning over vegetable booths and fish stalls. Not the ones run by old men or other women, but those tended by masker tradesmen whom we've exempted from military service – or else booths owned by minor Atarite officials. There was no stopping these women.'

'In that case,' Gabriel Elk laughed, 'your choice of disguises could have been wiser.'

Arngrim Blaine ignored this. 'That night a pack of children – turned loose by their mothers, I've no doubt – ran into the thoroughfare beneath my offices and began chanting a litany to Maz, asking Him to blow Himself up and Ongladred, too, so that we might at least die in the light.' The Chancellor permitted himself a wan smile. 'We had no success either in catching the children or in driving them away; the ones whom the guards did catch were inevitably replaced by others, all crying together, "Maz, Maz, destroy us in light. Preserve us from the slime of the sloak and the knives of barbarians. Let the lie die." A litany drummed into them by women.'

'Your sleep was spoiled,' Bethel Elk commiserated.

'Oh, that episode has its amusing aspects; I'm not blind to them. But that same night some hysterical person, or group of persons, set fire to a row of dwellings on Lunn's south-western outskirts. The houses all burned, and several people died, including children, Mistress Elk. A violet pall of smoke hung over the rooftops, quite lurid under the Shattered Moons, I assure you. And yesterday the wail of keening women filled the streets – issued from every house – from dawn until long after nightfall, a general lamentation the likes of which I've never heard in Lunn. I'm surprised you didn't hear it out here.

'Then yesterday – since the keening doesn't by any means end the matter – a procession of old women, as many as two hundred or so, walked all the way from Lunn to Brechtlin, on the point opposite Mershead, and disrobed on the beaches. After that, they waded into the sea and kept wading until their strength gave out and they drowned. These were widows, unmarried women, grandmothers. None of the Mansuecerian population tried to stop them; that they be left alone seemed to be the unspoken desire of even their relatives. We dispatched a few Atarite guardsmen to turn them back, but the women wouldn't be reasoned with – and simple coercion failed, from want of enough men to restrain them. Into the water they went, naked pathetic creatures, obeying an hysteria beyond my comprehension, Mistress Elk. Even now they are being buried, all the washed-ashore corpses no one will come forward to identify.

'And these things – the arson, the keening, the senseless suicides – are *not* amusing, friends. They betoken the depth of our citizenry's fear.'

A different kind of silence filled the study then. Arngrim Blaine had reasserted his dignity. The four of us sat there, self-conscious, in its palpable aura. At last Bethel said, 'And you believe that *Agon* and *Anabasis in Spring* are responsible for these things, Chancellor?'

'In part, yes.'

'I would like to think you are right,' the old man said.

'May I ask why?' the Chancellor said curtly.

'Certainly. Everyone requires a degree of power, no matter how minute.'

'Of this sort? Power to cause suicides and arson?'

'If one is weak, yes. However, I'm not a weak man, Chancellor, and that's not what I require in power. I see in these atypical patterns of behaviour – this hysteria – the potential for something constructive. It's that germ of constructiveness I would like to think my neuro-dramas help nourish. In all the negative acts of the last three days there is a thin, affirmative thread.'

'Very thin.' The Chancellor's lips hardly parted. 'Very thin.'

I said, 'The best explanation for this behaviour is not the neuro-dramas, but the news from Firthshir.'

'That figures prominently,' Chancellor Blaine said. 'Certainly I don't dismiss it. In fact, I ought to tell you that the Pelagan forces have pushed out of Firthshir into Eenlich Province, driving Field-Pavan Barrow's army before them.' He paused. 'There's no word of casualties. As far as I know, Gareth and Coigns are alive. On this point I can't say any more; I don't know any more.

'Messages have described the retreats as "strategic," but the fact remains that we're losing ground daily. Fields are being burned, early crops destroyed, animals slaughtered, and small hamlets overrun and subsequently abandoned. The enemy supplies himself at our expense. This is changing, however. A runner from Pavan Barrow reports that our people have begun to destroy any goods that may be useful to the Pelagans; the procedure now is burn and fall back, burn and fall back. We want to force the barbarians to be dependent on their own supply lines – in the hope that we can establish an unmoving front and then interdict at sea, destroy their own naval logistics system. But their troops have been reinforced almost three times a week, and we now estimate an invading army of almost twenty thousand men. If they continue to advance at twelve to fifteen kilometres a day, they will reach Lunn before the month is out. Ongladred will fall.'

'Why have you made a special trip to Stonelore to tell us these things?' Bethel Elk asked. 'Surely, Chancellor, you don't hold the neuro-dramas responsible for the Pelagan invasion?'

'No, not that, Mistress Elk.' He turned to Gabriel. 'Do you remember the conversation we had here at Grotto House after Bronwen Lief's recital, before the reivers murdered Josu Lief?'

'I remember it,' the old man said. 'You're not going to offer me the command of a Mansuecerian vessel again, are you?'

'No. That's not the portion of the conversation I'm referring to.'

'Then which?'

'You and your son argued strongly that societies fail when their leaders fail. You cited inflexibility as the most dangerous sin of command. Do you remember?'

'I remember.'

'And do you remember that Our Shathra Anna told you that one day you would have to include yourself among the number of Ongladred's leaders?'

'Yes, that too – more or less. Although I believe we made a distinction between intellectual and political leadership.'

I almost laughed, but Chancellor Blaine was manoeuvring craftily, as if born to the Socratic method; I watched him with genuine interest. Gabriel Elk, his large hands on his knees now, was also intrigued, a man ensnared in spite of himself.

'Distinctions such as that blur,' the Chancellor was saying, 'when the enemy plants his boots on our own soil, Sayati Elk. See me here before you,' spreading his hands self-deprecatingly, 'I am trying to bend. Our Shathra

Anna bids me remind you that in these times we must all bend, particularly the leaders among us. If you feel that Ongladred is worth preserving, either for its own virtues or in preference to the barbaric code that would supplant our own, you too must bend, Sayati Elk. You must—'

'There will be no more performances at Stonelore this season, Chancellor. At least for a while.'

Slowly Arngrim Blaine closed his mouth, cut off in mid-harangue. I, too, was surprised; the old man had said nothing to me about discontinuing the neuro-dramas. He had not even hinted at it. It was a course he had only just decided upon, it was his own pre-emptive strike – a means of regaining the initiative. And yet he struck out of belief, not out of wounded pride or insecurity; that his decision nonplussed the Chancellor merely increased his cold, grey delight in affirming a conviction. Elk leaned back; his hands came off his knees.

'Good,' Blaine said. 'That was easier than I expected.'

'I don't do it to please you,' Gabriel Elk told him, 'but because Ongladred is threatened and I am not a fool. I had hoped that Field-Pavan Barrow and our ships in the channel would save me a decision like this one, but that's past recall now – a dead hope. The news you've brought tonight, Chancellor, wounds and frightens me, me a man almost inured to pain and too old to get very frightened anymore. Therefore, Stonelore closes.'

'But what else does the Chancellor wish?' Mistress Elk asked. 'Will you place Gabriel in command of a galleon?'

'No. That would be too little, Mistress Elk, a mis-application of talents. Our Shathra wants something more.'

'A weapon,' Gabriel Elk said.

Again Arngrim Blaine looked surprised, almost in-credulous. He uncrossed his legs and extended them straight out before him. 'Yes,' he said. 'An unconventional weapon, something that can be developed in twenty days or less, easily transported, and deployed in the field.'

The old man looked at the ceiling and laughed, a sardonic yap. I started, so unexpected was this noise. Then Elk folded his hands in his lap and scrutinised them like a sculptor taking mental notes. 'A weapon,' he mused.

'That's principally why we want Stonelore closed,' Blaine said, 'so that you can devote your time to this project – although my own feeling is that secondary benefits will accrue, the foremost among these being the return to calm of Lunn's populace. Our Shathra Anna wishes you to begin at once. Will you?'

'Why don't you put your Atarite scientists to work on this, Chancellor? They have the Old Knowledge, the materials, the technological capacity – or at least its potential.' Elk clasped his huge hands together. 'Why do you trek out here to ask of me this pretty little enormity?'

'Oh, we have the technological capacity to do everything you have done, Sayati Elk. We also have the materials, the physical resources. It's the psychic capacity that we lack. Were it not for this inhibition, an inhibition programmed into us by the Parfects several thousand years ago, the People touched by Fire would have created self-propelled carriages, atomic-driven ships, mechanised communication systems, even vehicles that fly – all of these things we would have developed long ago. The knowledge is there, but we don't permit ourselves to use it; we are inhibited, *psychically* inhibited, and even our recognition of this fact doesn't cure us, Sayati Elk. In this case, self-awareness is not power. We have heated and lighted the Atarite palace, and a number of Atarite lords have done the same with the houses on their estates – but beyond that we haven't ventured, we haven't *wanted* to venture. What you have done at Stonelore and Grotto House doesn't confound our intellects, it confounds our sense of propriety, it mocks something innate and immovable in our natures. That's what we've come to you for, Sayati Elk. Those are our reasons. Do you understand?'

'Yes. I'm an aberration.'

'That's a pejorative term I would not have used. Please don't try to attribute it to me. What I mean is that you are not inhibited in the way of either those Accustomed to the

Hand or those Touched by Fire. Your aggressiveness is intellectual as well as physical.'

I said, 'You're Ongladred's superman, Sayati Elk, Zoroaster's übermensch.'

Ignoring this, Elk said, 'The Parfects re-created Man in a strange, divided image, Chancellor Blaine. They did not want us to kill ourselves, but they didn't want us to die, either. Mansuecerians. Atarites. A strange, divided people struggling together to subdue Ongladred. Then, a thousand years ago, we divided again, and what the Parfects tried to provide against is happening once more. We're killing one another, but even as we do we excuse ourselves on the grounds that it isn't yet genocide, the extinction of the species. Neither the Pelagans nor the ruling order in Ongladred has essayed a genocidal weapon; something in our shared unconscious will not allow the attempt. And yet today, Chancellor, you ask me to commit myself to the development of the first such horror on the road to just that end, the end of being able to destroy utterly, without mercy or discrimination.'

'Because you have the skill,' Blaine said. Then added killingly: 'And the temperament.'

'The temperament!' Bethel Elk said.

'Yes, Mistress Elk. The temperament that conceived and raised the miracle of Stonelore out of the dust of this upland arena.'

'Oh come now, Chancellor. Your language apotheosises my husband.'

'Its intention, Mistress, is quite the opposite. It's because Sayati Elk is more "human" than we,' keeping his face composed, decorously humble, avoiding even the hint of smugness, 'that we ask this of him.'

'My difference from the members of the Atarite Court,' Elk said, 'is not so great that it frees me from the sanctions of our shared unconscious.'

Arngrim Blaine sighed. Then he pulled his tradesman's clothes together, smoothed out the wrinkles in his breeches, and stood. 'Very well. Then I'll tell Our Shathra Anna that although Stonelore is closing, you

172

cannot bring yourself to do something no Atarite will attempt.' I was impressed, then, by Blaine's fairness; he might have said something as self-servingly crass as 'cannot bring yourself to *save* Ongladred,' but he had not: Conscience had prevailed.

'Sit down,' Elk said. 'Tell Our Shathra Anna that in twenty days – with the help of those Atarite lords who can supply me with information and materials – I will give her what she wishes.'

Blaine eased himself back in his chair. 'You have the complete co-operation of the court, Sayati Elk.'

'Then I must also have your promise to return the weapons to me when we have defeated the Pelagans. The weapons will be small and deadly – but in themselves they'll fall mercifully short of any sort of doomsday weapon. Still, I want your word that afterwards, after our victory, the weapons will come back to me – without fail.'

'You have it, Sayati Elk.'

'Good. Then let's stop talking and have something to drink. Ingram, will you serve us.'

I said that I would; got up; went down the hall to the kitchen. I could not believe that the evening would not find Gabriel Elk and me helmeted, wired and perspiring in our swivel chairs in the comptroller room. Before I returned to the study, I had a solitary drink of haoma and let several scenes of *Anabasis in Spring* play through my mind. I would never see them again, except in my mind. Somehow that struck me – for reasons I then refused to consider deeply – as a poignant loss.

And that evening we turned away a crowd of masker women, children and old men, telling them the amphitheatre had been closed. Unprotesting, they went back through the upland grasses, down to the Mershead Road, and returned from whence they had come – to tell their friends the news.

# Thirteen

The following day Gabriel Elk began work. He used the facilities in the programming room under Grotto House. Bethel handled the correspondence that the project required, writing letters in her small, looping hand and sealing them with purple wax and the impress of Chancellor Blaine's ring. I carried the letters. To the homes of the landed Atarites, to the offices of our scientists, I rode. Always I returned to Grotto House; and soon wagons of materials — chemicals, metals, precious stones, boxed unknowables — began rattling up into the dusty arena and leaving behind their cargoes. On several occasions men whom I didn't know arrived with stern or expressionless faces, disappeared into the programming room, remained a day or two, then emerged and departed, not to be seen at Grotto House again.

Ten days passed. I found myself thinking that if not for the Pelagan invasion, we would have just concluded our second neuro-drama and begun preparations for the third.

*Omega Thwarted*. Appropriate title, it seemed. I had not even read the play, had no idea what sort of end it would mark to Elk's trilogy or which corpses he had hoped would carry the burden of its theme; for the moment, they all lay inviolately frozen in their preservators, darkness and ice weaving about them a smoky, blue shroud. In dreams, I saw the faces of the corpses growing a fine, web-like covering of hair, their eyes simultaneously narrowing — until they all resembled the reivers who had attacked us so many nights ago. Then I woke to the nightmare in the north.

Field-Pavan Barrow's forces had begun to slow the Pelagan advance — but the countryside through which they retreated, burning what our own people had built or planted, stretched away to the White Sea like a desert of ash. So our runners said. Firthshir, Eenlich, and Vestacs provinces had been transmogrified into the Fields of Astivihad; they were diseased deathscapes in which charred tree trunks and unfilled graves lay desolate under a thin sun and no birds broke the silence with their songs. At sea, several more of our galleons had been sunk, and even in Lunn we could feel the breaths of an animalish people hot and rank on our faces. The enemy was only a little more than a hundred kilometres away, momentarily stalled. Or so our runners told us and so we hoped . . .

The fighting continued. Even young Atarite men were being sent to the front (those who could command were already there), and I expected at any hour to hear my own summons. At times I wished for it, so futile and anticipatory did my own privileged role seem. What was Elk doing? Though I slept in his house, I seldom got the chance to talk to him. At the front, I imagined, there would be continuous conversation of a lethal kind, the bass imperatives of cannon and the high-pitched yawping of rifles. Old, damn-near falling-to-pieces Yorkley rifles.

What kind of advantage was Elk going to give us?

On the sixteenth day after Arngrim Blaine's second visit to Stonelore, two empty, closed wagons arrived at the arena. Gabriel Elk directing, we spent the late morning and all the afternoon carrying equipment out of the programming room to the wagons. Up and down in the elevator, back and forth through the stone corridor. I worked with four masker labourers, handicapped men who had not been inducted; I struggled to preserve my dignity before them, sometimes attempting to lift more than I was able. Not long past, hadn't I come from these people?

Elk and I rode horseback (on creatures provided by the Atarite Court, animals which Elk eventually bought outright) beside the wagons on our way to Lunn. At sunset we reached the Atarite Palace and drove through the cobbled court to the great, white-stone recreation building.

Here we unloaded our materials, setting them up in the vast athletic hall exactly as Elk told us.

Once, as I passed him, the old man said, 'Your fire-touched friends will have to forgo their genteel pellet-ball and fencing for a day or two, Ingram.'

The hall was fiercely illuminated, the electric flambeaux rippled with the energy coursing into them, and the palace (as far as I could judge, outside, from the evidence of its muted windows) was almost dark by comparison – as if the recreation hall were draining some of its power away. Before we had finished unloading, Arngrim Blaine himself came out of the palace and approached the recreation hall; he came with two of the men who had been to Grotto House during the early stages of Elk's work. For the first time, their faces wore looks of ill-concealed excitement.

The wagons rattled away. In the shadow between two great buildings, we five men conferred. Chancellor Blaine said, 'Master Gordon and Sayati Snow have told me nothing about this enterprise, Sayati Elk, except that it progresses. Does it?'

'No further, I hope, than it has already.'

'What have you developed?'

'A device I call a photon-director. And I have merely developed it, not created it. The Old Knowledge preserved for us by the Parfects contains an incomplete and deliberately cryptic "description" of the instrument and an abstract of its theory, including a list of applications. The applications are all benevolent – from precision measurement to the healing of retinal lesions.'

'Then . . .?'

'Don't fear, Chancellor. I haven't been working these last sixteen days to manufacture a machine of mercy. The Parfects explicitly told us nothing, nothing at all, about how to murder one another by such a device. But the information's there for minds profound enough to dig it out.' The old man spoke as if each word scalded him. 'Profound enough,' he reiterated. 'And *flexible* enough. In times such as these flexibility is a cardinal virtue.'

'And genius,' the Chancellor said placatingly, sensitive to Elk's tone. And between Blaine's parted lips, the carnelian gleam of that tooth – a little tusk, a knife of discoloured bone. And then the lips closed.

'Genius is a hag who flies in the heart,' Elk said. 'This was different, this was a toad squatting there.'

'But it works?'

'It works. Master Gordon and Sayati Snow will demonstrate them for you in the morning, Chancellor. At first light.'

'They know how to operate this . . . photon-director?'

'Yes. And they aided me immeasurably in their construction – there are three, you see. Three photon-directors. Apparently the Atarite inhibition against conceiving and developing an advanced weapon doesn't extend to mechanical matters like assembly and use, Chancellor Blaine.'

'It's been rumoured that I have Pelagan ancestors,' Sayati Snow said. He was a man of my own age, a mathematician and abstruse theorist. His smile surprised me.

'And I,' Master Gordon said, not smiling, 'don't like being ruled by enzyme tags, plastic viruses, tampered-with chromosomes, any of that business. So I help with this.' Gordon was an artisan, a stocky, dark-complexioned man with violet eyes.

'At first light, then,' Chancellor Blaine said. He led the others to their rooms in the palace, and I found my own gloomy bachelor's quarters, deserted now since long before spring (with the exception of the nights I had spent there after bringing the Pelagan captive in from Stone-lore), two rooms in the low building opposite the recreation hall. Amid the smells of musty quilts and stale air, I slept.

At first light Gordon and Snow demonstrated one of the photon-directors in the recreation hall. Gabriel Elk stood to one side, with Chancellor Blaine and me, and watched. While his terrible, sleek, streamlined machine burned holes of various shapes and sizes in several different target materials against one of the building's wall, the old man talked:

'The old name was laser,' he said, 'and oddly enough it was perfected on Earth *after* the weapon that twice – in Holocausts A and B – levelled the civilisations of mankind. That the Parfects chose even to hint at its existence suggests that they looked upon it as a device chiefly beneficial. Necessarily,' he said, making the word sound evil, 'we are going to pervert it to our own ends.'

We watched as Sayati Snow triggered the device and a beam of intense, ghastly red light shot through the hall and burned a hole in a cuirassed dummy suspended from the ceiling. Godon turned a small wheel on the side of the machine's casing and manually directed the beam to inscribe a valentine on the cuirass' left breastplate. When he had finished, a heart-shaped plug of bronze smouldered there. For a long time the plug did not fall; it was as if the metal didn't even know that it had been severed from its own contoured matrix, the torso of our hay-filled warrior. This inscription the photon-director made without even setting the strawman afire. At last, realising its separateness from the cuirass around it, the plug fell and rang hollowly on the stone floor. Then Sayati Snow triggered the machine again and a brief stream of ruby light ignited the effigy. The dummy burned madly, and the breastplate, no longer having anything to support it, dropped to the floor with a hot clang of its own.

From where we stood we could still feel the heat the machine had generated and the scalding backwind of the destroyed dummy.

Then, after a time, Blaine: 'And these will save us?'

'Unless the Pelagans are more cunning monsters than we,' Elk said. 'I suggest that you send Master Gordon and Sayati Snow, each with a photon-director, to the front. Then, position each man on a flank of Field-Pavan Barrow's line of defence. Ingram and I, with the third machine, will go aboard a warship to the northern run – to halt the barbarians' supply fleet.'

'Why not a direct assault on Orland and the Pelagan

capital?' Chancellor Blaine asked. 'That would be surer. Much surer than trying to intercept the supply fleet in the White Sea fogs – with one vessel and a dubious weapon.'

'The weapons are far from dubious, Chancellor, and I'm requesting two escort vessels in addition to the warship carrying the machine itself. As for the *lasers*, they're to be used only defensively.'

'And returned to you?'

'And returned to me.'

'Very well, Sayati Elk.'

That afternoon, accompanied by a guard of Atarite retainers, Gordon and Snow left Lunn for the northern provinces. Elk and I rode in an unguarded wagon to the little port of Brechtlin and there, as two old masker stevedores carried our boxed weapon aboard the warship *Paradise*, watched the landward gulls flashing their wings in the day's last light.

A seaman pointed out to Elk and me the stretch of beach where the widows, grandmothers, and spinsters from Lunn had waded into the indifferent water and drowned themselves.

# Fourteen

We sailed in the morning. Around the southeastern cape of Ongladred we went, passing the village of Mershead and picking up an escort of two heavily armed galleons. The weather was good, the wind blew from the south, a late maloob, and our sails bellied out like so many linen-shirted paunches. For nearly fifty kilometres we followed Ongladred's coast, staying within the line of defensive warships positioned ten kilometres off the land at intervals just permitting each captain to see the vessels on his flanks; then we were swept out in the Angromain Channel and journeyed northward as a trinity of solitary free-lancers, glorified reivers, our task the crippling of our enemy's supply efforts, a task we would have to accomplish amid an archipelago not of rocky, knife-edged islands but of glittering, tabular icebergs, all of them peril-ously in movement. Through the Angromain Run we sailed, into the cliff-littered White Sea.

On this trip Gabriel Elk taught me how to aim, activate, and control the beam of the photon-director, which we had mounted on the raised forward deck of the *Paradise*. I spent two hours one afternoon burning holes in the improvised sails of a dinghy being dragged at a safe distance behind one of our companion vessels; then I sank the dinghy, setting both its sails and hull ablaze. The sailors on the *Sea Drake* cut the little boat's tow line and waved cheerily at me. I think I grinned. The maskers at Stonelore had never reacted with even half the effusiveness of the seamen; not once. Those on the *Mandragora*, our other companion, even fired a canon. How much more powerful than this could one feel, I wondered.

'Good, Ingram,' Gabriel Elk said. 'Soon you'll use your new-found skills against the Pelagans.'

'Me? Why not you, Sayati Elk?'

'I've done enough, Ingram. This is for you.'

We did not talk about how Snow and Gordon were faring nor about how the forces of Field-Pavan Barrow were acquitting themselves. These were things out of our control. We could only hope that the Pelagans had not altered their manner of supplying their own forces and that we could intercept them in the White Sea. But although we didn't talk about the land war, it wasn't hard to see that Elk frequently thought of it. In more than one sense, his own blood struggled in that conflict, strove both to honour itself and to pulse for its nation – even though the old man and his son were driven more by abstract ideals than by any fanatic nationalism.

The wind continued brisk, and on our third evening at sea we entered the southernmost reach of the Angromain Run, that corridor of indigo- and vermilion-shot water between Ongladred's northern coast and the overarching scorpion's tail of the barbarian archipelago. Most of these islands are little more than rocks, and uninhabited. Of our voyage into this region I remember principally the bitterness of the night air and, off to port, the small, pearl-like fires burning on the coast. These were now and again visible when a jut of land, like the nub of a gigantic finger, poked out accusingly from our island-nation's usually unobtrusive shore. Parallel to Firthshir Province's eastern coast, we saw no more of these fires; the enemy had let them go out – apparently they did not fear the sloak, or had forgotten about it, or (the most likely alternative) had insufficient men to keep the fires going.

But even without the coastal bonfires the *Paradise* sailed on a mirror surface of rich, darkly rich light; the Shattered Moons illuminated the Angromain Run as if it were a floor of marble and swirled the icy water with deeper indigos, more elusive vermilions. Was it really true that in the wake of the Pelagan advance our country was becoming a gutted ashpit? At sea, it did not seem possible, for the moonlight had an aurora-like brilliance and the very air sparkled. At night I spent as much time as I could on the *Paradise*'s decks, just to see these things – the immemorial wheeling of stars, and of water, and of curdled satellites.

'The moons are brighter out here,' I told Elk on our third night.

'One or several of them are artificial,' he said.

'How do you know that, Sayati Elk?'

'The Parfects carried us out here six thousand years ago, carried us out here eight hundred light-years from Earth. At least one of the Shattered Moons, perhaps the minutest shard, is an instrument of observation, data-accumulation, and relay – the Eyes and Ears of the neopeople who attempted to re-engineer their own progenitors. Mankind was given genes for morality. You and I, then, are integers in a modestly cosmic experiment, Ingram, and the Parfects therefore have a small vested interest in us – they would have wanted to see how their experiment turned out, they would have made provision for monitoring this hemisphere of Mansueceria, at least.'

'But how do you—?'

'It doesn't stop there. They would have wanted a means of interfering in our affairs, of altering the balance of historical forces in Ongladred – if the need arose. Their satellite or satellites among the Shattered Moons fulfill this purpose, too.'

'Robin Coigns told me once that he believed the Parfects would return and repair our botched world at the third coming of the sloak. Surely you don't believe that, Sayati Elk?'

'No, Ingram. One property that we can't lease out is the equivocal terrain of our fates.'

'An epigram,' I said with a cruel inflection that surprised even me.

'If you like, Ingram. But true for all that. In spite of the Parfects, we're alone, and we are also accountable.'

'But this instrument in the sky, the Eyes and Ears of the Parfects, how can you be so certain it exists? What proof have you?'

Sayati Elk looked up at the curling, night-darkened sails; then, grinning like a sly adolescent, he said, 'Faith.

Simple faith, Ingram.' And he went down from the forward deck to his own private cabin.

On our fourth morning we were in the White Sea, travelling northwest out of the Angromain Run. Since we had no idea into which of the many sinuous fjords at the top of Ongladred the Pelagans were running their supplies, our little fleet stood well out to sea and waited. Eventually the barbarians' hideous ships would have to sweep down the arc of the Angromain's scorpion's tail and reveal themselves – or else, for want of provisions, our invaders would soon have to plump out their bellies on ash and gunpowder. Several kilometres out from the coast we tacked about and faced to the east, our three vessels now strategically placed and separated in order to cover the wide, white mouth of water out of which our enemy must sail, dragon-prowed and sinister. *Evil* was the word I thought, knowing that Sayati Elk would have merely laughed at the literalness of my imagination.

We had nothing to do but wait. Nothing but wait and watch the icebergs drift down from Mansueceria's polar cap, sedate and reflective – like hermetically sealed, buoyant cities of crystal. Or like imperturbable monsters of glass.

We saw five icebergs on our first day of waiting, none so close that it posed a danger to the *Paradise* but all near enough to incite our wonder. The closest to us had inlets and firths like an island, although its sides rose up from the White Sea so steeply that none of these afforded a landing place; an eerie sucking roar emanated from the iceberg's caves as the sea rushed in, and a reverberant echo followed each guttural shout. The ice itself was a thousand different colours, mostly shades of blue that purpled the water beneath the iceberg and, as the evening drew on, turned the sky behind it a brittle cobalt. Maz went down early, but not before we saw this nearest leviathan calve and heard the thunderous groanings of her birth pangs as the ice tore apart. Another night to wait, but our first night to worry about ramming the progeny of a multicoloured and fecund ice-creature.

Captain Chant, apparently, had seen service in the White Sea before, and we survived the night intact.

The fifth morning greeted us with cottony banks of fog, all of it rolling down from the archipelago's last few islands. The *Sea Drake* and *Mandragora* disappeared, faded away into the gathering gauze as we watched – like apparitions becoming once more invisible. We were enshrouded, we were made a bobbing universe to ourselves. Now our fears were that the icebergs would demolish us or even worse, that the Pelagans would glide by us in the murk.

Again, we could do nothing but wait, muffled in this hanging fog. Maz was a wan dream somewhere on the other side of our anxiety, and fog drooped down on us from the masts and spars like a ghostly moss. Then night fell, a night that sealed us into ourselves.

All that reminded us of the worlds beyond our own was the intermittent ringing of the *Sea Drake*'s and the *Mandragora*'s ships' bells. The bells' notes, blurred by the fog, drifted through the darkness to us like parachutes of iron sound. Where did they come from? How did they reach us? And then I realised that the *Paradise* had a bellman of its own, that he was on the forward deck (by Gabriel Elk's canvas-covered machine), and that our bell, too, occasionally sent out peals of hollow warning.

'Aren't we just giving ourselves away to the Pelagans?' I asked a masker seaman on the *Paradise*'s main deck. I nodded forward.

'Oh, the bell. Perhaps, Master. But it's better than banging up against our sister ships, and the Pelagans – if they're out in this – have most likely ceased to run, so as to let the soup blow off. They've got fellows with passable heads, too, you know.'

I said: 'Our bells won't keep the icebergs off. They don't listen.'

'If we bump we bump, Master. It may mean giving up a sail or two, but we'll pull her by. So, too, the *Drake* and the *Mandragora*.'

His confidence was pleasant but not contagious. I went below decks and tried to sleep.

# Fifteen

On the sixth morning the fog was shredding. Shredding into a series of staggered curtains, some of them standing open, some of them closed but for a hairline of blue where sea and sky parted them. Our sister ships became visible once more. Ahead of us, still partially veiled, the mouth of White Sea water from which our enemy would have to come. Feebly Maz was parting the veils, revealing the icy glitter, the stretch of predatory sea, that had been curtained from us.

A voice cried out: 'Dragons floating! Six in flight!'

Gabriel Elk came by me, wrapped in furs. Sailors began moving on the *Paradise*'s decks.

Paralysed, I watched, watched everything.

In a crush of moving bodies the old man halted, twisted his wide face towards me, said, 'Up here, Ingram, up here,' and strode purposefully through the swarming men, a distinct and preeminent figure. I watched him climb to the forward deck. His stocky form teetered above me, disappeared. Then it was at the head of the ladder again, gazing down on me – though I couldn't see the old man's eyes, only the light pouring down over his shoulders and through his akimbo arms. 'Ingram, get up here, damn you! Is all the fog in your head now?' These words overmastered the confusion; somehow, though spoken in an almost conversational tone, they were audible.

In only a moment I was beside Gabriel Elk.

Looking forward over the prow of the *Paradise* I saw nothing – nothing but twinkling water and, slightly to our left, a single iceberg. No other icebergs were visible, only this one rectangular block whose length was several times that of our ship's. It loomed, loomed just out of our intended course. Again, the cry from aloft: 'Dragons floating! Six in flight!' And I wondered if the man up there weren't simply reading his own apprehensions into the facets of this solitary iceberg. Maybe the dragons floated in his mind, nowhere else.

'There,' Elk said, pointing, and I saw the sail: the first sail.

It seemed to rise up out of the White Sea like the wings of a pelagic, half-frozen pterodactyl, crisp and crimson-brown. Fog scattered as these wings beat through. The prow rising up beneath the Pelagan vessel's sail was carven into the shape of a horned, reptilian head – like that of a dragon, or a fire-lizard, or even an ancient Earth saurian. Exact identification hardly mattered. The impression was that of the entire ship's having emerged hungry from a long sleep in the cold sea. Now the monster was hunting, and the only prey in its path was the galleon on whose forward deck I stood.

One by one the other five sails breasted the horizon, popped into view as if propelled upward from the White Sea's bottom. We saw them, they saw us. And the other five Pelagan ships were as hideously accoutred as the first, bright banners streaming above their dried-blood-coloured sails.

On the *Paradise* orders were called out. Gabriel Elk tenderly and quickly drew the piece of padded canvas off the photon-director. It hit me that I was going to operate the machine, I was going to trigger it, I was going to control the intensity and the direction of its scorching needle-flare. More orders were called out; I didn't know where or from whom. The old man said something to me, bumped me into place. My gloved hands were on the photon-director's obscenely neutral-looking controls, a curved trigger and a simple metal wheel. And out in front of me: water like frozen milk, a single bluey-green berg drifting towards us several hundred metres away, and the distance-dwindled but still terrifying Pelagan warships. The only fog I saw now was peripheral, every wispy curtain drawn into the wings of our theatre of battle. Inside my heavy gloves my hands were sweating.

'Are we in range?' I somehow asked, the words at-tremble with two different kinds of cold, my voice hoarse as if from shouting.

Elk said, 'Only a target beneath the horizon is safe, Ingram.'

'Do I fire?'

'Did you hear Captain Chant?'

I looked at the old man – at his face under the fur cap, at the iceberg-green eyes, at the snowy sideburns standing away from his cheeks. How long had I known him? Why was he talking to me?

Quietly, guardedly, he was saying, 'Captain Chant wants you to wait – to see if they'll turn now that they've seen us, turn and go home.' *Was this true?*

Absently I said, 'I didn't hear that order.'

Then, from aft, I heard a megaphoned command. 'Commence firing, Master Marley. COMMENCE FIRING!' The order echoed aloft, the air reverberated with it, the immense northern sea swallowed the echo.

Gabriel Elk pushed me away from the mounted machine, pinioned my arms. 'Captain Chant, Captain Chant, I've decided that this man will fire at my word! At no other word but my own!' Then he released me and shoved me back into place.

My hands gravitated to the laser's controls – and I was very conscious of the sharp rippling of the highest fore-sails. My gums burned with the otherworldly chill, my ears throbbed acutely, and the *Paradise* seemed frozen by Sayati Elk's legitimate, but irregular, usurpation of the galleon-captain's command role. No one moved. Captain Chant's megaphone was stilled.

The Pelagans' little supply fleet had indeed begun to turn – but not out of either fear or surprise. Two of the dragon-prowed ships were manoeuvring away from the other four, off to the west. The remainder continued to run towards us, but with their starboard hulls slightly open to us and cutting across the wind. Like ours, the ships were all three-masted, but the sails differed from ours in being serrated and ornamented. Each topgallant bore the yin-yang symbol which Elk had once told me the barbarians had appropriated from legendary Cathay. I stared as ships and sails alike came on.

'Do you know what to do, Ingram?'

I nodded. I could tear cloth with the photon-director, I could burn clean holes, I could set lacerating fire, I could incinerate men on deck, I could sear off mastheads, I could open ragged vents beneath the ship's water lines. What could I not do?

—Turn the barbarians back with a shouted word, with a wave of the hand. No hope of that; none.

Therefore, I would wield Elk's re-created machine as if it were a funnel for all my frustration and rage.

'For Maz' sake, Sayati Elk,' Captain Chant called out from the pilot's deck, 'let the young master fire!'

'Stay your hand yet,' the old man whispered fiercely in my ear.

Numb, I obeyed. I saw a puff of smoke appear as if by magic on the starboard side of the foremost Pelagan vessel. Momentarily I feared that I had triggered my weapon by mistake. The puff of smoke tattered into greasy threads and blew away on the wind; a roar followed, pinched-sounding at this distance. Then, about fifty metres out to sea, a spout of water suddenly kicked up in front of the *Paradise*; air and water vibrated with the shock. It was as if someone had poured liquid mercury into my ears, that painfully deafening.

Another puff of smoke, followed rapidly by another; two muted barks in succession; then the shock of impact as the milky sea broke under the weight of Pelagan cannon shot and water spiralled up in two separate fountains off our bow. I could see individual drops glistening in the midmorning air, miniature prisms tracing their own kaleidoscopic parabolas of descent. Altogether numb, I watched.

'Sayati Elk!' Captain Chant was shouting. 'Let him fire!'

'Fire, then,' the old man said in my ear.

I pulled the trigger with my gloved finger, then released

it. The machine's needle-flare blazed out over the White Sea like a radiant, resilient thread snapping from one point to another – as if its light had originated at the target point and then simply reeled the instantaneous beam out of the photon-director's tubular throat: *Fffffthup!* An obscene, rapid sucking. Afterwards the air seemed changed – but the beam itself shot past the enemy warship; was bewilderingly absorbed by the changed, electrically cold air.

Had my finger touched off this raylike lightning, this gone-astray miracle of fire?

Bursts of smoke formed and dissolved on the sides of two of the Pelagan warships; spray kicked up all across the bow of the *Paradise*, the noise was almost insupportable, water leapt up to us on the high forward deck so that we were drenched with its lashing fallout.

'Again, Ingram!' Elk shouted at me. 'Again!'

I swivelled the laser on its mount, I pressed the trigger and held it back with all my will. Rage, frustration, bewilderment, longing for power, impotence, hatred, pride – these and more spun out of me in the swift embodiment of the photon-director's luminous, ruby ray. Almost blinded, I swivelled the machine, turned the wheel controlling the beam, and, teeth achingly clamped, willed the disintegration of everything that was not Ingram Marley.

I stitched the sails of the first Pelagan ship with fire, I sheered off all three masts above their topgallants, I scorched a line of black piping along the middle of its starboard hull. There were drops of water on my eyelashes, tears of half-frozen spray, and the red lambency of the emotions streaming out through the tube of the photon-director was reflected a thousand excruciating times in these tiny beads of ice.

The cannon aboard the first Pelagan ship ceased firing; no more innocent-looking puffballs of smoke. Aboard the *Paradise* we could hear men screaming, men shrieking like the winter ghost-wind. Their full-voiced terror was ludicrously out of phase with the placidity of the northern sea.

We could hear the splintering crack of wood; we could see the severed mastheads toppling, catching, and ultimately tearing through the adjacent sails to crash against the warship's decks, indiscriminately crushing men and equipment alike. The hull of the Pelagan ship was filling with water and ineluctably beginning to capsize – sails hanging and aflame, banners altogether scorched away, the dragon-prow glaring balefully out of one burnt-out eye and nodding ever seaward.

Finally I released the trigger, stopped swivelling the photon-director.

The booming of cannon growled over the water again, but this time from the *Mandragora*, which lay a little behind us and over a hundred metres to our right. A hollow booming, full of antiquated fury. Spray began geysering up in front of the enemy vessel that I had already effectively demolished, a line of violent punctuation marks. They added nothing at all to the unequivocal statement of the photon-director.

'They're jumping,' Gabriel Elk said. 'The Pelagan seamen who are still able to, Ingram, are jumping. They won't last ten minutes in the White Sea. If that long.' The old man was not looking at me, but at the sinking warship. 'If that long,' he reiterated.

I remembered something. 'Where's the *Sea Drake*?'

'There.' He gestured off to port. 'Those two warships that split away from the main contingent are bearing down on her, trying to use that iceberg as a screen between her and us.'

They were moving west, but because of our position I had to look north to see them. Already they had got behind the iceberg's striated, azure-and-rose cliffs and, in a moment, were cannonading the *Sea Drake* – a cacophonous, echoing barrage. At the same time, the three remaining vessels assaulting us and our other companion continued to come on, undeterred by the demolition of their leader or the ungodly shrieking of half its crew. Apparently no effort was being made to pick up the overboarded sailors; the Pelagans knew what Gabriel Elk knew, that they were dead men. Three warships, then, bore down on us; their two fellows attacked the *Sea Drake*.

Captain Chant was shouting orders again; masker seamen scrambled about frantically on the *Paradise*'s main deck.

I was drained, trembling.

'What should I do now, Sayati Elk?'

'Take the ones closing in on us, Ingram. I see nothing else for it.'

Swivelling the photon-director, I aimed at the Pelagan vessel negotiating its way towards us from behind the wreckage of the first. In ten minutes I had reduced it to a smouldering shell, masts down, hull precisely stove in. More men were in the water, and smoke trailed away to the north like a tattered banner. Even through my gloves I could feel the heat coming off the casing of Elk's machine. Inside my fur clothes I was sweating, profusely sweating. My face felt hot – but in my eyelashes, those frozen beads in which I could see the distorted reflections of the scene before me! No longer was I firing out of rage, or frustration, or hate; cold resolve sustained me, that and Sayati Elk's droning, almost perfunctory encouragement. For these things I had created wreckage.

'Now the third, Ingram; now the third.'

I destroyed the third ship, even though it had finally begun to turn away from the conflict; its captain had witnessed enough. No doubt he died with a terror in his heart more dreadful than that his ship's painted sails and grotesque dragon-prow had ever provoked in his enemies.

The fourth Pelagan warship fled. Successfully.

'Let it go, Ingram. Let it go. Someone must carry word of this back to the archipelago, back to Orland.'

Off to port, off to the northwest, the *Sea Drake* was suffering the methodical onslaught of the barbarian ships shielded by the now seemingly immobile iceberg. Their cannonade continued. The booming was deceptively melodic, deep and sweet. We could already see, however, that the *Sea Drake* would not survive the encounter; her foremast and several of her staysails were down, and she was returning fire only rarely, a tacit acknowledgment of her doom. Neither the *Paradise* nor the *Mandragora* had taken a direct hit.

'Can you help her?' Captain Chant shouted.

'Can we?' I asked.

'If you can burn through that berg, Ingram, if you can split it up and give yourself an aisleway to your targets.'

'Can I do that?'

'Probably not. I don't know. Its volume may be too great.'

Again, I swivelled the laser on its mount. Again, I adjusted the intensity and width of its beam, allowing for maximums in both. Again, I pulled the trigger back and held it in place.

At once the iceberg erupted in an almost volcanic billowing of steam, white clouds pouring over its table-top and sweeping off like thin gas. Hissing and creaking accompanied this eruption. When I finally released the trigger, the photon-director had done little more than bore an uneven tunnel whose depth I couldn't gauge.

Ships fell to this weapon more readily than did the calves of Mansueceria's polar cap. Still – with time – I might have won through. It was just that we didn't have the time . . .

The *Sea Drake*, gently capsizing into a foam scarcely whiter than the surrounding sea, slid out of our sight; gently she went, incredibly gently. If her crewmen were screaming, we did not hear them. Maskers often die without even a sigh of protest, and the officers of Ongladred, the Atarite elite, must emulate their stoicism, even in death. We watched our sister ship go down, we watched her slide with broken but commanding dignity into the indigo-riven deeps. And all on the *Paradise* were silent, stilled by our comrades' last end.

'Wait for the bastards,' the old man told me. 'Wait for them, Ingram, until they have to pull out.'

Fetched up with the *Mandragora*, we waited, we waited for the Pelagan renegades to sail out from behind the iceberg. I am certain that they knew we were waiting, that they had seen what we had done to the rest of their fleet.

A half-hour went by, then forty-five minutes. And when the barbarian ships came out they came out on opposite sides of the azure-and-rose ice plateau, cannons booming, their captains apparently determined that one crew would sacrifice itself for the other.

The water was pockmarked with shot, deliquescent with spray.

'Incinerate them,' Gabriel Elk said. His voice was flat.

Working first on one ship, then on the other, I did just that. I alternated until they both went down, blackened husks crumbling into ash on the waters. We were not hit. When it was over, Gabriel Elk walked away from me, descended to the main deck, strode the length of the ship, and without a word to anyone ducked into the passageway leading to his cabin.

I looked on my work: the sinking ruins; the flotsam of boards, boxes, and men bent double like shrimp-things, all bobbing hopelessly in the White Sea; and the smoke curling and dissolving above it all.

Then, the photon-director. On its swivel it sat: a slender, single-eyed beast no more remorseful than the snake that strikes and soon afterwards sleeps. I covered it with a piece of canvas. That way I could continue to look at it.

I looked at it for a long time.

# Sixteen

That evening as we sailed southward, the sky still smoking behind us and the *Mandragora*'s masts and sails silhouetted against that sky's brownish flame, I went below decks. I knocked on the door of Gabriel Elk's cabin. He had not been seen after our victory over the Pelagans; he had not joined Captain Chant and the other Atarite officers in the mess. So I went to Sayati Elk's cabin, and knocked.

'It's open,' he called, his voice still disconcertingly flat.

He was sitting on a stool in the middle of the small room, and over him leaned a middle-aged masker seaman with a razor. A basin of sudsy water rested on the writing surface next to Elk's bunk. The masker, a thin little fellow with no eyebrows, was shaving Elk; he grinned at me when I opened the door, then went back to work.

'This is Gnot,' the old man said. 'Yukio Gnot. He's a barber as well as a yard-trimmer and buntline-tender.'

I squeezed past the two men and sat down on the narrow cabin's bunk, a sort of wall cot. The little masker bowed. The hand holding the razor was extended gallantly out behind him. He recited,

> *'I am Gnot, the man*
> *You think I am,'*

and resumed work for a second time; all this he did completely humourlessly, with dead-pan seriousness in fact.

Elk was wrapped to the throat in a khaki-coloured apron, his face partially lathered, unnaturally pink where Gnot had already shaved him. Then I noticed that on the desk next to me, as well as the barber's soap-filled basin, there was a pair of heavy shears. What did all this mean?

194

For a time we listened to the groanings of the *Paradise*:
Elk in his khaki tent, Gnot concentratingly ignoring the
sway of the ship, and I somehow excluded from the inti-
macy of shaver and shaved. Between groanings I thought
I could hear the almost frictionless scraping of Gnot's
razor; it was as if the razor were scraping at the wet inside
of my skull.

Would no one speak?

'I'm sorry I deserted you, Ingram,' Gabriel Elk said.
'I'm sorry I made you do what I made you do.'

'You did desert me, didn't you?'

'Yes. But no more certainly than I deserted myself after
we closed Stonelore – and created again that thing out
there.'

'That was for a cause, Sayati Elk. What about this
morning's desertion? What about leaving me?'

'For the cause of my own sanity, Ingram. As the gold-
hearted beauty of the Stews once said, "It's nothing personal, Master, nothing personal a' tall." But I regret the
desertion mightily for what it seemed to imply.'

'Why are you being shaved at this hour?'

'An ablution of sorts,' puckering his mouth as Yukio
Gnot scraped at the grizzled whiskers near his Adam's
apple. 'Perhaps I should be bled clean. Gentleman Gnot,
an extra mithra if you go into the jugular neatly.'

The masker stepped back. 'There's nothing neat about
that operation, Sayati Elk. As for the mithra, I'm Gnot for
nothing and all's for Gnot in this barbering. You owe me
nothing, for all the pleasure's mine.' It was patter, amusing but sadly hollow. The little man leaned over Gabriel
Elk again, his browless eyes naked and vulnerable – like
ripe, peeled grapes.

His hands flashed expertly. Then I saw that he was
shaving away Elk's sideburns.

I said, 'Gentleman Gnot, was that requested?'

Elk threw me a sidelong look, the whites of his eyeballs
like little quarter moons. 'All of it's requested, Ingram.
Jaw, cheeks, and skull. All of it.'

'The masker mourning cap,' I said. 'What for?'

'For today.'

'You aren't one of the People Accustomed to the Hand,' I said, 'and you haven't lost a relative. Did you do this when your two eldest sons died?'

'I didn't, Ingram – because I wasn't a Mansuecerian, though born of them, and their customs weren't mine. Today I revive the custom of the mourning cap. Why? Because I mourn and don't know how to express it, the expression of it's gone out of me, all of it out. Today was a day I relearned everything but its expression, Ingram, and I turned to Gentleman Gnot for help. I'm no longer young, I'm nearing death, in fact – but I've never understood the element of affirmation that may exist in mourning, though I know that it *does* exist.

'The Atarite practice of mourning has always struck me as defeatist; the Mansuecerian, as cold and ritualised. But today – a day of my own making – requires this atonement at least. Already a kind of feeling flows in, behind Good Barber Gnot's fashioning of my cap. The outside will teach the inside. What say you to that, Ingram?'

'Nothing. Nonsense from Our Genius.'

'Exhibitionist nonsense?'

'Your words, your doubts.'

The old man shifted under the khaki barber's cloth. The wall candles flickered together; the cabin filled with interlocking shadows, most of them pooling and ebbing around the two men in the centre of the room. Delicately Yukio Gnot wiped the lather from Gabriel Elk's face; the old man's face was then naked, as if newborn. I wondered if I would have been able to recognise Elk if I had not seen the transformation. 'I'm a dramatist and poet,' he said confidently. 'Introspection and exhibitionism have been my trades. No doubts whatever in that, Ingram. This that I do now has nothing to do with my trades, however. It has to do with my humanity and mortality. How the world interprets it, I little care.'

He gestured at the spry, shadow-tattered barber and said, 'Proceed.'

Gnot took the heavy shears off the cabin's writing desk

(I had to move my feet for him) and began sclip-sclipping at Elk's massive head, the ring-curled, silver-white hair tumbling over the shears' blades like wool. Satyr's wool, I thought: Elk was smiling cryptically. Like the parings of old dreams the hair fell. In the shadow-filled cabin it almost floated, each curl a fleck of time, of coil-wound chronology, cut and discarded. Individual hairs clung to the drab bib or laced the floor with their dead, frightening beauty. I could not help thinking that this was something more than a simple barbering: I thought of the Parfects, I thought of the Pelagan reiver I had murdered, I thought of denatured animals and the resurrected performers of Stonelore. A sense of elation; a sense of loss. And the hair kept curling away from the blade, emphatically white.

When Gnot had finished with the shears, he lathered Gabriel Elk's shorn head, stropped his razor, and began scraping away the stubble. 'Harvest time,' Elk said. He sat perfectly still under the little masker's hands. Then, the operation complete, Gnot laid the shears aside and washed his patient's liver-spotted skull. Strangely, Elk did not look ludicrous – maybe because his bald head didn't shine like a tunic button, but more probably because his face, in its runnelled candour, green eyes hemmed in like a tortoise's, was already humorous at its own expense.

'Done, Sayati Elk. You needn't pay me. I'm Gnot for nothing.'

'I'd rather, Gnot,' Gabriel Elk said, shaking the apron out on the floor and giving the barber a few coins.

The barber bowed; he grinned. 'Oh, that's amusing, Sayati Elk, that's amusing how you put that. I'm appreciative, I am.'

I said, 'I'm doubled with laughter myself, tied up in a Gnot.'

'Oh, Master Marley,' he said, looking at me, 'you, too. You, too. All's for Gnot, it is. All's for Gnot.'

In disgust, I looked at the floor.

'I'll clean up, Gnot,' Elk said. 'You needn't feel obligated for that, too. You're a seaman and a barber, not a mercenary in the broom brigade.' This time the *not* wasn't a pun; the old man's voice had changed.

'Oh, no. I must do it, you know.' He took a small horsehair brush from the inside of his jacket, knelt, and swept the fallen hair into the barber's apron, which he had spread out on the floor as a receptacle for hair, dust, and any other oddments he could rake together. Speedily done, he pulled the four corners of the apron together and tied them up as best he could, careful not to spill either dirt or severed curls. He slung the resulting bag over his shoulder. He bowed to Gabriel Elk; he bowed to me. He looked like an archetypal gift-bringer, but one whose generosity has dissipated him into a posturing – and anaemic – clown.

'Take a few of those shavings,' I suggested, 'and paste on some eyebrows.'

The masker, alerted to something *unkind* in my tone, stared at me in utter incomprehension; his nonexistent eyebrows were quizzically raised. Elk opened the cabin door for him, let him into the hall.

'Thank you, Yukio,' I could hear him saying. 'You're a skilful man, and a good one. Let's hope we find our country and families safe when we put in at Brechtlin.'

'Yes, Sayati Elk. Let's so hope.'

Elk returned to the cabin. He sat down opposite me pulling his stool around as he sat. His naked, gravely humorous face was as unfamiliar as a map of Austermere, the Brobdingnagian continent sprawling over a quarter of Mansueceria's southern hemisphere. The naked, unfamiliar face looked at me, simply looked at me.

At last I said, 'Oh, that wasn't so bad, Sayati Elk. I've sunk five ships today, drowned nearly eight hundred men in an icy sea. Insulting Gentleman Gnot was one of my less murderous sallies of the day.' I wanted to cry. Instead, I pulled in my bottom lip and tried – tried very hard – to stare the old bastard down.

'A Mansuecerian, Ingram. A simple masker—'

'Why are you trying to shame me?'

'Oh no, Ingram, I don't mean to shame you, just to

explain that his shaving my head was my idea, not his. To explain that he speaks as he does because he's a simple, untouched creature.'

'But the banality of it, Sayati Elk, the endless banality of it.' And my eyes filled with wet candlelight, diamonds of melting, detonating colour that washed the old man's unfamiliar face away. I couldn't control my shoulders. *'The terrible, utter banality . . .'*

Then I could smell the old man's lather-sour warmth, feel his heavy arm and strong hand pulling me like a child into his side; he was sitting on the bunk next to me, a reality that had swum through my blurred vision to assert its realness. The voice was warm against my face. 'It's a banality which touches us all, Ingram – and we all attempt to transcend it, in whatever ways we're able. Even Yukio Gnot. Even the maskers who come to Stonelore.' His huge hand squeezed my biceps. 'But for pushing you to this, I'm sorry. My mourning is for you, too.'

'Will what we've done make a damn bit of difference?'

'That's hard to gauge.'

'Won't the Pelagans send more ships, and more, and more?'

'One escaped today. That one will return to Orcland, and the news its captain gives of his compatriots' end will soon be broadcast throughout the archipelago, both as rumour and warning. Or so I hope.'

I pulled away from the old man. In the melting-diamond light I found my feet and crossed to the door. 'Goodnight, Sayati Elk.' I went out without waiting for his reply. Inside my fur-lined parka my shoulders became a part of my body again, settled almost comfortably into me.

In the cold I found my way to the forward deck. There I directed two masker seamen to take the photon-director off its mount and carry it to my cabin. Under close-hauled sails, tarnished-tin stars, and the shadow-pocked moons, they did so.

They put the machine on the floor in the centre of my cabin, and I sat on the edge of my bunk for a long time looking at it. Then I extinguished my lamps, undressed in the dark, and lay down under several ragged quilts.

(Pulling them up, I remembered a quilt with blue flowers embroidered over its silken squares.)

The *Paradise* groaned, gently rocking. The shadow of the photon-director, the sinister bulking of its silhouette, drew my attention, and I stared at it as if compelled to wrestle with the implications of its shape. I was past crying. I lay in the dark and relived the morning and early afternoon, oh, eight or a thousand times. Then was rocked into dreamless nightmare, a series of floating images without correlatives . . .

# Seventeen

On the morning that we rounded the southeastern cape of
Ongladred, a strange thing happened. Captain Chant was
wringing the very air for wind, so motionlessly still was the
day; our sails were expertly trimmed, the yards finically
dressed, and we were moving homeward – but only just.
The *Paradise* rode the shallow, almost nonexistent waves
sluggishly, and the *Mandragora* had fallen back half a
kilometre in our languid wake. Aloft, our banners scarcely
fluttered.

Because the sailing was so poor along our island's coast,
we rounded the Mershead Cape well out to sea – far
enough out so that land was no longer visible. Although
we were now in waters lapping quiescently against unin-
vaded territory (the civilised heartland of our nation), we
saw only five or six ships of all of Ongladred's fleet, and all
of these out of hailing distance.

It was an odd morning, a subdued and lonely sort of
homecoming.

Gabriel Elk and I stood with Captain Chant and his
helmsman on the pilot's deck. Maz shone with a thin but
elemental vigour; He did not seem a likely one to nova, to
explode us all back into primordial plasma. Therefore
none of us wore parkas or overtunics; we basked in the
uncommon autumn mildness. And wondered at the absence of wind and the tranquillity of the sea.

'Where are all our ships, Sayati Elk?' I asked.

'On a day like this,' Captain Chant answered, 'their
captains would hope to be in harbour. Perhaps that's
where they are today.'

'But we ought to see a few. A precaution against the
Pelagans.'

'The Pelagans, Ingram,' the old man said, 'are defeated. I know it. Last night – and the night before – we

saw the bonfires on the coast. Having beat back one enemy, our people are turning their energies again to the threat of the sloak. Like Captain Chant, I believe most of our ships to be in harbour.'

'But the sloak,' I said, 'is no threat at all; a superstition.'

'Perhaps not a superstition,' Gabriel Elk said. His uncovered head struck me again as shamefully naked, a violation of character. Captain Chant's eyes caught mine once and their irises seemed to surround a question.

But our desultory talk continued. Meanwhile, on the *Paradise*'s decks our sailors worked with quiet, insectlike efficiency keeping the sails open to whatever breath of wind they could smell or intuit in the listless air. We were bound for home, we were bound for home, and only that mattered. The strange thing that happened that morning came too late to be an ironic comment on my refusal to see the sloak as a threat; too much time had passed to underscore my words with irony. Or so I tried to convince myself.

This is what happened:

Suddenly, with no warning, the sea beneath the *Paradise* – and everywhere else around us, insofar as we could judge – began to heave and surge, surge and heave, lifting and dropping in great, vaguely peristaltic swells. Our masker seamen turned their faces to the skies in disbelief, shouting to one another, checking braces and halyards. Captain Chant roared unintelligible orders over their shouts and scufflings, his megaphone jutting out before him like a supernatural trumpet. Officers on the other decks trumpeted these misheard orders back and forth over the sailors' heads, and the whole ship was atremble and ajostle with split-struck confusion.

Great slappings of water pounded our hull. It was as if a team of ocean-breathing giants – seaweed for beards and driftwood for bucklers – were playing at toss-the-blanket on the bottom of the Angromain Channel, oblivious to depth and pressure as impediments to their play. The flap-and-fall of their monumentally water-logged blanket translated itself into the lift-and-plunge that we aboard the *Paradise* were experiencing, into the running swells everywhere around us. It had to be giants. Since there was no wind, since our banners were still hardly billowing, this quaking of the sea, this ferocious faulting, had to originate from *beneath* the surface. I think that even I realised that, even I was aware of the odd nature of the channel's intransigence – and could do nothing but pray that the giants grow weary and desist. But, with Sayati Elk, I remained on deck, watching.

'The sloak!' I heard a voice cry out.

'Aye, the sloak!' in answer.

'The sloak it is!'

'The sloak!'

I grabbed Gabriel Elk's arm and shouted, 'I don't believe that! This is some kind of tidal anomaly, isn't it?' I had to repeat my words, but I got the old man to face me.

'I've never seen a tide like this, Ingram!'

'What about sea-bottom volcanic activity?'

'Who can say, Master? Who can say?' He was revelling in the surge of the waters, the cry and scuffle of our sailors. Me, he had no immediate concern for; I couldn't question him while this untoward pounding made our bilge echo and our masts passionately thrust and fall back. Men were mocked in this, their tenderness and pride both mercilessly battered, and the old man laughed and drank it all in. Every haughty wave.

I shouted, 'Do you – do you believe it's the sloak?'

But he didn't answer me, refused to hear me. Beside him on the pilot's deck I waited for an immense mythical creature to capsize and drown us on a transcendently fair day. The masker seamen, hauling line and climbing, kept us afloat, and then, in a split-struck instant, the seas calmed and the *Paradise* settled into a gently bobbing element scarcely even foam-flecked. The giants had wearied of blanket toss and gone on to more delicate amusements.

—*Like subduing boarnoses to their clammy hands*, I thought. I could imagine the sleek, sharklike creatures undergoing training.

After we had ridden for a time on the freshy stilled

waters, I began to force my questions on the old man. We stayed aboye decks in the midmorning sun, a little away from Chant and his helmsman. 'Was that really the sloak, Sayati Elk? Not freak vulcanism nor a quirk of the tides, but this creature you and the maskers call the sloak?'

'I believe so, Ingram.'

'Why?'

'Because that answer, to my mind, is the only one that truly works, the simplest and most legitimate.'

'Then do you expect this gelatinous monster to smother the coastal bonfires – haul itself irresistibly over our island – and destroy Ongladred for a third time? That seems to be all we can hope for?'

'Ingram, I am past expectation. Past prophecy and vision. But I don't think Ongladred will be destroyed again. At least not by an entity as remorselessly out-of-nature as the sloak.'

'If you believe in the thing, why not?'

'Because what we've just experienced, Ingram, was meant as caveat and warning, it was directed specifically at us aboard this ship and the men on shore who witnessed the turbulence's batterings, the men of our nation.'

'Caveat and warning,' I said incredulously. 'From whom? The sloak?'

'No, but from those who control it. It's a thing out-of-nature, Ingram, an anomaly in its own right, a product of smug and juridic intelligence. It has no will of its own; it executes the judgments of this "higher", all-ruling intelligence and does so in the guise of an apocalyptic but wholly natural phenomenon. The sloak exists, Ingram, but it's a lie.'

'I don't understand you.' —Although this argument was somehow familiar. I had heard it before. In Stonelore. From a haggish old woman in one of Elk's neuro-dramas.

'I'm speaking of the Parfects. The sloak is a quasi-organic creature, a biological construct which the Parfects have twice before activated in order to pull us back from forbidden knowledge. For them, the Old Knowledge is the limit of what we may know; the sloak, the unweaponlike weapon by which they fix the parameters of our knowledge. Once again, Ingram, we begin to encroach on the boundaries of the permitted: We have employed technology – proscribed technology – to kill. Hence this warning, a warning especially vivid to us on the *Paradise*, wielders of stolen fire.'

'Your interpretation, Sayati Elk, hardly seems the simplest and most legitimate; it's infinitely complicated.'

'It's the simplest explanation that accounts for the arrogantly directed history of our island, Ingram, and by "arrogantly directed" I don't mean to imply that we – Atarite and Mansuecerian alike – don't share in the shame of our failures and the simple pride of our glories, only that we have been measured against an alien standard and made to suffer unduly for the squalid aspects of our nature – even though They have altered that!' He delivered this little oration heatedly, as if it had been rehearsed a thousand times but never before spoken.

I said, 'Aren't you seeking a scapegoat, Sayati Elk, a scapegoat external to ourselves?'

'I absolve humanity of nothing! At the same time I refuse to designate humanity itself as a scapegoat, as the Parfects decided six or seven thousand years ago it must be so designated. That view is abhorrent to me, as abhorrent as the utter denial of our guilt. —I resent the suppression of humanity, I resent the Parfects' self-undertaken Sitting in Judgment.'

'And if humankind destroys himself?'

'He must be free to do so, even if he does it over and over again until the last sterile coupling of the species. Or until he learns.'

'And if he doesn't learn?'

'Then his viability as a creature worthy of the cornucopian gifts of chaos has proved altogether too weak and he must die – cursing himself, mind you, not that cruel but munificent chaos. His passing will have, must have, the grandeur of tragedy. That much is evident, Ingram, that much is clear.'

I looked away from his intent, naked face. Ahead of us,

off to the right, the hazy blue line of Ongladred's southern coast was becoming visible; we had successfully rounded the cape. The ships in harbour at Mershead and Brechtlin must have had to endure the shock waves of the pounding we ourselves had ridden out at sea. Now, however, the clear sky and the windless air mocked our memories; the planet basked.

'Could your sloak – whether native or quasi-organic – have caused an upheaval like the one we just survived, Sayati Elk? Legends have it that the thing's so thin its body has almost no width at all.'

'The legends are legends, and even if true, the activation of the monster's biocybernetic consciousness from the Parfects' orbiter would generate enough energy both to thicken the sloak's immensely attenuated membrane and to stir up the sea in the process. Once drawn together for its assault on Ongladred, the sloak becomes as formidable a sea beast as any that has ever lived – either in Mansueceria's oceans or in Earth's.'

'For everything, you have an answer.' *Didn't Sayati Elk's resurrection of the dead for the purposes of his dramaturgy have a kind of parallel, a kind of affinity, with the Parfects' 'activation' of the sloak (assuming of course, that the old man's hypothesis was correct)?* That was a question which I didn't ask, but which I decided to think about. There were a great many questions that I would have to think about in the days, the years, ahead.

'No, not answers, Ingram, *theories* – all of which I intensely believe in, since they are better than all others and since they are mine.'

Gabriel Elk said this without a hint of haughtiness, but I wanted to deflate him somehow, wanted to disabuse him of his own intricate but annoyingly logical theory. I asked, 'What about the two-thousand-year cycle of the sloak? Isn't that too regular for an expedient that you claim is punitive? Does humankind reach the brink of forbidden knowledge with so inhuman a precision each two thousand years?'

'The sloak has come only twice before, even according

to legend. How can we compute its cycle with any accuracy? Besides, Ingram, this – the Year of the Halcyon Panic – is not the only year that men have predicted the return of the sloak, the destruction of the species. Men are superstitious beings; they read numbers into everything. Eventually their mystical numbers become the basis of a numinous science. Oh, it's beautiful and frightening, this becoming, Ingram, one which always unworks itself only to evolve again. The cycle of the sloak? It is science and superstition compromising their separate integrities through the mediation of numbers.'

'Dear Maz,' I said. 'Spare me more of this. Spare me.'

Gabriel Elk threw his head back and laughed, laughed with hearty abandon, as if his breath would puff our sails in the breathless day and billow us jauntily into Brechtlin's harbour – a galleon of heroes ready for their gallons of haoma, a crew of gallant murderers hoping to inundate their crime in the masker panacea.

Amazingly enough, in two hours Captain Chant and our seamen, having wrung the air for its faintest stirring, took us into the recently wave-lashed but now silent harbour, and after fifteen days at sea we disembarked upon our native soil. Behind us, a sky full of masts and sails. Before us, the port, a road, and all of Ongladred.

In the flush of this excitement I forgot that it was I who had incinerated the enemy, nearly eight hundred human beings – until, as I left the *Paradise*, I saw Gentleman Gnot staring after me.

# Eighteen

Gabriel Elk and I rented a wagon in Brechtlin, had the photon-director loaded into it, and drove not to Lunn but along the coastal road towards Mershead. 'The weapon is mine,' the old man told me. 'I don't have to take it back to Chancellor Blaine; he'll discover soon enough, without our telling him, that the *Paradise* is in harbour.' It was dark when we reached Stonelore. Oddly, I felt that I had come home too; that this arena of rock and sand and artificial light belonged more certainly to me than did any of the tract on which the Atarite Palace sits.

Bethel and Robin Coigns met us in front of Grotto House. That there were only the two of them was in itself an ominous thing.

Bethel kissed her husband. Then she stepped back from him, her hands still on his shoulders, and said, 'Gareth is dead, Gabriel.' Then she ran her hand slowly over her husband's head, backward from the brow. 'Someone has told you already?'

'No. You are the first.' He pulled his wife to him, and they embraced – a silent, undemonstrative, somehow expressive embrace. Coigns and I stood apart, not so much excluded from this sharing as simply incapable of comprehending its intensity. Then Gabriel Elk drew his wife with him towards the house, the woman almost an extension of himself, he almost an extension of her, the two of them incomprehensibly and reproachfully whole. 'Ingram,' he said, 'Robin, come with us.' We followed. Silently.

Later, in the arras-hung dining chamber, we talked – while the beardless Gareth's almost tangible presence hovered in our words and breaths. The stone table was between us like a funeral slab; the Atarite Palace and the provinces of Ongladred were reduced in our minds to ghostly greys on a battle chart. Before a single dead loved one, the concepts of civilisation defended and honour reaffirmed dissolve into fume and blow away, like cannon smoke. Even with no one of my own to mourn, I knew that much; the knowledge had grown in me.

'He was killed four days ago,' Robin Coigns was telling us. 'Those machines that Sayati Snow and Master Gordon brought up to below Firthshir had turned it all around, the fighting, you know, and the Pelagans had started back up north, all the way through Vestacs and Eenlich, too, it looked like. The boy he was killed in the per-suit Field-Pavan Barrow ordered right after the machines turned 'em around. Then, when he sees they can still kill us, you know, while we're per-suing 'em, ole Barrow calls it all off and we just let 'em go, just let 'em run – but Gareth he was already dead, Sayati Elk, he was already lost, along with a mess of others, all of 'em on-the-line fellows, too.'

There was silence.

Bethel Elk sat with her hands folded in her lap, regal in her silken green gown as I had ever seen Our Shathra Anna. Gabriel kept his gaze down, apparently directing it at his heavy, rope-veined hands.

Then he said: 'An irony, Robin. An almost maudlinly predictable one. Irony, a part of my trade; a philosophical joke to work on my creations. Now it comes home to haunt me.'

Bethel said, 'Forget that, Gabriel. We will mourn awhile.'

The old man looked up; he looked at Robin Coigns. 'Where is Gareth? Was he buried in the north?'

'He's under,' Robin said simply. 'He's in the tunnel 'twixt Grotto House and Stonelore.'

'Here?'

'Aye, Sayati Elk.'

'How?'

'He took a rifle ball in the throat, sir, through the Adam's apple so his wind was cut; the ball lodged there, you see. It wasn't meant for me to be beside him then, I guess. Others came running for me and took me back, but by then our officers knew him for your son and called for haomycin to go into his blood so as to get him back here 'fore he stiffened. I was shunted off to one hand, Sayati Elk, and most near cried, and watched 'em do what they had to. Gareth he lay in the midst of all this scrambling, you know, and bled the life all out and couldn't see me no more than if he was blind, his eyes gone back and his face just as still as old milk. He got home 'fore I did, Sayati Elk – *preserved*, sort of. They took him off that way, with nothing for me to do but watch. I near cried, sir.'

'We put Gareth in a preservator, Gabriel,' Bethel said.

'Which one? They were all full.'

'They're empty now, Gabriel. Except for Gareth's, and Bronwen Lief's. After you left, I had some men come out from Lunn and give the other dead ones their second funerals. They were burned, our actors, all of them together – in the place we always burn them – at the end of the summer. I couldn't leave them sleeping in that heartless ice, Gabriel.'

'Why did you spare the girl?'

'I don't know. Because she was new – newer than the others. Because I had seen her dance.'

'I want to see Gareth,' the old man said.

I asked, 'May I go with you?'

After an almost imperceptible pause the old man said, 'Please, Ingram.'

We excused ourselves. Bethel and Coigns permitted us to go without them. They had seen the boy, and they knew Gabriel's wish for what it was, a plea for one last, unhampered moment of communion. Perhaps I was less sensitive than they, for I knew this, too, and should not have gone with him – but I felt that he would have refused to let me go if my presence had threatened to throw up a wall between him and his dead son. I had to go with him. Down into the programming room, into the dark tunnel, into the dormitory room for corpses. Sensing my need to accompany him, Elk had said yes.

And so we left the dining chamber, walked down the

hallway of luminous panels, and rode the elevator into the very womb and bowels of Grotto House. My sensation of going home grew more pronounced, more and more uncanny.

Then we were in the icy preservator room, among the ranked coffins and the upended storage tanks of lox. A faint musical seething played in my ears. Our breaths took shape in the air like dreamlike sails; we had voyaged into a numinous place, a world whose deities were enshrined in ice and plastic. Four of the shrines were empty, but in the two closest to the door we found the daughter of Josu and Rhia Lief and the newly slain son of Gabriel and Bethel Elk. These young people were the numens of the preservator room, guardian spirits whose frozen youth mocked their guardianship. Were they not too primevally vernal for such a custodial godhood? I stared through crystal at first the woman, then the young man – whose throat was swaddled in a wide bandage.

Bronwen Lief looked different to me. Her face was not a whit altered from the first time I had seen her, long ages ago, back before the spring had come. But the smirk I had then read in the twist of her mouth seemed not at all sinister now; it was not even a smirk, it was instead a wholly natural flaw, human and therefore reassuring.

As for Gareth, he looked no different, no different at all – except that his sparse, adolescent beard had matured into stubble. If Bethel had had him shaved before committing him to the preservator, then even in death his facial hair had continued to grow. So: His corpse's features were fresh and youthful, but touched with the beginnings of a revivifying weariness.

Wearing frost-gloves, Gabriel adjusted the cryostat on Bronwen Lief's preservator. With the cryostat he could take the temperature within each coffin up and down a limited scale of cold in a very brief time, although the preservator room itself remained at a constant 0°C. in case of separate cryostat malfunctions. As the temperature in Bronwen's unit rose towards that of the room itself, the old man leaned over his dead son and studied the boy's face. 'He was growing into himself, Ingram. He was just on the verge of growing into the wholeness of himself.'

My hands, for warmth, were in my armpits. I was behind the old man, and as he leaned over the preservator I noticed for the first time an angry red gleam on the back of his head, his mottled, naked skull. It was a nevus, a birthmark, a magenta discoloration just to the right of and a little above the brain stem. Before I could stop myself I had reached out and touched the tiny mark.

Gabriel Elk turned slowly and looked at me. I withdrew my hand, the image of the nevus clearly before me even though the old man had turned. 'You have a mark back there,' I said.

Briefly his face was inscrutable. Then he smiled and his eyes crinkled into almost Mongoloid slits: a pleasant, joy-etched smile. 'Ingram, I'd almost forgotten the mark. When I was little my father used to brush my hair aside there and tell me that I'd been branded by the Evil One, by Ahriman himself.'

'Yes,' I said. 'It's like a scorpion, a little scorpion with its stinger raised.'

'My father always told me of the blemish with a smile, as if joking, but he upset me more than he knew, and for a time I dreaded his touch – his reminder to me of something I knew was back there but couldn't actually see for myself. My father was a Mansuecerian, Ingram, a masker, and I knew that I was somehow different from him. For a long time I believed the difference lay in the scorpion mark, that it and only it was what set me apart from my family and everyone else.'

'That mark probably made your father uneasy, Sayati Elk. It's frighteningly perfect, it might almost be a tattoo.'

'He told me that, too, Ingram – though not in those words. And when I reached adolescence I ceased resenting his uneasy banter about the birthmark; I understood his uneasiness, his ill-expressed love. I understood what I was and how the differences in what we were didn't finally matter. But I kept waiting for him to express – in

212

some uncharacteristically flamboyant way – the love he didn't know how to articulate.' Gabriel Elk rubbed the spot I had touched. 'Oh, those are mostly good memories, Ingram, almost from another life, they're so far away.' He rubbed the spot and smiled.

Then he abruptly turned and began disconnecting some of the apparatus affixed to Bronwen Lief's preservator. Apparently he was not going to let those memories overwhelm him. As we had done several times during the summer, he pulled the coffin on its coaster-like wheels out of its moorings and pushed it towards the door. He gave me a pair of frost-gloves.

'What are you doing?' I asked.

'Going back to work. Will you help me?' He returned to the young woman's preservator after giving me the gloves and began to roll it towards me. I opened the door for him, and together we pushed the gleaming white fuselage through the tunnel and into the programming room. I couldn't believe that it was beginning again, I didn't know how to react.

Once inside the programming room, however, the old man said, 'Go upstairs and go to bed. Take Gareth's room. I want you to have it.'

I hesitated. 'Sayati Elk, I can't tell Mistress Elk I'm taking her son's room. Not now.'

'Tell her. She'll understand.'

'Are you going to stay here?'

'For a while. Go on. Go upstairs. Go to bed.'

Reluctantly I rode the elevator up. Alone in the main hallway, I felt like a figure in a photographic negative, like the light-blackened obverse of myself. Then, in her silken green gown, Bethel Elk came towards me out of the glare of the corridor's wall panels and restored colour to the microcosmic world of Grotto House.

I told her what her husband had told me to tell her. She put her hand on my arm. She led me to Gareth's room. The door opened for me. She said, 'Go in, Ingram, and sleep well.' The door closed behind me. And momentarily I felt again like a black figure on a white ground – until I brushed against a wall panel and a flood of yellow light reversed things once more.

The room was exactly like the one I had slept in before Gareth's death – except that at various places about the room Gareth had put on display pieces of his idiosyncratic statuary. Sinuous trees carved out of stone, every piece a gnarled and leafless tree. I picked up the sculpture next to my bed. It was unfinished, almost as if the boy had realised that no matter how expert his hands became or how exemplary his vision, in execution his trees would inevitably be dead and petrified before he could complete them; as if he had realised this and given up the attempt as foolish.

The tree I was holding may have been the last one he ever worked on. I set it down and stretched out on the dead boy's bed.

# Nineteen

The next day Arngrim Blaine appeared at Stonelore. His arrival coincided with Robin Coigns' departure for Brechtlin in the wagon we had rented the previous afternoon; the ostler was going to return the wagon and ride back to us on the horse following the wagon on a short tether.

As Coigns left the upland arena and joggled on the wagon seat down the dusty hillside, we saw the Chancellor's equipage approaching from Lunn. In a red billow, wagon and carriage passed each other. Only two Atarite guardsmen rode beside the Chancellor, and they did not venture into the arena with his sleek, ebony coach; instead, they halted and took up positions outside the rock wall, as had the charioteers on that night when Bronwen Lief danced and the reivers drew down on us from their blind. Had we learned nothing? But the war was over, I reminded myself, we had successfully beat back the bringers of ruin. I had murdered a few myself.

'Welcome,' Sayati Elk said when Chancellor Blaine stepped down from his coach. 'Once again, we're honoured.'

The man with the roan tooth tilted his head and clasped the old man's hands in his own. 'It's I who should extend the welcome, Sayati Elk. Welcome home to Ongladred. Your countrymen and your countrymen's rulers have proved to be more flexible than many' – the Chancellor gave me a significant look – 'felt to be possible. Our Shathra Anna has fathomless reservoirs of flexibility: she ordered me to pay you a visit when it became apparent that you weren't going to come into Lunn of your own volition.'

'An inconvenience to you,' Gabriel Elk said, 'for which I apologise.'

The three of us were crossing the arena, walking slowly. I said, 'Why exactly did she send you out here, Chancellor Blaine?'

He didn't answer at once. But finally he did say, 'To offer both congratulations and condolences, Sayati Elk. And these tasks I undertake willingly. Don't speak of inconvenience. There is none, none whatever. I'm only sorry that your son's death diminishes the joy you must feel in your homecoming.'

Elk said nothing. He opened the wrought-iron gate across the foyer to Grotto House and led us inside. Bethel joined us, and since the day was fair and unseasonably warm, we went through the foyer to the house's open, central courtyard. All of us but the old man took up seats on the stone benches there. Elk, his bald head absorbing rather than reflecting the sunlight, stood with his back to us. I could not help looking at the scorpion mark above his runnelled nape. It focused my attention.

I heard him saying, 'Robin tells me that Sayati Snow and Master Gordon swept the enemy before them with the ease of minor deities. And that we pursued our retreating enemy.'

Blaine responded, 'And Captain Chant tells me that Master Marley destroyed six Pelagan warships as if they were soap bubbles waiting for the lance.'

'Five,' I said.

'Was that pursuit necessary?' Bethel asked, picking up a dropped thread.

'That's a determination only Field-Pavan Barrow could make, Mistress Elk. I am no tactician.'

'Where are the photon-directors that Snow and Gordon used?' Gabriel Elk asked. 'They must be returned to me, Chancellor, that was a principal stipulation of our agreement.'

'In safekeeping at the Atarite Palace, Sayati Elk. Where is the one you and Master Marley used aboard the *Paradise*?'

'Beneath Grotto House. Coigns carried it down for me last night, and I removed its chemical power source.' Elk turned and faced us. The leaves of the blood lily behind him caught the sunlight and showed us their velvet, crimson under-bellies. 'It's a disembowelled machine, Chancellor. Dead.'

'Well, while it lived, it revelled. So be it.'

This remark seemed to me inordinately tactless. I stood up. I walked for a few paces down one of the stone paths in the courtyard. Then I halted, still within speaking distance of the others. Around me: blood lilies, autumn azaleas, the hard yellow berries of the ahura-wood, the inner walls of Grotto House. Gabriel, Bethel, and the Chancellor formed the points of a triangle which excluded me – until I realised that I had simply extended the geometry of our disenchantment. I was a fourth point, I meant too.

'You've offered congratulations and condolences,' Sayati Elk said. 'Surely that doesn't comprise the whole purpose of your journey?'

'Actually it does. The only other thing Our Shathra asked me to do was to bring Ingram back to Lunn with me. He's handled his responsibilities capably, and we desire to reward him.'

'Then let me stay here,' I said.

Arngrim Blaine looked at me as one looks at a presumptuous child; but for the carnelian flash of his tooth, his smile would have been fatherly. 'A decision such as that is out of my hands, Ingram. Nor could Our Shathra Anna make it without knowing Sayati and Mistress Elk's feelings.'

'Does Our Shathra Anna seek to reward me, too?' Gabriel asked

'Certainly.' The Chancellor's eyes blinked rapidly.

'Then I ask as my reward that which Ongladred owes me. A son. If Ingram Marley wishes to stay here at Grotto House, we wish him to stay as our son.'

Bethel said, 'Grant Ingram his request, Chancellor Blaine, and you have granted ours as well.'

'Ingram is rather old to be acquiring parents, Mistress Elk.'

'Oh, indeed yes,' she said.

'Besides, it's not only for his personal qualities that I wish him to stay here,' the old man added. 'A fortnight from now I intend to present a neuro-masque in the Stonelore amphitheatre, and Master Marley will be of invaluable assistance to me in the comptroller room. Tell Our Shathra Anna that she is invited, that the masque will commemorate her reign in dance and song.'

And so it happened in that exchange of words, that I gave up my place in the Atarite Court, my status as a dirt-runner, my incompetently executed duties as a member of the Eyes and Ears of Our Shathra Anna. As the Chancellor and Sayati Elk and Mistress Elk talked, my past fell away.

I looked up at Maz. I was conscious of the fluttering colours of the courtyard, leaves peripherally afire with burnt red and smoky emerald, and of the wan circle of the sun shedding its summer scales down the sky. My past had fallen away, even that part of it including my sojourn with the Elks. It had not disappeared; it lay at my feet like dead leaves or shed scales, and I had the power either to collapse into it or to stride out of its alluring, brittle debris. I was still held, but the coils were off, the colours were golden.

The conversation of the others went on around me as I tried to read the future in Maz' outlines, to adjust to the new skin that I still had no right to. The morning passed, the afternoon passed, and somewhere in this evanescent progression Arngrim Blaine found a moment in which to bid us goodbye and depart.

Before I could think what had happened to me, to all of us, I was in Gareth's bed once more, hypnotised by the tangled shadow cast upon the wall by one of the young Elk's meticulously carven stone trees. I could not sleep. My mind was in the branches of the shadow. I lay tangled in the flown, leafless day. Too many things had happened, but the only one who seemed aware of their significance was I. Then, faint footfalls began to resonate in the shadow's branches. It was an illusion. The footfalls were

218

coming from the hallway, from the corridor outside my door. I lay listening to them even after they had gone. A long time later I got up and left Gareth's room. Down the illuminated corridor I walked placing my feet in the shadows of the footfalls that had preceded me.

I was in front of the elevator. I rode the elevator down.

In the programming room I found Gabriel Elk bent over the corpse of his son, working with liver-spotted and untrembling hands to turn the boy into an actor. As he worked, he talked. He talked in a low, almost emotionless monotone whose very lack of coherence was poignant.

Beside the table on which Gareth lay was the pre-servator I had seen him in the night before. It stood open and empty, like the casing of one of those fabled bombs that had so long ago virtually destroyed our spawning place, making our planet the home of a preemptive neo-human species that had exiled us, masker and Atarite, to the darkling islands of a northern sea on a world eight hundred light-years from Earth. The whirring of a small computer and the tiny hands sweeping across each tube in an array of cathode-ray tubes (these last on the face of a toposcopic unit opposite the table itself) made the room an eerie place. Gabriel Elk's voice droned on above the sound of the computer; his hands continued to wire, and probe, and snip, and hover, lingering now clinically, now out of something profoundly unscientific.

Before the old man could see me, I turned and left the programming room. Upstairs, the boy's inert trees were waiting for me, frozen in time, tangled in my own nascent memory.

# Twenty

I have been at Stonelore almost two years. The sloak has not returned to Ongladred, and the bonfires on the beaches have long since been allowed to go out. Perhaps there is not any such creature; perhaps the Parfects – in their infinite, condescending wisdom – have granted us their penultimate reprieve. I don't care any more, I live as if my fate were in no one's hands but my own. When I look at the night sky, I see only the Shattered Moons, nothing sinister, nothing quietly malign – and I hold my breath and genuflect before their random, concerted beauty.

The photon-directors that Sayati Snow and Master Gordon used against the Pelagans have still not been returned to us. Our Shathra Anna and Chancellor Blaine have each been to Stonelore twice since the morning I was granted my freedom from the Atarite Court, and they now assure us that the weapons were dismantled in Lunn.

I don't know how we should accept this news. Gabriel Elk doesn't believe it, he thinks Blaine is lying.

As for our enemies, they have ceased to attack our goods and people even in the small reiving parties for which they have always been famous. For what purpose, then, can our rulers want a weapon like the photon-director?

We know. We are not naïve.

But uncertainty about the final handling of the ones wielded by Sayati Snow and Master Gordon still plagues us. It is impossible to demand of Our Shathra Anna any sort of clarification.

Gabriel Elk, however, has clarified a point that used to deprive me of sleep. Why a place like Stonelore? Why the agony and the frustration to which he yearly subjects himself?

'Because one day I am going to make them weep, Ingram, one day I am going to make them weep.' Until that day, despite the old man's and Bethel's undoubtedly justified reproaches, they will continue to be maskers to me. Not Mansuecerians; maskers. But they will weep, that day will come – I'm certain of it. And when it comes the citizens of this island nation will cremate the dead when they die, and I, since I have no talent for dramaturgy or sculpture, may become the first living actor in all our history.

Nevertheless, the day is coming when they will weep.

# A Selection of Best Selling Science Fiction from SPHERE BOOKS

## Deathworld Trilogy

| | |
|---|---|
| **DEATHWORLD 1** | *Harry Harrison* 65p |
| **DEATHWORLD 2** | *Harry Harrison* 65p |
| **DEATHWORLD 3** | *Harry Harrison* 65p |

| | |
|---|---|
| **TWO TALES AND EIGHT TOMORROWS** | *H. Harrison* 65p |
| **NOVA 4** | *Harry Harrison* 65p |
| **PRIME NUMBER** | *Harry Harrison* 85p |
| **THE STAINLESS STEEL RAT** | *Harry Harrison* 75p |
| **THE STAINLESS STEEL RAT'S REVENGE** | *Harry Harrison* 75p |
| **THE STAINLESS STEEL RAT SAVES THE WORLD** | |
| | *Harry Harrison* 75p |
| **FLOATING WORLDS** | *Cecelia Holland* £1·50 |
| **THE MAN WHO AWOKE** | *Laurence Manning* 85p |
| **DRAGONQUEST** | *Anne McCaffrey* 85p |
| **TO RIDE PEGASUS** | *Anne McCaffrey* 85p |
| **THE ICE SCHOONER** | *Michael Moorcock* 65p |
| **RINGSWORLD** | *Larry Niven* 95p |
| **INCONSTANT MOON** | *Larry Niven* 85p |
| **SPACE VIKING** | *H. Beam Piper* 85p |
| **GUNPOWDER GOD** | *H. Beam Piper* 85p |
| **SF: THE GREAT YEARS** | *F. & C. Pohl* (Eds.) 75p |

## Illuminatus Trilogy

| | |
|---|---|
| **1: THE EYE OF THE PYRAMID** | *R. Shea & R. A. Wilson* 95p |
| **2: THE GOLDEN APPLE** | *R. Shea & R. A. Wilson* 75p |
| **3: LEVIATHAN** | *R. Shea & R. A. Wilson* 95p |

| | |
|---|---|
| **JOURNEY OF JOENES** | *Robert Sheckley* 85p |
| **TO OPEN THE SKY** | *Robert Silverberg* 85p |
| **NIGHTWINGS** | *Robert Silverberg* 85p |
| **UP THE LINE** | *Robert Silverberg* 85p |
| **MEN IN THE JUNGLE** | *Norman Spinrad* 95p |
| **TO LIVE FOREVER** | *Jack Vance* 85p |
| **TYRANOPOLIS** | *A. E. Van Vogt* 85p |
| **THE WORLD OF NULL-A** | *A. E. Van Vogt* 65p |
| **THE PAWNS OF NULL-A** | *A. E. Van Vogt* 65p |
| **THE BEST OF A. E. VAN VOGT** | *A. E. Van Vogt* 60p |
| **THE SECRET GALACTICS** | *A. E. Van Vogt* 75p |
| **THE UNIVERSE MAKER** | *A. E. Van Vogt* 75p |
| **EARTH'S LAST FORTRESS** | *A. E. Van Vogt* 85p |
| **THE WINGED MAN** | *A. E. Van Vogt* 85p |
| **MISSION TO THE STARS** | *A. E. Van Vogt* 75p |

All Sphere Books are available at your bookshop or
newsagent, or can be ordered from the following address:
Sphere Books, Cash Sales Department,
P.O. Box 11, Falmouth, Cornwall.

Please send cheque or postal order (no currency), and allow
19p for postage and packing for the first book plus 9p per
copy for each additional book ordered up
to a maximum charge of 73p in U.K.

Customers in Eire and B.F.P.O. please allow 19p for
postage and packing for the first book plus 9p per copy
for the next 6 books, thereafter 3p per book.

Overseas customers please allow 20p for postage and packing
for the first book and 10p per copy for each additional book.